THE ARABIAN NIGHTS

BLACKIE & SON LTD., 5 FITZHARDINGE STREET, LONDON, W.1
17 STANHOPE ST., GLASGOW
BLACKIE & SON (INDIA) LTD., BOMBAY; BLACKIE & SON (CANADA) LTD., TORONTO

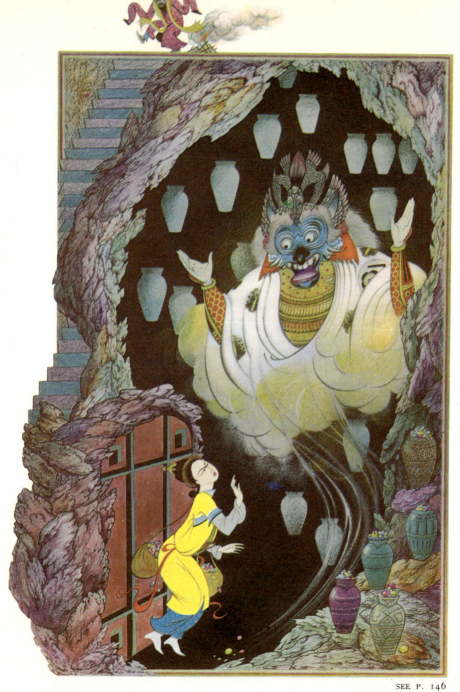

SEE P. 146

There appeared a hideous Jinnee which glowed horribly

THE
ARABIAN NIGHTS

Stories retold by Amabel Williams-Ellis

Illustrated by Pauline Diana Baynes

BLACKIE
LONDON AND GLASGOW

First published 1957 Reprinted 1958, 1960, 1962

Printed in Great Britain by
Blackie & Son, Limited, Glasgow

CONTENTS

CONTENTS

ILLUSTRATIONS

To my Mother

 HENRIETTA MARY AMY STRACHEY

who taught me to love fairy tales

WHO
TOLD THE STORIES?
or
THE TALE OF
QUEEN SHAHRAZAD

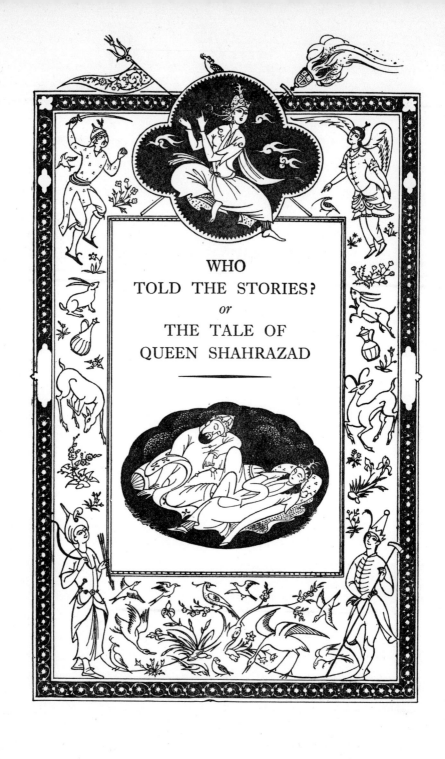

WHO
TOLD THE STORIES?
or
THE TALE OF
QUEEN SHAHRAZAD

*In the name of Allah, the Compassionate, the Merciful,
Creator of the Universe, Who has raised the Earth without Pillars.*

THERE LIVED LONG AGO A KING NAMED SHAHRIYAR.
He was married to a beautiful Queen who appeared
to love him as dearly as he loved her. One day he
discovered that, in spite of her sweet words and smiles,
she had been for many months conspiring with his
enemies to kill him and to marry somebody else. Then
King Shahriyar fell into such a terrible rage that he was
almost mad and, in his fury, he killed his Queen with his
own hand.

"Never again," said he, "shall wife of mine deceive
me!"

Then, still in his rage, he made a vow that, whenever he
wanted to, he would marry some unfortunate young
maiden and, on the very next day, have her beheaded.

For some time he kept his mad and wicked vow. At last
the people of the country began to steal away with their
daughters and go to other countries, so that, after a while,
there was hardly a young girl left in any of the cities round
about. Indeed there were soon only two—they were
sisters, the daughters of his Grand Vizier or Chief Mini-
ster. Their father soon began to feel that he, too, had
better have gone away—in spite of his being Grand Vizier
—for he loved his daughters and could not bear the idea
that the terrible fate which awaited any wife of the King
should fall on either of them.

So, when the King next said that he wanted a wife, the
Grand Vizier told him that there were no more maidens
to be had. At this the King became furious and swore that

13

if the Vizier did not immediately bring him a maiden—
and a young and beautiful one!—he should be beheaded
at once. When he heard that, and saw the fury of the King,
the Vizier returned sadly to his house.

Now his elder daughter was a lovely
girl named Shahrazad. She was not
only beautiful but accomplished, and
she loved reading stories, histories
and adventures, so that she knew no
less than a thousand wonderful or
funny tales. When Shahrazad saw her
father's sad face and noticed that he
would eat nothing, but sat with a bent
back like someone weighed down with misery, she said:

"Why do I see you so sad, O dear Father? You sit
weighed down by some burden of grief."

At first the Vizier would tell her nothing, but at last,
when she had coaxed him, he told her about the anger of
the King and its cause, and that he was sad because the
King meant to kill him the very next day.

"By Allah, O my Father, give me in
marriage to this King!" said Shahrazad. "For either I shall die, and so shall
save your life and that of yet another
daughter of the Moslems, or else, in
spite of all, I shall live! If I live, I shall
save the lives of many other maidens.
I shall save you, too, and my dear
sister!"

For long the Grand Vizier would not be persuaded, but
at last (guessing, too, that Shahrazad had a plan, though
she would not tell him what it was) he began to make pre-
parations to take her to the palace the next day. Before

14

they left she asked her father for one thing more. This was that her younger sister, who was called Dunyazad, might come with her, and to this her father agreed.

Shahrazad—the elder daughter—was beautiful. Her face was round like the full moon; her hair was the colour of night and hung to her waist. Her eyes were large and dark and veiled by silken lashes; her teeth were like pearls set in coral, and her shape was slender. So when, next morning, she had been dressed in her bridal dress—in

cloth of gold, decked with jewels and with a perfumed veil of the finest silk—she looked so lovely that the attendants wept to see such a beautiful maiden go into such danger. Only Shahrazad herself kept up her courage and no tears fell from her great dark eyes. But her father was almost dead with grief as, at last, he brought her to the palace.

In an outer room Shahrazad took leave of her younger sister and, as she did so, she said earnestly:

"Dear sister, companion of my childhood, I shall need your help! I am going to ask the King to allow you, to-morrow morning, to be admitted to the inner rooms. An hour before the dawn you must come in as if you meant to take leave of me. But you must not do so immediately. Instead you must present a cup of delicious sherbet to the King and another cup to me. Then I want you to say: 'Tell me, I beg you, as you have so often done, some strange story, so that we may the better enjoy the cool hour before the sun reddens the sky!' Do not fail in this, dear sister, for our lives may depend upon it!"

So the next morning, an hour before the dawn, just as Shahrazad had asked her, Dunyazad, the younger sister, came in, cups of cooled sherbet in her hands, and she said to Shahrazad:

"O my dear sister! Do as you have so often done! Tell some strange story to beguile the cool hour before the daylight reddens the sky."

"Most certainly," replied Shahrazad, "if this noble King allows me?"

The King, being restless, was pleased that the cool hour should be passed in this way, and so he gave his consent, and Shahrazad began to relate a story, which she called "The Story of the Merchant and the Jinnee."

Now this was a strange tale. It was about a merchant who, journeying to a foreign country, sat to rest under a tree in a deserted but shady garden, there to eat a piece of bread and a date. When he had eaten, the merchant threw away the date stone. Now in throwing it away he ought to have called out 'Destoor!' which is to say, 'By your leave', but, as he was alone, he did not say it, but just threw away the little stone. No sooner had he done so than there appeared before him a terrible Jinnee of enormous size, who had a drawn sword in his hand, and who, in a voice of thunder, accused him of having just killed his son by hitting him on the chest with the date stone!

The merchant wept bitterly and begged the Jinnee to spare his life. "Allah be my witness," said the unfortunate merchant, "I meant no harm, it was only a date stone! I am not ready to die! I have a wife and children that I love, also I have not yet paid my debts nor set my affairs in order!"

But the Jinnee only answered that he must die. So at last the merchant promised that, if the Jinnee would spare him for a while (so that he could appoint guardians for his children and pay his debts) he would come back on that very same day next year to that very spot; after that the Jinnee could do as he liked with him. To this bargain the Jinnee at last agreed and the merchant went sadly home, set his affairs in order, told his wife and children what had happened, and, taking his grave-clothes under his arm, said farewell to his weeping household, travelled sorrowfully back to the deserted garden and, punctual to the very day, kept his promise to the Jinnee.

But when she had got as far as that in the story Shahrazad broke off, saying, with a sigh, that there was no time for more, for the sun had now risen.

" But what happened to this unfortunate merchant?" asked her sister.

"Ah!" said Shahrazad. "The things that happened were very strange! Indeed this is nothing to the next part of the tale, which I would gladly tell—if only I had time."

"By Allah," said the King, "I, too, should like to know whether that evil Jinnee did indeed kill the honest merchant."

"To-morrow, if the King spare me," Shahrazad replied, "I will tell."

So the King got up, and he went as usual to sit in judgment on his throne in the great court of the palace.

Now all that night the unfortunate Grand Vizier had spent mourning in his lonely house, too sad to eat or sleep, and, next morning, when he came, as usual, to prostrate himself before the King where he sat upon his throne, he had brought grave-clothes for his daughter. The King said nothing at all about Shahrazad but, as was his custom, received ambassadors from foreign lands and sat in judgment, and all without telling the Vizier one word of what had happened to Shahrazad. Yet, as he had not been given the body of his daughter, the old man went home with a little hope that perhaps she still lived.

In the palace next morning, an hour before the dawn, Shahrazad's younger sister once more brought in cups of sherbet cooled with snow and, once more, she begged her sister to go on with the story of the Merchant and the Jinnee.

Shahrazad asked the King's permission and, when it was granted, she went on with the story. She told how, as the merchant sat sadly in the deserted garden, which was the place where he had to meet the Jinnee, he was joined by a handsomely dressed man who led a gazelle by a golden cord, and then by a second man who led two black hounds on chains of silver. They both sat down to rest

and began to ask the merchant why he sat alone in the deserted garden and why he looked so sad. No sooner had he finished telling them what had happened, than the Jinnee appeared, looking more frightful than ever and with his sword ready in his hand. The two strangers now begged him not to be in such a hurry, and offered to tell the tales of why the wife of the one had been turned into a gazelle and the two brothers of the other had been turned into black dogs. If the Jinnee liked the stories and thought them strange enough, they would make a bargain with him; each would ask as his only reward half the life of the merchant! When he had listened to the stories, the Jinnee was so astonished that he was quite ready to agree to spare the merchant's life and said that he did not regret his bargain.

When she had got as far as this Shahrazad again stopped.

"I perceive," she said, "that the sun has nearly risen! I wish, O dear sister and my Lord the King, that there were time to tell you also the story of the Fisherman and the Brass Bottle, for it is really much better and more wonderful than this tale of the Jinnee and the Merchant."

"By Allah," answered the King, "if it is an even better tale, I must certainly hear it! You shall begin it at the same hour to-morrow!"

Once more all happened as before. The King went out and sat on his throne in his Hall of Judgment, but once more he said no word to the unfortunate Grand Vizier.

However, this time, Shahrazad managed to send word secretly to her father to tell him that she was still alive and had good hopes that her plan was going to succeed.

Now, as was said before, this excellent Shahrazad knew and remembered a thousand tales and she was also parti-

cularly cunning in her way of telling them. Sometimes she would tell them so that one adventure was tangled in another, so that the King could not be sure of hearing what happened in one story unless he first listened to several other shorter tales. At other times her plan was to tell her stories in such a way that, because of the rising of the sun, she had to break off just at some particularly exciting place in the story. She took care, for instance, in the Sindbad story about "The Valley of Diamonds", to stop at the point when that huge bird the Roc had just flown up with Sindbad tied to its leg, and just when Sindbad might (the King would think) at any moment drop off and be dashed to pieces, or when some ship that Sindbad was on seemed to be on the point of sinking. Another time it would be just when the copper door of the treasure cave had shut, leaving Aladdin alone in the dark, or when the Caliph was most enjoying the trick he was playing on Abou Hassan, or else when Abou Hassan, in his turn, was laughing at the Caliph! She stopped when the young prince had just mounted the flying horse, and, in the story of "The Pomegranate of the Sea", when the strange Uncle had just taken the new-born baby in his arms and had plunged into the water with it.

Each time she did this the King declared that he could not rest unless he knew what happened next.

21

And so, for a thousand nights, Shahrazad told her tales, and, in this book, the choicest and best of her stories are told again.

As for what happened on the thousand and first night to Queen Shahrazad herself, that also shall be told—at the very end. And now comes the extraordinary tale of The Fisherman and the Brass Bottle.

THE STORY OF
THE FISHERMAN AND
THE BRASS BOTTLE

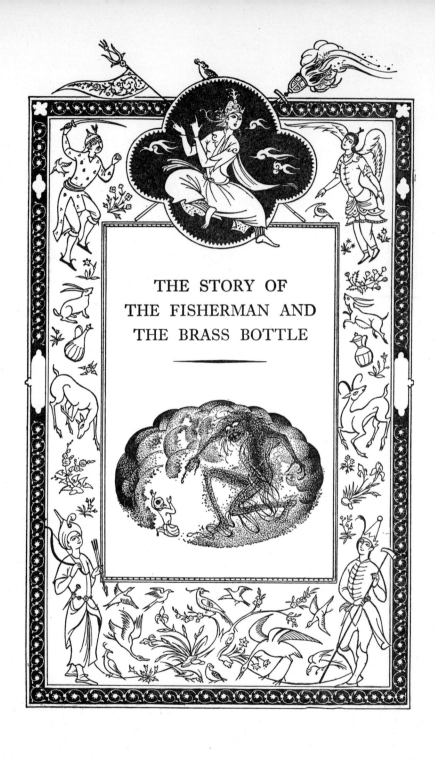

THE STORY OF
THE FISHERMAN AND
THE BRASS BOTTLE

THERE WAS ONCE A CERTAIN FISHERMAN, WHO had a wife and children. Though he was very poor, it was his custom never to cast his net into the sea more than four times on any one day. One day he went down to the shore and, for the first time that day, he cast his net. He threw it out and waited until it rested quietly in the water and, when he drew it together by its strings, he found that it was heavy, so he naturally began to hope he had got a good catch.

He pulled as hard as he could, but it was so heavy that he could not draw it up; so he took the end of the cord, knocked a stake into the shore, and tied the cord to it. He then stripped off his clothes, swam round the net, and pushed and pulled until he got the whole net into shallow water. But, alas! when he got it right out, and could see what he had got, what was his disappointment when he saw that it was only a dead donkey!

Getting rid of the wretched donkey, he wrung out his net and exclaiming "In the name of Allah!" he cast it again. Once more he pulled, but it was now even more difficult to raise than before. But he was disappointed again, for this time he found in it only a large broken jar clogged with sand and mud. He got rid of the jar, wrung out his net, and went back to the edge of the sea for the third time, and again threw his net. But, alack! as before, it had nothing in it but worthless rubbish.

Upon this he raised his head towards heaven, and said, "O Allah, thou knowest that I never cast my net more than four times; and I have now cast it three times!" Then, for the last time, he tried again, and again had great difficulty in getting his net out. This time, however, at the very bottom, was a large and strange-looking bottle made of brass. He pulled it out and, looking at it carefully, saw that

25

its mouth had been closed with an ancient stopper of lead and that, on this lead, had been stamped the magic seal of Solomon the Great. At this the Fisherman began to feel more cheerful, for, said he to himself, "I can sell this old brass bottle in the market. It may even be worth ten pieces of gold!"

When he had put on his clothes again and had picked up the bottle, he noticed how heavy it was and said to himself, "I had better open it and see what is in it. Whatever it is, I can store it in my fish basket before I sell the bottle."

So he took out a knife and began to pick away carefully at the seal, easing off the lead until he had pulled it all away in one piece. Then he shook the bottle and laid it on the ground, so that whatever was in it might pour out. What was his amazement when there came out nothing but smoke!

This smoke seemed never-ending; it rose towards the sky and then it began to spread out.

Soon it began to collect together, and at last he could see that it was taking the form of a Jinnee so huge that its head was in the clouds, though its feet rested upon the ground. This Jinnee's head was like a dome; its legs were like masts; its mouth was like a cavern; its teeth were like stones; its nostrils like trumpets; its eyes like lamps; and it had long, matted, dust-coloured hair.

27

When the Fisherman saw this dreadful sight he was so much afraid that it seemed to him that the day had grown dark. The Jinnee, as soon as it saw the Fisherman, seemed almost as much frightened as he.

"There is no God but Allah; and Solomon is his Prophet!" it exclaimed. "O Prophet of Allah, kill me not; for I will never again oppose you in word, or rebel against you in deed!"

"O Jinnee!" said the Fisherman, who was shocked at this. "It is not Solomon, but Mahomet who is the Prophet of Allah! Solomon has been dead a thousand and eight hundred years!"

At that the Jinnee seemed to be very angry and answered in a voice like thunder:

"Here is news for you then, O Fisherman!"

"News of what?" asked the Fisherman.

"Of your being instantly put to death!" the Jinnee answered.

"O Master of all the Jinns!" said the unfortunate Fisherman, "I have done you good! Why do you threaten to kill me? For I have let you out of that bottle and rescued you from the bottom of the sea!"

But the Jinnee only answered:

"Choose what kind of death you will die."

"But what is my crime," said the Fisherman, "that death should be my reward?"

"You will understand when you hear my story, O Fisherman," the Jinnee replied.

"Tell it then," said the Fisherman, "but be short, for my soul has sunk down to my feet with fear!"

"Know then," said the frightful creature, "that I was one of the Jinns who rebelled against Solomon the Great. To punish me he called for this bottle and imprisoned me in it, and closed it with a leaden stopper, and he stamped the lead with the Most Great Name; and gave orders that the bottle should be thrown into the sea. I said in my heart, 'Whoever sets me free, I will enrich him for ever.' But a hundred years passed over me and no one liberated me, and then there began another hundred years. Then I said, 'Whoever sets me free, I will give him the treasures of the earth.' But no one came; and four hundred years passed over me. Then I said, 'To whoever sets me free I will give three wishes.' But still no one liberated me. Then I fell into a violent rage and said, 'Whoever sets me free now, I will kill! And I will only allow him to choose in what way he will die.' So now, O Fisherman, choose!"

When the Fisherman heard this he called on the name of Allah, and began once more to plead with the dreadful creature, saying that he had acted kindly to it and that it was wrong to reward kindness with cruelty.

But to this the Jinnee only shook its great head.

Then the Fisherman began to think. 'Certainly,' thought he, 'this is a most fearful and gigantic Jinnee and I am only a man. All the same, with the art and reason that Allah gave to man I will plot against the horrible creature just as it has plotted against me!' So he spoke to it again.

"Very well! If I must die—die I must! But by the Most Great Name engraved upon the seal of Solomon, before I die I charge you to answer one question! Will you answer truly?"

On hearing him speak of the Most Great Name, the Jinnee replied:

"Ask and be brief!"

"This is my question. How can you possibly have been in this bottle? It is not large enough to hold your hand or your foot; how, then, could it ever have held your whole body?"

"Do you not believe, then, that I was ever in it?" asked the Jinnee.

"No!" said the Fisherman. "And I will never believe anything in your story until I see you in it again!"

"See then!" said the Jinnee. Then it shook itself and was again turned into smoke. This smoke once more rose to the sky, and then, little by little, it poured back into the bottle.

No sooner was it all inside than the Fisherman snatched up the leaden stopper and, clapping it over the mouth of the bottle, cried out in triumph, "Now, horrible creature! Choose what manner of death *you* will die!"

The Jinnee tried to break the seal, but The Name on it prevented this. Then it began to beg for mercy:

"Oh set me free! Show kindness, and reward evil with good! I vow that I will never do you harm, but will show you a marvel which will enrich you for ever!"

"No!" answered the Fisherman. "I shall now throw you and your bottle back into the sea and, what is more, I shall build a house here so that I can watch and I shall warn any other fisherman who happens to come here never to cast a net in this place! I shall tell him that here lives the vilest, filthiest, most ungrateful and most disgusting of all Jinns!" So saying, the fisherman took up the bottle and held it as if to throw it.

But still the Jinnee begged in a humble voice:

"For the love of Allah the Merciful let me out, O most excellent Fisherman! In the next world, those who return good for evil are sure of a reward! And in this world you shall have a reward that will benefit both you and your children."

At last, after making the creature swear by Allah, Solomon, Mahomet and all the other prophets that it really would do him no harm but give him the promised reward, the Fisherman (though he trembled as he did it) again opened the bottle. Once more the tall column of smoke rose up, once more it collected itself into the form of the monstrous Jinnee.

Its first act was to kick the bottle into the sea!

"That is not a sign of good!" thought the poor Fisherman, but aloud he said to it:

"Now perform your promise, O Jinnee!"

At that the Jinnee gave a loud laugh.

"Take your net and follow me," it said, and so saying it set off inland. So the Fisherman took his net and followed, though he still trembled for fear. The creature led him out of the city. They went over a mountain, and beyond that, down again into a flat and desert valley which the Fisherman had never seen before. Beyond were four black moun-

tains and in the middle of the valley, which was wide, was a large lake. When the Fisherman came near he saw swimming in the water crowds and shoals of strange-looking fish, such as he had never seen before; some were white, some blue, some yellow, and some red.

"Cast your net," said the Jinnee. "But, however many fish you catch, take out of your net only one of each colour and put the others back. Take the four fish to the Sultan, give them to him as a present, and he will reward you. You can come back, but be careful not to take fish from this lake more than once a day, and never more than one of each colour. And now, O Fisherman, that advice is your reward! Excuse me from doing more for you! For remember I have been in that bottle for one thousand and eight hundred years and know very little about the world and have no better ways of performing my promise."

So saying, the Jinnee stamped hard upon the ground, which instantly opened and swallowed him up.

Thanking Allah for the fish (and also that he seemed to have got rid of that abominable Jinnee) the Fisherman made his way back to the city, went to his house, took a bowl from the shelf, filled the bowl with water and put the fish into it. They were still lively and splashed about in the water. Then, with the bowl on his head, the Fisherman set off for the Sultan's Palace.

When he saw these four extraordinary fish the Sultan was astonished and, just as the Jinnee had foretold, gave the Fisherman an excellent reward. So that night, having now more money than they had ever had before, the Fisherman, his wife and his children all sat down to a good supper.

SEE P. 45

Raising his sword the Sultan killed him with a single blow

2. The Fisherman and the Mysterious Fish

Now, AS HAS ALREADY BEEN TOLD, THE SULTAN WAS delighted with the present of the four beautifully coloured fish that the Fisherman had brought to him. It so happened that this Sultan had also had another present, only three days before, and that, too, had been one that had greatly pleased him. The other present had been a charming and good-natured black girl, who was famous for her good cooking and who had been sent to him by the King of the Greeks, who well knew that the Sultan liked good food.

So now, when he had got the fish, the Sultan decided that he would make one experiment of it and try both the new cook and the strange fish. So, as he sat on his throne doing justice, he called to his Vizier and ordered him to take the fish to the black girl, who was to have them ready as soon as the Sultan had finished the day's work of settling disputes.

The Vizier took the fish and went and found the black girl.

"The Sultan," said the Vizier politely as he handed over the fish, "says he has at last a task for you worthy of your skill! He asks you to cook these remarkable fish so that he may have a specimen of your excellent cookery!"

The black girl was delighted, for she wanted to show her new master what she could do, so, as she cleaned the fish and made them ready, her white teeth were like pearls in her smiling black face. Then with a fan made of palm leaves she blew up her little fire of charcoal till it glowed, and arranged the fish on the frying-pan. Then she sat watching till they were nicely cooked on one side. When

3   33   (H112)

she was satisfied, she carefully turned each fish so that it would cook on the other side. No sooner had she turned the last than, to her amazement and terror, the solid wall of the kitchen parted as if it had been a curtain and, through the opening, stepped a tall and beautiful young lady, richly dressed and with a long rod of Indian cane in her hand. The mysterious damsel touched the frying-pan with this rod, saying:

"O Fish! Are you faithful to your promise?" This she asked twice, and on her asking it a third time the fish raised their heads from the frying-pan and answered:

"Yes! We are faithful!"

On this the damsel immediately overturned the frying-pan so that the fish fell into the fire. Then she took a step back, upon which the wall of the kitchen closed again.

Now when she saw and heard all this, and especially when she heard how the fish in the frying-pan spoke, the poor black girl fainted, and when she came round it was to find that the fish were burnt as black as the charcoal.

"Alas!" cried she in despair. " The very first time the Sultan commands me to show my skill, I am obliged to fail him!" As she spoke she saw that the Vizier was standing behind her and heard that he was telling her that the Sultan was ready for his fish. Weeping for disappointment, the poor girl told the Vizier what had happened. Fortunately the Vizier, who was an excellent man, believed her.

"These can have been no ordinary fish!" exclaimed he, and immediately went off to tell the strange tale to the Sultan, who also, fortunately, believed it.

So next morning the Sultan sent for the Fisherman and asked him if he could bring to the palace four more such fish. The fisherman agreed that he could and, setting off again for the lake with his net, he once more caught one fish of each colour and, when he brought them to the palace, the Sultan again ordered him to be richly rewarded.

But this time the Vizier himself watched while the black girl prepared the fish and, once more, began to fry them. As the Vizier watched, exactly the same thing happened. Again the kitchen wall parted, again the richly dressed damsel appeared, again she asked her question three times and, at the third time, the fish again raised their heads from the frying-pan and answered as before. Neither the black girl nor the Vizier was able to prevent her from, once more, overturning the pan and disappearing.

Once more the Vizier went to the Sultan and told him everything that had happened.

"This is a marvel that I must see with my own eyes!" exclaimed the Sultan. Again the Fisherman was sent for and brought four more fish—red, white, yellow and blue —and for the third time he was well rewarded.

35

"Now," said the Sultan to the Vizier, "these fish shall remain here in my sight and shall not go to the kitchen at all. Bring a charcoal brazier and cook them yourself before my eyes!"

"To hear is to obey," answered the Vizier.

The charcoal brazier was brought, the fish were arranged on the pan.

But no sooner had the Vizier cooked the fish on one side and had begun to turn the last fish than the wall of the Sultan's apartment was split in two, just as the kitchen wall had been. But this time it was not the beautiful damsel who stepped through into the room, but a huge negro, as big as a bull, and this huge creature had in his hand the branch of a great tree. In a clear, loud, terrifying voice the negro spoke the very same words:

"O Fish! Are you faithful to your promise?" said he. At the third repetition the fish again raised their heads and said, "Yes! We are faithful!" upon which the negro upset the frying-pan and disappeared, and once more the fish were burnt as black as charcoal.

At this the curiosity of the Sultan knew no bounds. He sent for the Fisherman and questioned him, and the Fisherman told him that the fish had come from a certain lake which lay in a valley with four mountains beyond.

"How long is the journey to this lake?" asked the Sultan.

"My Lord, it is a journey of less than an hour!" said the Fisherman.

At this answer the Sultan became still more puzzled, for he knew his dominions well and yet he had never heard that such a lake lay so near his city.

Then he ordered out his horses and his bodyguards and his tents, and the Vizier rode behind him, and the Sultan commanded the Fisherman to guide him there immediately.

At this the Fisherman cursed the Jinnee in his heart, for he feared that no good would come to him from all this. However, he could only do his best, so he guided them over the mountain that hid the lake from the Sultan's city and, sure enough, there lay the wide and treeless valley just as before, and there in the middle of it glimmered the lake, and in the lake there swam, as before, many fish of four colours—red, blue, white and yellow. But the Sultan and those who rode with him could not restrain their astonishment that a valley which was utterly strange to them, and a large lake that they had never seen before, should lie so close to the city!

"Have any of you ever seen this lake and this place before?" asked the Sultan. And each answered that not one of them had ever seen it or so much as heard of it.

"By Allah," said the Sultan, "I will never rest till I know the true history of this lake and of its fish!" and so he ordered the camp to be set up. As soon as he had eaten and sat resting in his tent, the Sultan sent for his Vizier and told him that he himself meant to go out alone that night to see what more could be discovered, and especially to see what lay behind the four black mountains on the further side of the lake.

"Perhaps," said he, "I may be away from the camp longer than one night. But, however long I am away, you must sit at the door of my tent and say to everyone who comes, 'The Sultan is sick and has commanded me to let no one come to him.'"

Now the Sultan was no longer a young man and the Vizier, who loved his master, feared for his safety if he went off thus alone and so he did his best to persuade him not to go. But it was all in vain. Presently, when it was dark, the Sultan disguised himself, slung on his sword, and went off alone into the darkness.

And, in the next story, which is "The Story of the Young King of the Black Mountains," is told the strange history of what the Sultan found and how, in the end, he did learn the history of both lake and fish.

3. The Fisherman, the Sultan and The Young King of the Black Mountains

As the sultan began his dark and solitary journey, he soon began to think that the mountains that he had seen from the camp must be much further off than they had seemed, and indeed, when day came, he had not reached their cooler heights. But that did not make him any less determined. Soon, as the sun rose higher, the heat became very great, the sun blazing down and the heat striking up from the sand, so that his feet were almost blistered and his eyes were dazzled.

At last the Sultan saw, far in the distance, something high and black and, as he began to get nearer, he saw that it was a huge palace, all built of black stone and with a black roof. As he got closer he saw that its great entrance-gates were half open. With the hilt of his sword he knocked gently at this half-open gate. But there was no answer, so he went on knocking, more and more loudly, till the sound of knocking echoed through what he began to think must be a deserted palace.

The Sultan's curiosity was growing and, at last, he went boldly through the great black door. His way seemed to lead through one deserted echoing courtyard after another and, thinking that perhaps all this might be a trick to ambush him, he kept calling out as he went, saying that he was no robber, but only a traveller, who needed water. Still only the echoes of his own voice and his own footsteps answered him. At last he found himself in a fine inner court  which, though its walls were black, like the rest of the palace, had in the middle a golden fountain, round which flew a number of beautiful birds—the first living things that he had seen. Looking up, he saw that over the whole of this courtyard a net had been spread so that the singing-birds could not fly away. The water and the birds made him believe that the palace must not long since have been inhabited.

At last he sat down on the steps of the fountain and drank some of the clear, bubbling water, and, as he sat, it seemed to him as though, as well as the tinkling of the water and the singing of the birds, he could also hear a mournful human voice, singing softly—as people sing when they are alone. Listening intently, the Sultan began to be able to make out some words:

> "Where shall I hide myself from fate
> When she I loved has brought me to distress?
> Alas I did not guess
> That all her love had changed to hate!
> And now that I know all
> My tears fall.
> And with the fountain I cry out
> 'Too late! Too late!' "

The melancholy voice seemed to be that of a young

man. The Sultan, wondering at such words, now began to walk softly across the courtyard in the direction from which the voice seemed to come. He found a small archway, which was closed by a curtain, and no sooner had he

raised it than he found himself face to face with a handsome young man who sat, richly dressed, upon a couch, but with a face as sad as his song. For a moment or two the Sultan and this unhappy young man looked at each other in silence.

"O honoured traveller," said the young man at last with a deep sigh, "I would rise to greet you if only I were able!" And with that he buried his face in his hands and wept.

The Sultan wondered why the young man should be all alone in such a place and should moreover be so filled with sadness. So he came nearer, spoke to him kindly, and asked him why he wept.

"Who would not weep if they were as I am?" replied the young man. So saying, he pushed aside the skirts of his silken robe and the Sultan saw, to his astonishment, that from his waist down he had been turned to stone.

40

Moved with pity at the sight, the Sultan, telling the young man who he was, and also that he had his army not far off, promised that, if the young man would tell him the cause of all the strange things that he had seen, he would do his utmost to help him.

"Know then, O Sultan," began the young man, "that I was once King of a thriving country and of a prosperous city. But of all the splendid things of which I was once master nothing is left me, and I am forced to sit here most wretchedly, day and night, neither alive nor dead." At this he fell silent again till the Sultan begged him to go on.

"I lived in this palace," he went on, "and I was married to a beautiful young wife who was moreover a distant kinswoman. I loved her dearly and she protested that she loved me so much that, if hunting or affairs of state kept me away from her side for a little while, she could neither sleep nor eat till I came back to her again.

One day (when we had been married for five years and, as I thought, both loved each other as tenderly as ever) as I rested in the heat of the day, I happened to overhear two slave girls who, thinking that I was asleep, were talking quietly to one another.

41

'What a pity it is,' said the first, 'that our young king's wife is deceiving him so cruelly!'

'She is a very wicked woman,' answered the other, 'to pretend, day after day, that she still loves our poor young master, when all the time she cares for nothing but learning yet more spells and enchantments. I believe that she is plotting his ruin with that horrible old black sorcerer.'

'She means in the end to kill the young King—I feel sure of it! Then I suppose she will make that wicked black magician King instead—and a bad King he will be!' added the first.

'The drink that she gives our poor young King every night she mixes with some drug. He sleeps so deep that he never hears how she steals out to meet the sorcerer. That drink will be so strong one night that he will never wake again!' said the other.

'Yes,' answered the first slave girl, 'that is how she means to manage it!'

Now, though I had listened quietly to all this, I did not believe their words. All the same, that night I did not drink the cup of wine that my wife gave me as usual so lovingly and with such sweet words. Instead I poured it away secretly. However, I lay down as usual and soon pretended to be deeply asleep. Presently I heard her stir and it seemed to me that she watched me for a while and then I heard her say words that froze my blood:

'Sleep on, and never wake again! How I hate and abhor you! How weary I am of this pretence!'

I neither stirred nor moved, but only cautiously opened my eyes and watched how she dressed herself again and then how, catching up a sword, she crept quietly out of the room.

It is useless, O Sultan, to tell all that I saw and heard

that night as I followed her. Let it be enough to say that it soon became plain to me that she was certainly already a powerful enchantress for, as she crept along in the dark and silent palace, all the locks were loosed and all the doors opened when she muttered certain secret words.

The slave girls had been right in supposing that her purpose was to visit a horrible and filthy old black sorcerer and that he was her teacher in all wicked arts, and that these two were certainly plotting my ruin and that of the whole kingdom.

I climbed to the roof of the hut where this horrible black magician lay hidden, and when, in this way, I overheard what was said and discovered their purpose, I became so angry that, slipping down, I burst open the door and, seizing the sword that my wife had taken from the palace, I struck the old enchanter a hard blow on the neck. I struck so hard that I thought I must have killed him, but it was dark, so that neither could I see what I had done, nor could either of the plotters see who it was who had struck the blow. I slipped out of the door again without a word and went back to the palace with a heavy heart.

Now, as I have told you, O Sultan, I loved my beautiful wife and, believing that I had killed her wicked master, I was almost minded to forgive her, but when she said no word of repentance, but still went on with her horrible pretence of loving me, the time came when I could bear her deceit no longer. One day I came to her in a fury and told her plainly what I had seen and heard. Upon this she rose up and cursed me! Alas, her curse was a powerful one. No

sooner had she spoken it than I was turned half to stone—
as you see!

So now I lie here, neither alive nor dead, and every day
she comes to taunt me. She tells me that the blow that I
gave to the old sorcerer only wounded him, so that he still
lives and she still tends him. She whips me cruelly, and as
she does it she tells me how she has enchanted and ruined
my whole kingdom. She tells me with each stroke that she
does it in revenge for her wicked master's sufferings and
that when I cry out in pain it is a joy to that cruel wretch.
Such, O Sultan, is my story."

Then the Sultan, who had listened to all this in pity and
astonishment, exclaimed:

"Only tell me where this wicked woman and her master
in the black arts are to be found! I am determined to be
the means of freeing you!" And then the Sultan, in his
turn, told the young King about the lake and the fish and
how the whole kingdom was now only a desert.

As they consulted together they could see that the difficulty was that the two plotters could not be got rid of
directly, but that the wicked Queen must somehow, first,
be tricked into taking off the enchantment.

"Tell me where to find them!" said
the Sultan at last, "and I will think
of a way!"

The young King answered that the
wounded sorcerer now lay in a sort

of garden pavilion that the Queen had built for him, and that she tended him there but came every day to the palace to taunt and whip her helpless husband.

That night the Sultan searched round outside the great black palace and at last he found the garden-house. There he waited, hidden. In the morning the Sultan saw the wicked young Queen come out and knew that she must have gone to taunt and whip the unfortunate young King.

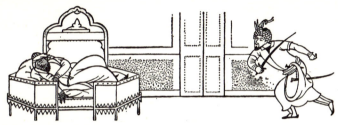

When she was out of the way the Sultan came out of his hiding-place and quickly opened the door. There was the old black sorcerer, lying on a splendid bed, and raising his sword, the Sultan killed him with a single blow. Then, taking the body on his back, he threw it down a well out of sight. Then the Sultan quickly dressed himself in some of the magician's clothes and lay down on the bed. All the time, while he was doing these things, the Sultan could hear the wailing of the poor young King as the vile enchantress tormented him.

Presently the Sultan heard her come back. "Speak to me, Master!" she said. "Say that you are a little better. See, I have brought you delicious food and wine."

Upon this the Sultan answered in a muffled, peevish voice:

"I shall never be well, foolish woman, while you go on as you do!"

"Oh what joy to hear you speak again, dear Master!" she answered. "What more must I do?"

"You beat that husband of yours too much! His wailing and crying disturb me! If it had not been for this I should have been better long ago."

"O dear Master! Why did you not tell me this before?" she answered. "I will go at once and set him free."

Then the Sultan pretended to groan and said in a disagreeable voice:

"Go! And be quick about it! I am sick of his lamentations!"

So the enchantress went off immediately to where the poor young King sat helpless. She took water from the golden fountain, said words over it, and as she spoke her powerful words the water bubbled and seemed to boil as if a fire was under it. With this enchanted water she sprinkled the young King as she muttered the words of yet another spell, and, as she thus spoke and sprinkled, he was at once restored. But she did all this as unkindly as possible and, when he had struggled to his feet, she spoke bitterly to him, telling him to get out of her sight at once and threatening to kill him if he delayed a moment. Then she went back to where the pretended black magician still lay on his bed.

"Come out of the darkness, O my dear Master," said she in her softest voice, "so that I shall not only have the

joy of hearing your voice again, but may see with my own eyes that you are better!"

"How can I possibly get up?" said the disguised Sultan, again speaking in a disagreeable voice. "You have not done nearly enough! Why did you turn all the people of the city into fish? You do everything to torment me! Every night they raise their heads out of the water and call down curses upon me. How can I possibly get well? Go and take off that enchantment also! When you have done it, come back and take me by the hand. Perhaps then, I may really have the strength to get up, for already I feel a little better!"

Though the one she thought was her dear master spoke so peevishly, the wicked Queen was filled with joy at these words, and she went down at once to the lake. As soon as she had finished with her spells, the fish became men and women again, the lake became a city with market places

47

and streets, streams began to flow through the desert land, and the parched and withered grass began to grow green once more.

Then the enchantress came back.

"Everything has been done as you have commanded, Master!" said she, as she stretched out her hand to help him to rise; the Sultan, seizing it, sprang up and killed her with a single blow of his sword.

The young King, who had been waiting, came at the Sultan's shout of triumph, and they embraced each other and rejoiced because these two wicked creatures could now do no more harm. The young King called the Sultan his preserver and thanked him a thousand times.

"Come, then, to my city so that we may rejoice together!" said the Sultan. "It is only two days' journey away!"

"O Sultan!" replied the young King. "Your city is not two days' but a full year's journey distant! It was because of the enchantment that you were able to come here in two days. Nevertheless I will come, for in truth I cannot bear to stay in this black palace where I have suffered so much. Indeed I love you as a father, O my preserver!"

"And I," said the Sultan, "love you as a son. I never had a son of my own, but now Allah has given you to me!"

And so it was agreed. The young King and the Sultan travelled for a whole year, and as they travelled they spoke of many things.

SEE P. 53

Kafur tells his story to the merchant and to his household

"Why," asked the Sultan, "were the people of your city turned into fish of four colours?"

So the young King explained that the people of his city had been of four religions—Moslems, Christians, Jews and Fire-worshippers from Persia, who all lived peaceably together. The Moslems wore white turbans and thus doubtless became white fish, and so on. But who the damsel, or who the huge young black man who asked the fish "Are you faithful?" were he did not know.

At last they came near to the Sultan's city and the good Vizier, overjoyed, came out with a great retinue to meet him, praising Allah and rejoicing, for he had given up hope of ever seeing his master again.

At last when they had rested, and when all things were restored to order, the Sultan sent for the Fisherman.

"O Fisherman," said the Sultan, when he stood before the throne, "listen now to the extraordinary history of your fish!" And when he had told the tale he added, "You, O Fisherman, were the cause of the taking off of a terrible spell and of the restoration of a whole kingdom and of a thriving city, and it is, therefore, right that your reward should be great!"

4   49

So the Fisherman's daughter was married to the young King of the Black Mountains, who, declaring that he could never again live in the black palace, was now made the heir to the Sultan's kingdom, while the Fisherman's other children were promoted to posts of honour. The Fisherman himself was given a great treasure, so that he was soon the richest man in the Sultan's kingdom.

As for the faithful Vizier, he was sent to be King of the Black Mountains, and they all lived for many years in peace and prosperity.

THE HALF-LIE

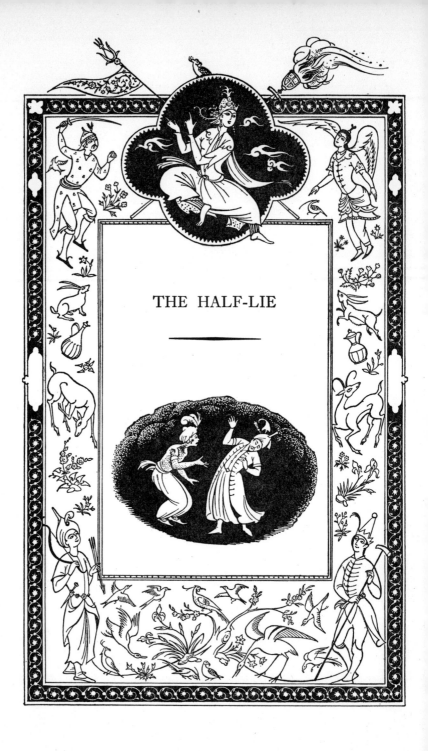

THE HALF-LIE

A MERCHANT WAS ONE DAY WALKING THROUGH the market in Cairo when he saw a negro slave for sale.

"How much is this slave?" he asked.

"Only six hundred pieces of silver," replied the slave dealer, "for he has a single fault."

"What's that?" said the merchant.

"Why," said the slave dealer, "he always tells one lie a year, and, if you buy him, you must put up with one lie each year."

Now the merchant loved a bargain. "Only one lie a year?" thought he. "That isn't much! Most slaves tell many more. So do I, for that matter." So he bought Kafur, as the slave was called, took him home and set him to work, and for some months all went well. Kafur was cheerful and obedient, and worked hard.

On New Year's Day the merchant and some of his friends rode out on their mules to a pretty flower garden a little way outside the city to celebrate. They took wine and fruit and sweet cakes with them, carpets to sit on, and musical instruments. Kafur went with them.

About midday the merchant said to Kafur, "Mount my mule and ride home. Ask my wife for more pistachio nuts and bring them back as fast as you can."

Kafur set off. But as he drew near the merchant's house he tore his clothes and began to howl out loud, "Oh, my master," he sobbed, "oh, my poor master! What will become of us all now?"

Many people—old and young—heard and gathered round him, and they all went along with him to his master's house. When the merchant's wife heard Kafur's cries and howls, and saw the crowd of people, she ran to the door.

"O mistress!" screamed the slave, the tears running down his face. "My poor master is dead! The old garden wall, in whose shade he was sitting with his friends, fell suddenly and killed them all!"

Then the merchant's wife wept too, and tore her clothes; and so did his daughters and all the women of the house, and all the women in the crowd ran in to comfort them. The merchant's wife ran through her home and, in sign of despair, she began breaking the windows and smashing the china—just to show how much she loved her husband, for that was how people often showed sorrow when the master of the house was dead.

"Come, Kafur, and help me mourn!" called out the merchant's wife, and between them they pulled down shelves, broke crockery, tore the rich hangings and smeared soot on the walls. Bang! went a blue and gold china coffee-pot upon the floor. Crash! and Kafur, with a

sob, hurled his master's precious coffee cups through the window. Smash! he threw a little ebony table inlaid with ivory after the coffee cups so that it broke in pieces in the courtyard, and all the while Kafur kept calling out, "Oh, my poor master! my poor master!"

Kafur and the merchant's wife tore the gold embroidered cushions and ripped up the divans. Kafur, with a great tug, pulled down the high shelves which ran round the kitchen just under the roof, and clatter bang! all the green and blue china and silver and gold bowls on them fell to the floor and broke.

Kafur worked with a will, and ran all over the house, till soon the whole place looked like a ruin, with broken china, soot and torn stuff everywhere.

"Now," said the merchant's wife, "let us go and fetch my poor husband's body!" So she ran out of the house, with all the women and slaves following her, and as they

went through the streets more and more people began to join in, while one of the neighbours made the crowd still bigger by running to tell the Governor of the city, who immediately sent workmen to the garden with picks and baskets to dig out the bodies.

Kafur ran in front of them all, still howling and weeping and crying out, "Oh, my poor master, my poor master!" Soon he had outdistanced all the others, so that he got first to the garden, with the huge crowd some way behind. Then, though he still howled and wept, he began to cry out:

"Oh woe, woe! Oh my mistress! My mistress! Who will care for me now?"

Soon his master, who was sitting peacefully with his friends, heard him.

"What's this?" said the merchant, standing up and looking very pale. "In Allah's name, what has happened?"

"Ah, Master," said Kafur, "when I reached your house I found that it had fallen down, and that everyone inside it had been killed."

"My wife?" said the merchant.

"Dead," cried Kafur.

"And the mule I loved to ride on?"

"Crushed, too," cried Kafur.

"And my son and my daughters?"

"All dead," cried Kafur. "And the sheep and the geese and the hens too! Cats and dogs are eating them even now."

Then the merchant beat his breast and tore his fine clothes. His friends, when they heard, wept too, and they all started off towards the city.

They had not gone far when, of course, they met the the merchant's wife and family, the huge crowd of neighbours and the workmen who had been sent by the Governor.

"Oh, my love, are you safe?" cried the merchant's wife.

"Oh, my life, how is it with you?" cried the merchant.

"Why, we are all right," said his wife. "But Kafur came weeping and with his clothes torn and told us the wall of the garden had fallen upon you as you feasted!"

"No!" said the merchant; "Kafur ran in here, weeping and crying, clothes torn and with dust on his head, and told us the house had fallen upon you and that you were all killed!"

Then they both turned on Kafur, who was still weeping and crying and beating his breast.

"How's this, you wretch?" said the merchant. "You black ill-omened son of the Evil One! You won't get off lightly, I can tell you! Just wait till we get home, and then you'll have a beating you won't forget."

"Oh no, master!" answered Kafur with a grin. "That would not be fair! You bought me cheap because I had one fault, and you said you would put up with the consequences of my telling one lie a year. So far this has only been half a lie! Before the end of the year I'll tell the other half."

The merchant was furious. But, all the same, all the bystanders agreed that it would not be fair for him to punish Kafur. But when he got home and found his house in such a state, and so much damage done, he remembered with horror that Kafur had talked about more lies before the year was out.

"Do you call all this only half a lie?"

"Yes, master!" said Kafur, grinning.

"Why, then, a whole lie of yours would wreck a city, or even two! You're not going to tell the other half here, I can tell you! I'd rather set you free! Be off out of my house at once!"

So Kafur became a free man, but he was a lazy fellow and knew no trade, and with no master to set him to work he lived as best he could as a beggar, and often went hungry.

SINDBAD THE SAILOR

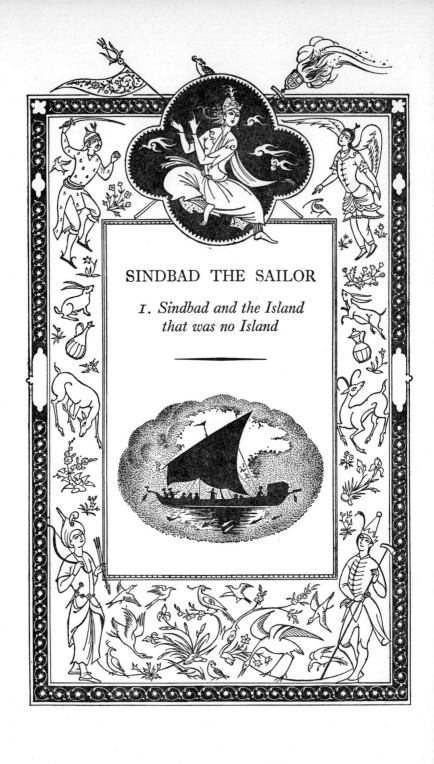

SINDBAD THE SAILOR

*1. Sindbad and the Island
that was no Island*

IN THE TIME OF HAROUN AL RASHID THE GLORIOUS, who was for long Caliph and Ruler over the Faithful, there stood in the city of Baghdad a house so fine and delightful that it was almost a palace. There was no dust before it, for here the way was always kept swept and watered. Through an archway that led in from the street could be seen, when the great doors were open, a garden full of shady trees from which came at all times the scent of flowers and the voices of turtle doves, nightingales and babbling water, and with these, at certain times, was mingled the sound of the lute and of voices singing.

Now this house stood on a narrow but busy street. Down this alley, in the burning heat, porters used to pass and repass all day long, carrying heavy loads of merchandise on their heads. Sometimes these porters used to stand resting for a while, looking in at the cool garden, thinking that some people have all the luck, and doubting whether the master, a handsome old man with streaks of silver in his beard, had ever known such toil and hardship as theirs.

On a certain day, when not only were there the sounds of lutes and singing but also the scent of the most delicious dishes from a feast which was going on in the garden, one of these poor porters set down his burden on a bench that stood outside, and leaning sadly in the archway began to make up some verses and murmur them to himself.

> "Allah made both of us, this man and me,
> Yet I must bear a heavy load
> While he goes free.
> Alas the diff'rence is like vinegar and wine!
> This lucky one has never borne a load like mine
> Or like me known the dust upon the road."

Hardly had he finished and, turning, with a sigh, had begun to take up his load again, when a handsome little page ran out from the garden and took him by the hand.

"O Porter, lay down your load. My Master calls for you!"

The master of the house and all the guests spoke kindly to the porter and made room for him at the feast. Rose-water was poured over his hands, which he wiped with a snow-white napkin. There were tender little birds wrap-ped in vine leaves. There were dishes of hot Indian curry, and others of cool dahl; there were sweet peppers stewed in curds. Even the rice was coloured red or green, and there were besides all kinds of sweetmeats and fragrant mint-tea. When he had eaten and drunk the master of the house addressed him in these words:

"O Porter, we heard your lamentation as you stood at the gate, but the thing is not as you suppose, for I too have known hunger, thirst, and toil and also much greater danger. Indeed my experiences have been very strange!"

Then all the guests assured the master of the house that no sound of lute, or fountain, or singing-bird would be sweeter to their ears than the story of his adventures.

So then Sindbad-of-the-Sea, or, as some call him, Sindbad-the-Sailor—for the master of that house was none other than that celebrated traveller—began to relate

his adventures, and they were so many and so strange that one evening was not enough, so that, not once, but many times, all who were at the feast that day met again in the cool garden to hear him. This was how Sindbad be-gan the story of his adventures.

My father was one of the richest merchants of all the city of Baghdad, but when he died I was still a heedless young man and it was not long before I had frittered away most of my fortune. I did not come to my senses till most of it had been wasted. However, I found that by selling my house and my farm-lands I had still enough money to buy merchandise—such things as bales of cloth and silk, fine carpets, brass-work and the like. With this merchandise I resolved to travel abroad and see if I could not perhaps mend my fortunes by selling it at a profit and at the same time see something of the world and its marvels.

So, one day, I and other merchants embarked on a ship with our goods. We sailed down the river to Basrah and then, putting out to sea, we traded prosperously from island to island and from shore to shore.

At last, after a long sea passage, we came to a small but pleasant island and, since we had been long cooped up on the ship, the captain, deciding to cast anchor, had the landing-planks put out and we all went ashore to stretch our legs. Some of the merchants and the sailors took with them washing-tubs and began to wash their clothes, some began to light fires to cook a meal, and some—of whom I was one—walked about to explore the island.

All at once there were shouts from the ship. "All aboard!" "In Allah's name! Quickly!" "Run for your lives!" "The Fish! The Fish!" shouted the sailors, and with that they began, in all haste, to heave short the anchor and then to pull in the landing-planks. Then we who were ashore felt that what had seemed to be the ground was shaking under us and I guessed that this was in truth no island but must be a gigantic fish on which, as it lay thus since times of old, sand and earth had gathered, and even trees had grown. But now the immense creature had felt the heat of the fires which we had lit upon its back. Still those who were in the ship shouted,

"Save yourselves! It will plunge to the bottom! Save yourselves!" So we all ran, leaving everything—food, cooking-pots, washtubs. Some reached the ship in time and some did not, and, in a moment more, the great fish plunged and, with a roar, the sea closed over the place where it had lain.

Alas, I was among those who had not time to reach the ship, and I sank in the sea with those who sank. But, by the mercy of Allah, when I rose to the surface again, I found, floating near me, the largest of the wooden troughs that some of the ship's company had used for washing. I seized it, managed to get astride of it and, tossed and buffeted by the waves, began, as well as I could, to paddle with my feet in the direction of the ship. But alas! In mortal fear lest the great fish should rise again, the captain had already ordered the sails to be hoisted. She was soon far away, I was unseen and my shouts were unheard, and before long her white sails were no more than a speck upon the waters.

SEE P. 64

Some reached the ship in time and others did not

When darkness covered the ocean I resigned myself to certain death and with the light of the next morning things seemed no better. But the wind or some current favoured me, and by the end of the next day I was in sight of another island with high cliffs, on which the waves broke and on which I supposed I and my washing-trough would be dashed to pieces. Yet Allah still favoured me, and I managed, more dead than alive, to haul myself out by means of the branches of some tall trees that hung clear of the breakers. It was with my last strength that, drenched and weary, I hauled myself out of the water and then let myself down from the branches to the ground. My legs were not only numb but bleeding from the nibbling of the small fish that had begun to attack me. Darkness was falling, I had no strength to go further, but lay all that night on the ground.

But next morning, when the sun rose, I found that I was not far from a spring of fresh water and from some trees that bore fruit, and, though my legs were still numb, I managed to crawl to them.

I remained thus, very miserable, for several days, but, my strength gradually returning, I began to walk about the island to see if I could find any sign of human inhabitants.

One day, as I thus walked on the shore in a part of the island far from where I had landed, I saw something in the distance that I took for a large wild animal or one of the great beasts of the sea. Walking towards it, I saw that it was no savage or dangerous brute but a beautiful mare, which moved quietly about cropping the grass. She did not see me and I came closer. Suddenly she caught sight of me and, startled, gave a loud neigh; this startled me in my turn, so that I took to my heels in terror, when, right in my path, I saw a man who seemed to have risen out of the earth.

"Who are you? What are you doing here?" he asked.

"Sir," I answered, "I am an unhappy stranger, a ship-wrecked voyager, a castaway!"

Then the strange man looked kindly at me, took me by the hand, led me to the cave from which he had appeared so suddenly and gave me food. When I had eaten, my soul became more at ease, and, when he questioned me, I told him all my adventures from first to last. When I had finished I begged him to tell me why he was living in this cave and to whom the beautiful mare belonged.

"I am," he answered, "one of the grooms of the great king Mahrajan and from time to time we bring the swiftest and most beautiful of his mares to rest and pasture for a while in this wild and solitary place. We shall soon be returning to the city, when I shall take you to our King and show you our country. Allah be praised that I found you, for otherwise you would have died in misery, none knowing that you were here!"

Upon this I called down blessings upon him, and that night I slept in his cave. Next day I awoke to find that more grooms had assembled from other pastures. They began to collect all the mares and—setting me on one of the most beautiful—they all mounted and we began our journey to the court of King Mahrajan.

When the King had been informed of how his grooms had found a castaway, he sent for me and, having heard my story, he also praised Allah for the mercy he had shown me, treated me with kindness and honour, and soon made me Comptroller of Shipping at his largest and most prosperous sea-port. Here it was my duty to enquire the names of the captains and the nature of the cargoes of every vessel that put in for trade and to give an account of them to the King. I used, of course, also, for my own sake, to ask the sailors and merchants of every ship if any on board had ever heard of the city of Baghdad or in which direction it lay. But alas! No one knew anything of Baghdad, the City of Peace! None knew of any ship which had ever traded there.

For a long while I continued in favour with the King and with his subjects. I earned the goodwill of the humble because I was always ready to tell the King of their troubles, and of the King and the merchants because I was honest in my dealings.

Indeed for one like me, who had determined to see the world and hear more of its marvels, it was a fine place. One day I would find that the King had in the palace a party of merchants from India, who told me of their country and of the seventy-two races and sects that inhabit it. Another day it would be a party of sailors who told me of strange islands. There was one such not far off, they said, where, all night long, could be heard wild cries and fiendish laughter with a beating of drums and the clash of tambourines.

Many strange things I saw for myself; for example, a fish two hundred cubits long and another with a head like an owl. But, with all this, I began to long for my own city.

One day, when I chanced to feel particularly sad, because there seemed no end to my absence from Baghdad, I happened to be standing on the wharf, leaning on my staff and gazing out to sea. As I looked, I saw a ship which appeared to have a large company of merchants on board and which was making for the harbour with a fair wind. Seeing her come in and that the sails were being furled and that landing-planks were being made ready, I came near, as was my duty as comptroller of the port. I brought out my register and, as the crew landed the merchandise, I began to enter it up. When they seemed to have done I turned to the captain and asked if everything had now been brought ashore.

"Not quite all, my master; I still have some goods in the hold, but the owner of them was drowned during our voyage. Take note of them separately, for I must sell them here and then take back the price to his family."

"And where did this drowned-one live?" I asked.

"In Baghdad, the City of Peace," answered the captain.

"What was the merchant's name?" I asked.

"Sindbad," answered the captain, and when I looked more closely at him I recognized him.

"Do you not know me?" I cried. "I am Sindbad! By the mercy of Allah I was cast up on this island, where I found favour with the King and became chief clerk of this port. These goods are my only possessions."

But the captain grew angry at my words.

"Is there no longer faith or honesty in man?" he cried. "By Allah! Just because you heard me say that I had goods whose owner was drowned, you are trying this mean trick so as to get them without paying!"

It was long before this honest captain and his sailors, who soon crowded round, would believe that this was no trick but the truth. "We saw him sink! We saw him sink!"

they all kept repeating. But I told them so many things about our former voyage —events from the day we left Basrah till we cast anchor on the island-that-was-no-island—that at last the captain and the others believed me. Then they all rejoiced and embraced me kindly.

"Allah," they said, "has granted you a new life!" Then the captain gave me the goods, and I found my name written on them, and so honest had he been that nothing was missing. So then and there I opened the best of my bales and selected a costly gift. The sailors helped me to carry it to the King and I offered it to him as a present, begging his leave to return home. The King was pleased at this end to a strange story and gave me a still larger present in return. The rest of my goods I soon sold at a profit and, with the money, bought the finest products of the island and with much joy re-embarked in my old ship.

Fortune served us, destiny helped us, so at last I found myself once more in my own city—and once more a rich man.

I soon forgot all that I had suffered and, once more, as I had as a youth, spent my time in feasting and pleasure.

To-morrow, if Allah wills, I will tell you of yet stranger adventures.

2. *Sindbad and the Valley of Diamonds*

AFTER A WHILE I BEGAN TO FEEL THAT I HAD HAD enough of this idle life of pleasure.

 Instead I began to think of the yet greater pleasures of seeing strange lands, peoples whose ways were new to me, and all the marvels with which Allah has filled the world.

So I shut up my house and, once more, I bought goods for trade. This time I sailed down the Tigris in a small river-boat with my merchandise to Basrah and there chanced to find a fine new sea-going vessel which was about to put to sea. She had new sails, a good crew and a pleasant company of merchants and, on the master agreeing, my goods were immediately stowed in her hold, I myself stepped aboard and we were soon off.

We had a pleasant voyage, calling at this island and that, and at each port at which we landed we met the merchants and grandees, the sellers and the buyers. And so, as we went, we increased our knowledge of the world, our honour and our profit.

At last we sighted a pleasant island, on which, as we sailed nearer, there seemed to be an abundance of fresh water, trees, fruit, flowers and singing-birds, but on which we could see no sign of human inhabitants.

We had been long at sea and, the master anchoring our ship, we all went ashore to get fresh water and to amuse ourselves with the sound of the birds, the sight of the trees and the murmurings of the brooks.

I had taken a little food with me and, having eaten and finding myself by a murmuring stream, I lay down upon the grass and, alas! was soon overcome by sleep. How long I slept I know not, but when I awoke it was to find myself utterly alone. My forgetful shipmates had sailed away without me! Not one of them had remembered me! Racing to the shore, I saw that there was no further hope. The ship was now only a speck on the vast blue of that lonely sea.

Overcome by despair, I threw myself down upon the sand. Once more I was a castaway and utterly alone. I remembered the proverb which says, "The jar that drops a second time is sure to break!" I blamed myself for my folly not only in going to sleep, but in leaving Baghdad at all. I thought of my wretched plight—for a second time without food or goods, for I had, alas! left everything upon the ship. I imagined, too, that the island might be the haunt of wild beasts or savages; indeed I was soon almost mad with despair.

At last, when I had recovered a little, I climbed up a tree to see if I could see anything more than the loneliness around me. But there seemed to be nothing but sky and sea, sand and trees, rocks and springs of water, and all I could hear was the cry of birds and the murmur of the wind as it gently swayed the branches of the trees.

But at last I thought that I could see, indistinctly through the trees, something different, something smooth and white. But, not being able to tell if it was large and far away, or near and small, I could not even guess what it might be.

Climbing down from my tree, I went cautiously towards this unknown thing and found to my astonishment that what I had seen was an enormous white dome, almost

71

as high as the dome of a mosque but resting on the ground.

I walked round it but could find no door, and it was so smooth that to climb it would clearly have been impossible. I made a mark in the sand at the place where I stood and, walking round the dome once more, found that I had walked fifty paces before I came to my mark again.

Now it was evening, but the sun had not yet set, but, as I stood, the evening light was suddenly darkened as if by a great cloud. I looked up and, to my amazement, saw a great bird hovering above me, and judged that it must be this bird's gigantic wings and enormous body that had darkened the sky.

Then I remembered a story which had long ago been told me by travellers. They said that in certain islands there lived gigantic birds called Rocs—so large that they feed their young on elephants. The dome before me must, I thought, be the egg of a Roc and the shadow above me must be the shadow of a Roc.

And now, as I stood wondering, lo! the giant bird alighted, so that it straddled the dome and, stretching out its legs on either side, seemed to brood over it with its huge wings and body much as a hen will brood over her clutch of eggs. Soon the bird, which had fortunately not seen me, seemed to sleep.

I stood there watching, and as I watched I thought to myself that this bird might perhaps have flown from far. Who knows, I thought, how far this great creature flies by day to find food? It may be that she goes to some other land where there are men and cities. Then, murmuring the name of Allah, who never sleeps, I made my resolve. I unwound my turban, folding and twisting it so that it became like a rope. I bound this rope securely round my

waist and then, as gently as I could, tied myself on to one of the great legs of the sleeping bird.

All night long I waited, keeping as still as I could, not daring to sleep, but holding on fast to her leg. At daybreak (when, as I supposed, she knew that the sun would once more warm it) the Roc rose from her egg, and with a terrible cry and a tremendous clapping of her enormous wings, she rose into the air. Up she soared, higher and higher, till it seemed to me that we must touch the sky. At last, after a long time, I could feel that the direction of our flight was downward, and she alighted. No sooner had she touched ground than I untied my turban from her leg, which was as thick as the beam of a house, for, though she seemed not to have felt my weight or to have known that I was there, I was so much afraid of her that I longed to get away. Indeed, once loose, I trembled so that I had scarcely strength to hide. No sooner was I hidden than I noticed that the great bird was looking this way and that, as smaller birds look for worms. Soon she darted off towards a great, black, long, coiling thing which lay near. Then I saw that this was an enormous, wicked-looking serpent! The Roc now seized the huge creature in her claws and with a great clapping of wings flew away with it.

As soon as she had gone I began to look about me and saw that I was in a desert place and on a steep slope. On one side towered a mountain which seemed as steep as a sea-cliff but very high, while below lay a wide, deep valley. The sun began to burn, there was no water, there were no trees, all seemed desert.

I blamed myself yet again and wished that I had stayed on the island, and I thought with despair how, every time I escaped from one danger, I seemed only to run into a worse.

However, since the mountain seemed unclimbable, I decided to go down into the valley, and what was my amazement when I got there to see that the whole ground seemed to be thick, not with common stones, but with the most splendid diamonds! But this was not all. Unfortunately the enormous and hideous serpent which the Roc had carried off was, it appeared, only one of thousands; the whole valley seemed to crawl with them as they made off to the caves in which they hid during the day. In a little while, indeed, every small hole seemed to hold a hissing snake, and every cave seemed to hide a serpent so big that it could have swallowed an elephant. "By Allah!" I said to

myself, "of what use are these diamonds to me? For my destruction is certain!"

All day I wandered without food or drink and watched how certain birds swooped and flew in the hot sky, spying out for any snake or serpent that had not yet hidden itself. These were birds not so great as the Roc, but greater than any eagle or vulture that I had ever seen, and it seemed to me that they all watched me and only waited for my death. So, most miserably, I spent all that day and, when night fell and the serpents came out once more, I found a cave and, thinking that if any serpent had it for a home, now that night had come it would at least be empty, I took refuge in it. Alas, it was indeed the home of serpents and I soon saw that one of them lay at the back, brooding her eggs. At this my hair stood on end for fear. But I dared not go out and so, the great and hideous serpent not moving, I spent the night there. Once again I dared not sleep, so that, when day dawned, what with sleeplessness, hunger and thirst, I tottered out more dead than alive.

As I walked along the valley where, once more, the splendid diamonds that lay all around shone in the light of the newly risen sun, I came near the steep cliffs of the mountain. Suddenly from these cliffs there fell right in front of me the skinned carcass of half a sheep. I wondered greatly at the sight, looked round, but could see no one. Then I remembered a story that I had been told long before by a traveller.

This man had told me that certain diamond-merchants who traded in India were in the habit of getting diamonds by a very strange trick. Unable to climb down into the Valley of Diamonds because of the steepness of the cliffs and the danger from the serpents, their trick was to climb the mountains above, slaughter a sheep, skin it, and then, from the cliffs, throw down joints of the meat still moist and fresh, so that some of the diamonds were sure to stick to them. By and by one of the great birds, which have their nests in the mountains, would swoop down on the meat and, taking it up, fly up to their nests with it. Whereupon the merchants would, with cries and a great beating of gongs, sticks and cooking-pots, scare away the birds. Then, before the birds could fly back, the merchants would quickly pick out the diamonds and leave the meat for the birds as they came back.

No sooner had I remembered this story than I thought of a plan of escape. Quickly filling my pockets and every fold in my clothes with the finest diamonds that I could see, I soon found another and a larger slaughtered beast. Taking off my turban, I once more twisted it into a rope, lay down on my back, shifted the carcase of meat on to my chest, and tied it on firmly with my turban-rope. I had not long to wait before one of these immense vultures, swooping down, grasped the meat firmly in its claws and, seeming not to notice my weight, flew soaring into the air. Alighting on the top of the great mountain, it was just about to make a meal of the meat when suddenly, from a nearby rock, there was a great shouting, clamour and banging of sticks, whereupon the startled bird flew off.

As quickly as I could I untied my rope and, soaked with blood from the meat, stood up. I know not which was the more frightened, I or the merchant who had thrown down the meat! He now began cautiously to come forward from behind his rock. He knew there was no time to waste, for the vulture would come back. Turning over his meat, he found not a single diamond, so, uttering a loud cry, he beat his breast and looked at me.

"O Heavy Loss! Allah defend us all from the power of the Evil One! Who are you? Why are you here?"

We moved off together and I soothed him as well as I could, telling him I was neither a devil nor a robber and offering him some of my diamonds.

"Accept them, I beg of you, for they are, I am sure, better than those which, but for me, might have been sticking to your meat!"

Soon, hearing voices, other merchants, who had also thrown down meat, came up with us and all were astonished at seeing me there. I told them that I had diamonds enough for them all but was now giddy and almost fainting for hunger, thirst and lack of sleep. So, without more questioning, they took me to their encampment, offered me no violence, but treated me hospitably. When I had eaten, drunk and slept a little I told them my tale; they were so pleased and astonished that they would hardly accept the splendid diamonds which I offered to them, though in truth I had enough to make us all rich.

So, when I had done, we all thanked Allah for his great mercies and they told me that, up to that time, no one had ever set foot in the Valley of Diamonds and come out alive.

Then again I slept in their tents for many hours. Next day we all set out and, though we had yet more mountains to cross, and though we saw many serpents and many still stranger sights, yet each night they contrived so well that we always pitched our tents in some safe and convenient place.

So at last, after a long but prosperous journey, we came again to the cities of men and the shores of the sea. I and the other merchants traded our diamonds at great profit, so that, when at last, crossing the sea, we came first to Basrah and then to Baghdad—the City of Peace—I was yet richer than at any former time.

3. Sindbad and The Old-Man-of-the-Sea

WHEN I BEGAN AGAIN TO BE WEARY OF THE PLEASURES of the shore and of its idleness, I still had ample money and I decided that this time I would buy a ship of my own, hire a captain and crew to work and navigate her, and let other merchants join me and pay me their passage money. There would like this be no chance, I thought, that I should be left behind on some island. No captain forgets his owner! So, at Basrah, I bought a fine new ship well equipped in every way, with tall masts and new sails.

Once more the beginning of the voyage was prosperous and, as before, I and the other merchants traded from port to port and from island to island and talked with men of many strange lands, hearing marvels and telling our own adventures.

One day we found ourselves near a large, uninhabited island and here I caught sight among the trees of something that I had seen once before—a white dome almost as

big as the dome of a mosque but lying on the ground. I, of
course, knew at once that this was the egg of a Roc. As the
island seemed pleasant, the passengers begged leave to
land. To this the captain and I agreed, but having some
business on board, I, unfortunately, did not land with
them. As soon as they were ashore they, too, caught sight

of the strange white dome. Not knowing what it was—not
knowing that at sunset that fearful bird would come back
to her egg—they began, just for sport, to throw stones at it
and to batter it. It was not long before it broke, so that
they saw the young Roc inside—almost ready to hatch.
The passengers were delighted and, then and there deter-
mining to have a feast, they lit fires, cut up the huge young
bird and, coming back to the ship for cooking-pots, called
out to me:

"Oh Sir! Come and see what we have found! The dome

was a great egg, which we have broken, and inside we have found a young bird almost ready to hatch. We are just about to cook it. Come and join the feast!"

At this I cried out in horror!

"We are all lost!" I cried. And I told them how at sunset, which was then not far off, one or perhaps both of the parent birds would be sure to come back. "They will be enraged to find what you have done!"

So I called out that we must now push off immediately. Scarcely had they begun to return to the ship when, as before, the sky was darkened and, this time, not one, but two Rocs appeared above us—circling before flying home to their egg.

"All aboard!" I cried, and they, too, were filled with fear. As the captain and crew began in all haste to bring in the landing-planks and weigh the anchor, we saw how the Rocs, flying low, had seen that their egg had been broken and their young one killed. With dreadful screams the great birds wheeled up again into the sky. With all speed we set the sails for the open sea. But too late! Once more the sky was darkened and the most fearful cries filled the air and we saw that both birds had begun to chase us and that each held a great boulder in its claws.

SEE P. 76

Seeming not to notice my weight the immense bird soared

The cock bird—the larger of the two—flying directly above us dropped his boulder, but the Captain, by clever steering, managed to make a quick turn which kept us clear, so that the boulder dropped beside us instead of on us. But so heavy was it that the great splash with which it fell almost swamped us. Then the hen bird dropped her boulder, and this one hit our stern so that the rudder flew into twenty pieces and a great hole was torn in the ship's planking, so that she immediately began to sink. Those who had not already been crushed by the boulder sank with her, and of these I was one, so that the dark and bitter waters closed over my head. But, as before, when I came to the surface again Allah was merciful to me. This time it was not a washing-trough, but one of the stout planks of the broken ship that was floating near me.

It was now almost dark and I passed a wretched night clinging as best I could to this plank, but fortunately the sea was calm and, when daylight came, I found that I had drifted in sight of another island. I paddled towards it as well as I could and crawled up upon an open beach.

After a while, although my fine new ship and all my goods were lost and my captain, crew and fellow-merchants drowned, I began to recover a little and determined to find out what sort of a place it was upon which Allah, in his mercy, had cast me.

I soon found that this was an island as beautiful as Paradise. Its trees bore ripe fruits, its rivers flowed between banks of flowers and the sound of singing-birds mingled with the murmur of many streams. So all that day I wandered about, refreshing myself with the fruits and at night I slept on a grassy bank. But all this while I saw neither man nor any sign of man.

Next morning, though I was still weary and disheartened, I resolved to see more of this land, for it seemed like a lovely garden, except that it was solitary. After a while I came to the bank of a small river, and on the bank I saw sitting a strange-looking old man. He seemed to be either ill or very feeble and to be clothed only in leaves. I thought that he might perhaps be another castaway and, seeing his sad looks and guessing that he was not only old but weak, I went up to him and wished him peace in the name of Allah. But he only replied to my greeting by a mournful nod. I began to question him, but soon supposed that he did not understand the language in which I spoke, for, to all I said, he only replied by signs. Presently I began to believe that he had a request and that this was that I should take him up on my shoulders and carry him across the little river.

Now Allah rewards those who do kindness, especially to the old and weak, so making signs that I understood him, I bent down and lifted him so that he sat on my shoulders, and was a little surprised to find him heavier than I had imagined. However, I waded across the stream with him. When we reached the other side I bent again, signing to him that he should now get down.

But, instead of slipping to the ground, the old monster wound his legs tightly round my neck. I again made signs as well as I could, thinking that he had not understood. Then I glanced at his legs as they clung more and more tightly round my neck and saw, to my horror, that they were not like the legs of an old man but as rough as the hide of a buffalo. The sight of them frightened me, so now I tried with might and main to throw him off. At this the old wretch only clung the tighter and now began to squeeze my throat so hard with his hands that soon I could no longer breathe, I felt that I was becoming dizzy, the world grew black in front of my eyes, and at last I fell to the ground.

And even now he would not let me be! Loosening his legs a little, he began to beat me over the head and I soon found that he had not only the weight but the strength of a young man. Once more I tried to get rid of him, once more this only made him cling more tightly so that I was almost choked. All this time he never said a word, but only beat me, exactly as a cruel rider might beat a horse. When he got me up again he soon began to force me to go in whatever direction he chose by pointing with his hands and then pressing with his legs.

I found that what he wanted was to make me walk under the trees on which grew the best and ripest fruits. Here the old wretch, sitting at his ease, high on my back, picked and ate as much as he wanted, but scarcely gave me a moment to get some too. If I disobeyed his signs or went too slowly, he would kick and beat me with his arms or his feet and legs so that I could hardly bear the pain.

All that day, weary as I was, I had to carry him and, when darkness came, he made me lie down with him, but the old monster only slept a little and never once loosed his hold, and now and then would kick me up again so that I had to stumble wearily along in the darkness.

"By Allah," I said to myself, "is being a slave to this old monster my reward for a good deed? I will never do good to any one again as long as I live!" It seemed to me that nothing that I had hitherto suffered had ever been so detestable as carrying this filthy old wretch!

After many days and nights of this miserable slavery I happened one day to come upon an open grassy place where many pumpkins grew. Some of these were dry, so I took up a large one, cut a hole at the top and cleaned it out. Presently, coming to a place where vines grew, I picked some of the ripe grapes and squeezed their juice into the now empty pumpkin. I then stopped up the hole at the top and put the pumpkin to lie in the sun. Coming that way again after a few days, I found that, just as I had hoped, the grape juice had fermented so that I now had a pumpkinful of strong and excellent wine.

Every day I used to come to this place again and drink a little of the wine, and this helped me to endure the misery of carrying my heavy monster of a master. Sometimes, indeed, when I had drunk a little I would almost forget my misery and my feet would move more quickly, so that he beat me less. The old wretch began, I suppose, to notice that my seeming more nimble and cheerful had had something to do with the pumpkin, for one day he put out his hand as if to take it from me, though I managed to put it out of his reach. Then, a trick coming into my mind, I began to pretend to be drunk and to dance and sing, and what I sang was the praise of wine. All this, of course, made him—as I had intended—want more than ever to taste what must, he thought, have been a magic potion. Next day, though making pretence of trying to keep the pumpkin for myself, I let him have it, and then the greedy old monster, instead of only taking a sip or two, drank all that was left in the pumpkin at one gulp. Now this wine, which had been at the bottom, was the strongest part, and soon he began to sway about on my shoulders and to make a noise as if he, too, were trying to sing. Soon his horrible legs began to go slack and I could feel that they were beginning to loose their hold. Now was my chance. Sitting down quickly, putting my hands under his feet and at the same time giving a violent jerk to my shoulders, I found that I was at last free!

As I saw the hideous creature lying senseless on the ground, bloated and filthy, my heart was filled with hatred for him and his vile ingratitude, and (partly also for fear of what he might do on waking) I took up the first stone I could find, and with it I battered in his wicked skull.

So that was the end of my tormentor! May Allah have no mercy on his soul (if he had one!).

For some days I was happy in my new freedom, for now I could roam as I liked, sleep when I liked, eat and drink of the delicious fruits and excellent water whenever I had a mind to. I had indeed hardly begun to long for human company again when, sitting one day on the shore, I saw a ship which seemed to be making towards the beach on which I was sitting.

Soon she had furled her sails and dropped her anchor, and the passengers and sailors began to come ashore with empty water-casks. When I ran down to meet them, they all gathered round me in surprise at seeing anyone on what they believed to be an uninhabited island and, soon, they were offering me all sorts of kindnesses.

When they heard my tale they told me that it was indeed a marvel that I had escaped.

85

"Know that the monster who rode on your shoulders was none other than The-Old-Man-of-the-Sea and that you are the first that ever escaped him. Praise be to Allah that you have been the means of destroying such a wretch!"

Giving me food and clothing, they took me with them in their ship and we set sail.

One more adventure I had before I again reached my home in Baghdad—the City of Peace—and if this adventure had not happened I should, this time, have returned a poor man for, as I have told, my goods, as well as my fine new ship, had been lost. But this adventure was the means of profit for me.

I had now no goods with which to trade, and though, no doubt, the excellent captain of the ship which had rescued me would have given me my passage home for nothing, he could not do this, for the ship was outward bound in quite another direction. So they could do no more for me than leave me at their next friendly port. So now, when the ship which had rescued me had left me ashore and had sailed on her way, I found myself wandering about the streets of a strange city trying to find some work in order to gain enough money for a passage home.

As I walked, I fell in with an excellent man who asked me what trade I knew. I told him that, unfortunately, having been a merchant all my life, I knew no skill such as that of tin-smith or leather-worker, or carpenter, or indeed any other trade by which I could now earn money. At that I began to lament, for it seemed to me that it would be hard for me even to live, and still harder to earn enough to be able to return to Baghdad.

When this good stranger saw that I longed for home and was heavy with sadness he thought a while. Presently he left me, telling me to wait, went to his house and came back with a large strongly made cotton bag, which he gave me.

"Take this bag, O my brother!" said he. "Go to the beach and half fill it with pebbles. In the morning you will see many men of this city, each with just such a bag of pebbles, and you will see that they go out of the city towards the forest. Go with them and do as they do."

I wondered at his words, took the bag and thanked him in the name of Allah.

Next morning it was just as he had said. Many men of the city had collected, each with a strong cotton bag half full of pebbles. The man who had given me my bag was there and said to the others:

"This man is a penniless stranger. Consent to take him with you and teach him what he must do, so that he may perhaps gain money enough to reach his home. If he does, those who help him will certainly gain a reward from Allah who—being merciful—loves those who show mercy." So they agreed and I went with them.

After walking for some time through the forest we came to a wide valley full of tall trees. Now these trees were very high and they had smooth trunks with not a single branch, and at their very top, which swayed in the wind, grew a great head of leaves.

Now we were many and we had not been silent as we went, nor had we crept quietly as hunters do, so that, as we walked, some talking, others singing, the many beasts, such as apes and monkeys, that lived in the forest had been frightened and had swung along in front of us, chattering and jumping from tree to tree. When we came to the tall trees all these apes and monkeys had climbed up to their tops. Then the men opened their cotton bags and began to pelt the apes with the pebbles. The apes became furious and soon, in their turn, began to pelt us. Then I looked to see what it was that the apes were throwing down. I saw that they were coconuts. So then I made haste and chose a great tree, on which many apes had taken refuge, and I did as the others did, pelting them with the pebbles I had brought, and they did as the other apes had done and pelted me with coconuts. Soon my large cotton bag was full of splendid nuts and, the others having also filled their bags in this way, we all went back to the city well satisfied.

I began to look for the kind stranger who had lent me the bag and who had persuaded the others to let me go with them, and when I found him I thanked him and would have given him all my coconuts. But he courteously refused them, saying that they were all for me and, instead, gave me the key of a little outhouse he had. Here he told me to store the best of my nuts, to sell the rest in the market, and next morning to go out again with the others.

The kindness and goodness of this man—may Allah reward him—was the means of my gaining not only enough money to pay the captain of an excellent ship to take me home, but also to get merchandise in the town where I was, and with this and a fine stock of my best coconuts I was able to set sail.

And so, once more, I was a merchant among merchants, exchanging my coconuts at one island for cinnamon, at another for pepper, at a third for Chinese and Comarin aloes, and at a fourth for pearls. All this I did at a good profit, so that when at last I reached home I was once more a rich man.

4. Sindbad and the Caliph's Command

AT LAST THE TIME CAME WHEN, COUNTING THEM UP, I found that I had made no less than six of these long and dangerous voyages. In each I had experienced, not only one, but often two or three extraordinary adventures. Once I was almost roasted and eaten for supper by a great black giant as tall as a palm-tree, whose teeth were as long as a boar's tusks, whose ears hung over his shoulders, and whose eyes shone like coals. I had been obliged to see him roast and eat several of my shipmates and had only saved myself by putting out his eyes and then, with much difficulty, had managed to escape his blind hands as he tried to catch me.

Another time I and all my shipmates were made prisoners by black apes, and once, having lived prosperously for some time in a fine city, I had been obliged to go to my own funeral, when having married a wife there who died, by a strange law of that land I was buried alive in a dismal cavern. Once I had managed to escape by making a raft hardly wider than a coffin, on which I had been carried at great speed and in total darkness round the narrow windings of a swift underground stream. When this stream reached daylight again I had seen that I was in worse danger, for it was about to dash with me down a fearful precipice. Fainting with terror, I had only been pulled out, just in time, by the kind hand of a stranger.

Now, in the course of the last of these adventures, I had found myself a castaway on the coast of the rich and beautiful island which is called Ceylon. Here I was taken before the King, who was an excellent ruler and who took pleasure in learning about the world. He listened with pleasure to the stories of all these adventures, showed me favour, and asked me, after I had told him my story, to tell him also about my own city, Baghdad.

I told him that it was a splendid city and that it was ruled over by the most splendid of rulers, the great Caliph who was named Haroun Al Rashid The Magnificent, and whose excellence I praised. After he heard me, the King of Ceylon soon determined to fit out a ship for me in order that he might send, by my hand, a letter and costly presents to his brother ruler, the Caliph. And so, in much honour, having carefully packed away his gifts and letter, I kissed the ground before the King of Ceylon and set sail. I had a prosperous voyage home.

The letter was sealed, but I knew that the presents were

magnificent. There were bundles of precious aloe-wood, a magnificent bed set with jewels such as emeralds and diamonds, and, most beautiful of all, a cup a span high that seemed to be made of a single ruby and whose golden stem was embossed with enormous pearls.

And so, having reached Baghdad, I went before the Caliph, delivered the presents from the King of Ceylon and his letter, kissed the ground before the Caliph, and returned to my own house and, this time, I resolved to adventure no more.

"Allah is merciful," said I to myself, "but he may not always deliver me! I am growing past the prime of life and have seen many wonders. What has happened is enough!"

And with that I determined to pass the rest of my life in tranquillity in Baghdad—the City of Peace.

One day, as I was sitting at ease in my garden, there came a knocking at the outer gate. My doorkeeper opened and one of the Caliph's beautiful young pages appeared.

"The Commander of the Faithful has ordered me to fetch you into his presence, O my Master," said the boy, bowing courteously.

"To hear is to obey," I answered.

When I had kissed the ground before the Caliph he told his attendants to make a place for me on the steps of the throne, and motioning for a scribe to come near he said:

"Hear, O Sindbad, the letter of the King of Ceylon."

Now the letter was written on the fairest parchment and the writing was in blue and the whole letter was sweetly scented and dusted with gold.

Then the scribe read:

"Peace be on thee, O Prince and Caliph! This greeting is from the King of Ceylon, before whom stand a thousand elephants and on the battlements of whose palace are a thousand jewels, and who is obeyed by countless princes and warriors."

"Stop!" said the Caliph to the scribe and, turning to me, he asked, "Is this true, O Sindbad?"

"It is true, most mighty Prince," answered I.

Then the Caliph motioned to the scribe to read again.

"We have sent thee some trifling presents. Accept them from a brother and sincere friend. The presents are not suited to thy great dignity, but we beg of thee, O brother! to accept them graciously, and to favour us with a reply and an acceptance of our friendship."

Then the Caliph motioned away the scribe and began to question me about this King of Ceylon and if what he said about his power, riches, and also his good intentions, was true.

"O my Lord," I answered, "this King is truly mighty! Whenever he comes out from his palace a throne is set for him on the back of a gigantic elephant. All his chamberlains and servants carry staffs of gold and the chief of these have, at the top of their staffs, emeralds so big that a man could scarcely grasp one in his hand. This King has a guard of a thousand horsemen who wear silk. His crown is of a splendour surpassing even the crown of Solomon the Great. Also he is a wise ruler. Indeed, he has long ruled his people so well that there is no need of judges in his cities, for the people themselves know truth from lies."

At last the Caliph said:

"Then it is plain that this letter must have an answer, and also that I must find means to send presents in return to this wise and magnificent king. Is it not so, O Sindbad?"

"The Caliph speaks well," I answered, and with that the Caliph dismissed me.

But he soon sent for me again, and when I had kissed the ground before him he said:

"Sindbad, I have a task for you! Will you do it?"

I answered respectfully:

"What task has the master for his slave?"

"I desire," said he, "that you should go to this King of Ceylon with our letter and our presents."

At that I trembled and said:

"By Allah the Merciful, O my Lord! I wish that you had ordered anything else! For I have taken a hatred to voyaging because of the many troubles, dangers and horrors that I have lived through. Indeed, my Lord, I have even bound myself with an oath never to leave Baghdad again!"

The Caliph was astonished and began to question me. But the time was not then long enough to tell him all my adventures as I have told them here, so that he sent for me again several times. At last, when I had told them the Caliph was still more astonished and said to me:

"The Mercy of Allah is great! Such marvels have never been heard since times of old! I understand your wish! May the word 'travel' never be mentioned in your hearing again! And yet, for my sake, O Sindbad, go out yet once more! Take my letter and presents to this great king and, if Allah wills, you shall return quickly and in honour. For it is not right that we in Baghdad should have this debt of honour and courtesy."

So I prostrated myself and answered only:

"To hear is to obey!"

So, with a heavy heart, I began to make ready to do as he ordered, and the Caliph sent me the presents and the

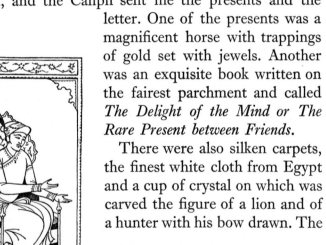

letter. One of the presents was a magnificent horse with trappings of gold set with jewels. Another was an exquisite book written on the fairest parchment and called *The Delight of the Mind or The Rare Present between Friends.*

There were also silken carpets, the finest white cloth from Egypt and a cup of crystal on which was carved the figure of a lion and of a hunter with his bow drawn. The

Caliph also provided me with a fine ship, with her captain, crew, and splendid provisions.

We had a prosperous voyage. When we landed in Ceylon, and when I kissed the ground before the King, he gave me a friendly welcome and presently asked:

"What is the cause of your coming again, O Sindbad?"

So I answered that this time I brought him a letter and presents from my master the Caliph, Commander of the Faithful, and when the slaves had brought in the presents and he had read the letter, the King of Ceylon was greatly pleased. In his delight he dressed me in robes of honour and treated me with the utmost friendliness.

After a few days I begged leave to go home, thanking him for all his kindness but urging my age and the many years that I had spent in travel and my longing to spend the end of my days in my own city. So, though the King pressed me to stay, yet in the end he gave me leave to go. So I set foot once more on board ship and we hoisted sail, and I prayed to Allah that our voyage home might be as swift as our voyage out, for now I had no more desire to trade or to see wonders!

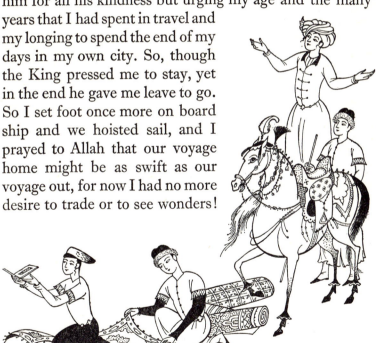

But alas! After sailing for several days with a prosperous wind and that wind continuing, suddenly our ship was surrounded by boats full of armed men—very demons they seemed and, if their hands were not full of bows and arrows, then they were full of spears, swords, or daggers. Those of us who tried to fight they killed and, having captured our ship, they turned her about and took the rest of us to a city they had nearby. Here they at once sold all those who were unwounded in the market place, but, because there was much treasure in our ship, the wretches did not even trouble to get a good price for us.

I was not as unlucky as some, for I was bought by a rich man and he took me to his house, gave me food and drink and, for a day or two, did not set me to any work. At last he sent for me and asked if I had any skill or knew any art or how to make anything.

"O my Lord," said I, "I have been all my life, a merchant. I am skilled in nothing else!"

Then he asked me if, at least, I knew how to shoot with a bow and arrow.

"Yes, Lord," I said. "That I do know!"

So next day he gave me a good, stout bow and heavy arrows and, mounting on an elephant, set me behind him. We went for some way out of the city and then into a thick forest and at last, where the undergrowth was not so thick, we came to a place of large and tall trees. He told me to take the bow and arrows and to climb up into one of the trees.

"Here," said he, "you must remain hidden all night, and in the morning, when a herd of elephants comes to this place, shoot at them with these long, heavy arrows. It is easy to hit but hard to kill, but, if you are lucky or skilful enough to kill, come back and let me know." Then he turned his elephant about and left me there.

When the first light of morning came, I could hear the noise of elephants and, not long after, the light increasing, I saw that a herd of these great beasts was now wandering about under the trees. As soon as they were near enough I shot my arrows at them as fast as I could and, with one of my last, was lucky enough to kill one, upon which the rest of the herd immediately made off. As soon as they had gone I slipped down from my tree, went home as fast as I could, and told my master. He was delighted with me, treated me with honour, and sent some of his other slaves to fetch the dead elephant, which was fortunately one with fine tusks. Next evening he told me to try again, and next morning I was again lucky. And so it went on for several days.

But one morning, as I sat in my tree, in the first light of the dawn, I heard that the elephants were coming much more quickly than before and that there must be many more. At last an enormous herd came plunging into sight, and they now began trumpeting and roaring, with their trunks in the air. Though I stayed perfectly still, it seemed to me that they must have seen me or got wind of me, for some of the largest of them began to form a ring round my tree. No sooner had they done this, than an immense elephant—the greatest I had ever seen—came straight up to my tree, wound his trunk round it and, some of the others helping him, it was not long before they had loosened all its roots. The tree fell and I fell with it. What

was my surprise when the great elephant, instead of trampling me to death, as I had expected, pushed aside the branches in which I was entangled, wound his trunk round me, and set me, quite gently, on his own back. Then, he leading, and the other elephants following, he plunged with me deeper into the forest.

I clung on as best I could, for if I had fallen the other elephants must have trampled me, and so difficult was it not to be tipped off by his great strides or swept off his back by low branches, that I could hardly tell in which direction we were going. At last, when we seemed to be in a clearing, he tipped me off his back and, in a moment, he and the other elephants were gone!

When my terror and surprise had left me a little, I began to look about me and saw, to my surprise, that, all around, were the bones and tusks of elephants. Then it seemed to me that the huge elephant must be the wisest as well as the largest of his kind. For he had left me where I could get as much ivory as my master could desire, and that without killing a single elephant!

Now, as I said, this was a huge beast and he had carried me a long way and in such a fashion that I had hardly been able to notice how we came! Because of this it was a day and a night before I was able to find the way back to my master.

When he saw me, he embraced me as if I had been his brother and told me how, when I had not come back at the usual time, he had himself gone to the place, seen the uptorn tree and the marks of many elephants, and had supposed that the beasts must have killed me.

"Tell me, then," he concluded, "what was your adventure?"

So I told him my tale and he rejoiced and wondered, and he asked me if I thought I could find that place again. When I said that I thought I could, he at once ordered out his elephant and a strong rope with it, took me up behind him and, without much difficulty, I was able to guide him to the place.

When he saw all the splendid tusks he was greatly delighted at so much ivory, and we gathered up a load, as much as we could tie with the rope, and then set it and ourselves on the back of his elephant and so returned.

As soon as we had stored away the precious ivory, he called me again and, embracing me, told me that I was now free. So I, too, rejoiced and told him of my longing to return to my own city. He answered that he would have kept me with him always in honour, but that he understood my request.

Now the season had come for a fair to which merchants from many countries came to buy ivory. I found among them merchants from Baghdad. So now the man who had been my master paid the captain of their ship for my passage home, and gave me many presents and food for the voyage.

And so at last we came to Baghdad, the City of Peace. And when I had rested a little in my own house I presented myself before the great Caliph Haroun Al Rashid and, having kissed the ground before him, I told him that, by the mercy of Allah, I had been able to obey his commands and taken his letter and his splendid presents in safety to the King of Ceylon.

"And what, O Sindbad," the Caliph asked, "happened

to you on the way back? For you have been gone far longer than the time to go and to come."

So I told him all that adventure—first and last.

"Allah be praised for his mercy!" said the Caliph. "This story is so strange that I shall order my scribes to write it all out in letters of gold."

And so I took my leave of him, begging him, most respectfully, that he would send me on no more journeys!

Ever since that day I have lived here in peace and so, I hope, I shall live till the end of my days, so that, if the mercy of Allah allow, the pleasures that I now enjoy may make up for the hardships and terrors of all these adventures.

THE GREAT
CALIPH HAROUN AL RASHID

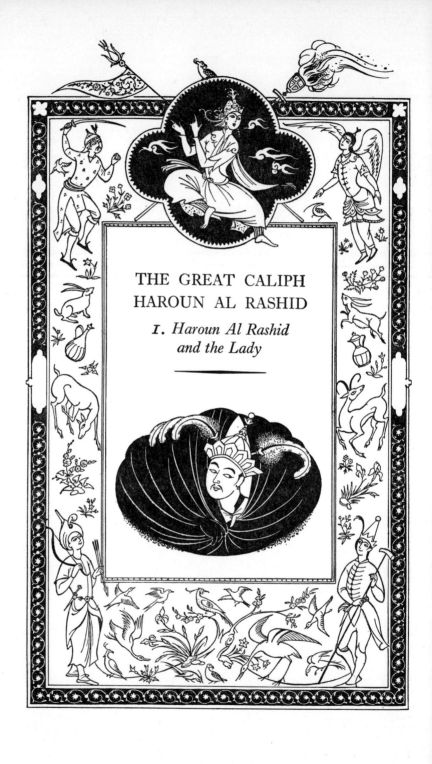

THE GREAT CALIPH
HAROUN AL RASHID

1. Haroun Al Rashid
and the Lady

IT WAS THE HABIT OF THE GREAT CALIPH, HAROUN Al Rashid, the Magnificent, Commander of the Faithful, to disguise himself and, at the evening hour, to go about the streets of his splendid city of Baghdad in search of amusement and adventure.

Sometimes the things that the Caliph heard and saw were merely laughable, but sometimes they seemed very strange and, if they had made him curious, next day, sitting on his throne, the great Caliph would summon his astonished companions of the night before and ask them for an explanation of what he had seen.

Sometimes, if they had done evil and had something to hide, being asked to explain before the whole court frightened them very much and they were doubly terrified to find that someone whom, the night before, they had thought was merely a beggar, a foreign merchant, a fisherman or a barber, had really been none other than the mighty Caliph. If, however, they had done no wrong, but were perhaps themselves being oppressed by some great man, they were sometimes very glad of an unexpected chance of telling their story to the Caliph himself, for, if they had shown themselves worthy, the powerful Caliph would usually manage to put things right.

One evening the Caliph, disguised as a foreign merchant and having pretended to be both hungry and weary, had been entertained in a fine house that was strange to him, and there he had seen sights which had greatly roused his curiosity. So next day, while he sat on his throne, he sent messengers to the lady who had seemed to be the owner of the house and bade her come before him. The messenger particularly ordered her to bring her two black dogs.

The Lady Zobaida—for that was her name—came

willingly, and when she had prostrated herself before him the Caliph said to her:

"It is easy to see that you are a virtuous and excellent lady. I now desire to ask you three questions. Why, last night when the feast over and the hour was late, did you say to your sister, 'Rise up, sister, that we may pay our debt?' That is the first question. Why were these two black dogs with golden chains immediately brought in, and why did you then, seizing a whip and rolling up your sleeves, beat them till your arms were tired and till they howled with misery? That is the second question. The third is: Why, after you had beaten them, did you then kiss them and press them to your bosom and wet their black coats with your tears?"

At this the Lady Zobaida was astonished, for she wondered how it was that the Caliph should know so much about her affairs. But soon she guessed that the foreign merchant, who seemed so hungry, thirsty and exhausted with his journey, and to whom she had given supper the night before, must in truth have been none other than the great Caliph himself in disguise. So she soon recovered herself, for she knew that she had done no wrong and that Haroun Al Rashid would not punish the innocent.

"O most virtuous ruler," said she in a sweet, low voice, "I will gladly tell you the whole story. But know, O Caliph, that it is a long as well as a sad one," and as she spoke she sighed deeply.

So then the Caliph told her to wait a little and presently, having cleared the hall of audience, he signed to the Lady Zobaida to take her seat upon a golden footstool near to his throne and told her to tell her story without reserve.

"O great Caliph," said she when she was seated, "I

must answer your last question
first. These two black dogs who
stand yonder are in reality two
of my sisters; that is why I
kissed and caressed them. As
for the reason why I spoke of a
debt and why I beat them so cruelly, you shall hear.

When our father died he left to each of us four sisters an
equal part of his fortune. I and my youngest sister remained at home, but my two elder sisters married. They
were both unlucky enough to marry husbands who
squandered their riches in foreign lands, and then leaving
my two sisters far from home, abandoned them.

When they managed to make their way back to our
house they looked so miserable that I did not know them,
but took them for beggars. But, as the Caliph perhaps
knows from experience"—and here the Lady Zobaida
smiled a little—"it is the rule of our house to be good to
those whom we believe to be hungry and thirsty, for so
Allah has commanded. So these two poor women were
taken in, clothed and fed, and when this had been done
I saw who they were and embraced them with joy. When
they had told me of their misfortunes I told them that they
must consider our house as theirs. From my own share I
gave them money, fine dresses and jewels, and for long
they remained with us in the house and—or so I thought
—in sisterly love and friendship.

Now after a while I decided that our wealth might not
always be enough for us all.

Our father having been a merchant, I knew something
about trading, and so I decided to fit out a ship and to try
to increase our fortune.

I asked my elder sisters if they would like to come with

me or to stay behind and help our youngest sister to take care of the house? They answered that they would come, saying that this was because they loved me so much that they could not endure to be separated from me!

So, with a stock of merchandise and a good ship, commanded by an honest and experienced captain, we set sail.

But, though our captain was experienced, after a while some changes of wind and current threw him out of his course, so we found ourselves in a part of the sea that was unknown to him; so for ten days we sailed we knew not where, though we had a calm sea and a pleasant wind.

At last an unknown city, standing on a low shore, loomed before us in the distance. The captain and I agreed that, since it seemed to have a good harbour, we should put in and see if we could trade with the people there. Even if this was not possible, we could at least, no doubt, get fresh water and provisions. Getting nearer, we saw that the harbour was a good and safe one, but that everything seemed to be deserted. So I begged our prudent captain to land first, take a look at this strange city, and bring us back news of what sort of place it was and what sort of people lived here. He soon came back to the ship in a state of great astonishment.

'Rise!' he said. 'Come ashore and see what Allah has done to this unfortunate city and pray to be preserved from his anger!'

So we landed. All was silent. As we walked up from the harbour we saw the market, with the gold and silver and all the other merchandise lying ready on the stalls. But as for the citizens, there seemed to be none, and then we saw that they had every one of them been turned into so many black stone statues.

After a while, when we had got over our surprise, our

party began to separate, each of us attracted by some
special thing among the wealth that lay in the silent and
deserted market stalls and shops.

As for me, I left the market and went up to what seemed
to be a walled citadel. Inside its high wall I found a great
and splendid palace. Going through a great arched door-
way and through many splendid rooms, I saw that a statue
that must once have been the King sat upon a pearl-
encrusted throne, surrounded by stone attendants, while
the stone Queen and her stone ladies were still in a beautiful room in the women's apartments.

This King and his Queen had crowns on their heads
and so many jewels that my eyes were dazzled.

Steps led up from the room where the splendid stone
Queen sat, near to the door of a magnificent hall, where the
daylight came through a diamond as big as the egg of an
ostrich. By the side of a magnificent divan lay a copy of
the Koran bound in gold, and in this room I saw the first

sign of life—lighted candles. I was encouraged by the sight of the sacred book, for I thought that where there are True Believers utter wickedness cannot flourish, while the lighted candles must mean that some living person must be near. So I stood still and listened attentively.

At first I could hear nothing. All seemed silence in the deserted palace. Then, far way, I heard a soft and pleasant voice reciting a chapter from the Koran. I went at once towards the sound and soon found myself in a small room lighted by more candles. On a silken prayer rug was the owner of the voice, and I had time to see that he was a young man, richly dressed and with a gentle face, but that his expression was sad.

At last I spoke—softly so as not to startle him—asking him in the name of Allah why he lived in the deserted palace and why he, alone, had not been turned to stone.

At that he turned, rose, saluted me politely, and begged me, also in the name of Allah, also to tell him how I came to be in the palace. So, together, we went back to the splendid hall. There, little by little we told each other our histories. Mine, O mighty Caliph, you have already heard; but his story will be as strange to you now as it was then to me.

This charming young prince now told me that he was the son of the king and queen who had been turned to stone. He remained alive because, when he was a child, he had been converted to the faith of Allah and his prophet Mahomet by an old slave woman who had been his nurse.

110

'She taught me,' said he, 'all she knew, such as to keep
the proper fasts and say the proper prayers, and also to
recite many chapters of the Koran, but all this she taught
me in secret, for my parents and all the inhabitants of our
city were Magians, that is, worshippers of the Sun and of
Fire, and they hated and persecuted all True Believers.

'Then one day a mighty voice sounded out, loud as
thunder, from the sky and the voice warned everyone in
the city that they must leave off worshipping Fire and the
Sun and stop their persecution of the Moslems, and that a
terrible fate would befall them unless they turned to the
worship of Allah. The people, hearing this terrible voice,
ran in fear to the King, my father, asking what they were
to do. But the King only told them not to be terrified, because their Fire and Sun gods were strong! Again the voice
rolled like thunder, saying once more that a terrible fate
awaited all those who did not heed and obey. Three times
this mighty voice spoke. Soon after the last warning, very
early, just after daybreak, a sudden hush fell on the city,
for, as each went about his business, everyone in our city
was suddenly changed into stone!'

Then the young prince asked me if I, too, was a Moslem. And, when I assured him that I was, he asked me
very earnestly if I could take him to
where he could meet other Moslems, so that he could learn more
about our faith, and added that
he had become weary of living in
solitude in the deserted palace.

I told him, O Caliph," went
on the Lady Zobaida, "how easy
this would be and that fortunately
I myself lived in your city of

111

Baghdad, where many learned saints and scholars of our faith are to be found, and many who have made the pilgrimage to Mecca, and I offered to take him with me to Baghdad as fast as our ship could sail. At this the good young man seemed overjoyed.

So then we left the palace together and went into the silent market-place. There we soon found the captain and the rest of my ship's company, who had been anxiously searching for me, and not long afterwards we set sail.

Now almost as soon as I had begun to converse with him in the lonely palace I had begun to love this charming young prince, and he me. As we sailed, my sisters spoke to me.

'And what, dear sister, do you hope to do with this handsome young prince?' they asked.

'I should like,' I said, 'to make him my husband.'

Not long after, it was agreed that we should be married as soon as we touched at a port where there were lawyers to make the contract. This was done, and when we had become man and wife we were very happy.

Now my sisters had pretended to be delighted at our happiness, but soon, either wanting the young prince for themselves, or being unwilling to share our wealth with him—I do not know which—they began to whisper together and plan evil. Unfortunately neither I nor the young prince suspected this.

One dark night, when we were asleep, they came stealthily to where we lay and the cruel creatures threw us both into the sea and, the captain suspecting nothing, the ship sailed on.

Alas, my young husband, who was unable to swim, was soon lost in the dark waters and drowned. As for me, I managed to struggle to the shore of an island. Not knowing

SEE P. 114

The Jinneyeh said that justice demanded their deaths

what had happened to him, I searched and called for him in the darkness, but, not finding him, I cast myself down weeping on the ground and slept for weariness and sorrow.

I awoke to find that the day had just broken and heard a rustling and hissing in some nearby bushes. Soon, from under them there darted out a small and pretty snake, which moved as if frightened and bewildered, and then chasing the little snake, out came a huge and hideous serpent with its mouth open, ready to swallow! Without thinking what I was doing, I took up a large stone and flung it at the serpent. My aim was good and the head of the great brute was crushed by the stone. What was my astonishment when, upon this, the pretty little snake instantly spread a pair of wings and soared up into the sky!

But I was so wretched and weary that I merely lay down again, and once more I slept. When I woke again I was surprised to find that a charming negro girl was rubbing my feet and had hung up some of my garments to dry. Half frightened at the sight, I sat up.

'Who are you?' I asked.

'Have you forgotten me so soon?' answered the beautiful black girl with a smile. 'You have just done me a great kindness by killing my enemy. I was the pretty little snake that you saved not an hour ago.'

I begged her to explain.

'I am a Jinneeyeh—a female Jinnee—and you have just saved me from my worst enemy, a wicked Jinnee who had taken the form of that horrible serpent. I already knew your story,' she went on, 'and, when I flew off just now, it was only to bring your merchandise, your good captain, and all in your ship safely to Baghdad—all, that is'—and here she frowned—'except your two most wicked and ungrateful sisters!'

'And the young prince, my dear husband?' I exclaimed.

'Alas!' said she with a sigh, 'I could not save him! He was already drowned, and over death we Jinns have no power. Death is mightier than we are!'

At that I again wept bitterly. But she spoke gentle words, reminding me that, since he was drowned when in search of a better understanding of the True Faith, I could be certain that, at the very moment of drowning, a beautiful Houri had carried his soul to Paradise.

'As for your ungrateful sisters,' the Jinneeyeh went on sternly, her eyes flashing, 'I have only waited to kill them till you yourself should say what dreadful death they should die, so that you should have ample revenge for the evil they have done to you!'

But I began to plead with her, saying that I did not in the least desire to kill them or to have revenge, for that would not bring me back my husband. At that the Jinneeyeh grew angry and said that justice demanded their deaths! At last the best I could do was to make a bargain with her; she agreed not to kill them, but to turn them into two black dogs, but she said that if, for a term of years, I did not beat them every evening with a whip until my arm ached, she would immediately turn me and my other sister also into black dogs! 'That is the debt you owe to Justice,' said she. I had to agree, and when I had promised punctually to pay the debt (as she called it), I immediately found myself safe and sound in my own house.

And so, O Mighty Caliph," concluded Zobaida, "you see the dogs here before you, and now you know the causes of the strange things that you saw and heard after supper last night."

Now all through this extraordinary story the Caliph had been gazing at the Lady Zobaida and, though she was veiled, her veil was a light one and he could see that she was beautiful. He could also hear that her voice was low and sweet, while he decided that her story proved her to be wise, brave and loving.

Giving her a present of a magnificent jewel, the Caliph Haroun Al Rashid sent the Lady Zobaida back in honour to her own house, and the very next day he sent messengers asking her, since her poor young husband was dead, if she would become the chief of his queens. To this she gladly consented, a good husband was found for the youngest sister, while, the term of years being up, she was no longer obliged to beat the two wicked sisters, though they never recovered their human form.

As the story of "Abou Hassan and Heart's Desire" will show, the Caliph grew to love her and the Lady Zobaida lost her melancholy and was able to play her part in the merry life of Haroun Al Rashid's magnificent court.

2. *Haroun Al Rashid and Abou Hassan*

THERE LIVED ONCE IN BAGHDAD, IN THE DAYS OF the great Caliph, a lively and pleasant young man named Abou Hassan, who, when his father died, decided to divide his riches into two parts. The smaller part he put carefully away, and the rest he spent on feasting with other gay young men.

Everyone said how witty and amusing Hassan was, and how delightful his hunting parties and picnics were; indeed he was one of the most popular young men in the town.

After a while, however, he found that, except for what he had put away, nearly all his money had gone. He had had a fine time, and so had his friends; but now he was obliged to tell them that, unfortunately, he couldn't afford to give any more feasts or hunting parties. He expected, of course, that his friends would quite understand and was also sure that, since those who had money would now invite him back, he would be able to go on living much as before.

Nothing of the sort! No one bothered about him any more. So poor Abou Hassan found himself sitting alone every evening. He felt bitterly disappointed with these false friends, for it now seemed to him that they must have loved his money and not him. His old mother sympathised very much, shook her head, and agreed that they were a worthless lot.

As for Abou Hassan, he felt so angry that he made a vow that he would never trust a friend again! However, as he hated to be alone, he decided on a very strange plan. He would go out every evening, pick out some interesting-

looking stranger, bring him back to his house, give him a
feast, but next day, if he happened to meet the man he had
feasted in the street, he would pretend that he had never
seen him before.

So every evening Abou Hassan went and sat by the
great bridge that crosses the river Tigris and, when any
stranger passed who looked interesting, he would rise,
salaam, and politely invite him to his house. There he
would offer him wine, there would be music, beautiful
girls would dance for their amusement, they would tell
each other stories and would feast merrily together; but
next morning Abou Hassan always kept his resolve and
would not so much as look at his last night's visitor.

Now, as everybody knows, the Great Caliph, the
Commander of the Faithful, Haroun Al Rashid the
Magnificent, often went about his kingdom in disguise.
One evening the Caliph and four or five attendants—all
disguised as foreign merchants—happening to come back
to the city across the bridge, Abou Hassan rose from his
seat and politely invited the one who seemed the leader to
his house.

A sudden invitation from an unknown young man was, of course, just the sort of thing that amused Haroun Al Rashid, so, hoping it would lead to some adventure, the Caliph accepted at once.

Abou Hassan's house was a fine one; in the courtyard spouted a fountain ornamented with gold; the wine and the food were excellent—a roast goose, fine white bread, sweetmeats such as fresh dates rolled in honey and spices, and perfumed wine to drink. While they ate and drank, a beautiful slave girl played and sang for them. The young man seemed so cheerful, polite and pleasant that the Caliph thoroughly enjoyed his evening and thought he would like to find a way of seeing the young man again. Presently, towards the end of the feast, he said to Abou Hassan:

"O young man, tell me your history, for to-morrow I should like to repay you for so much kindness."

At first Abou Hassan managed not to answer any of the Caliph's questions, but always made a joke, paid a compliment, or poured out more wine. However, the Caliph was determined, and after a good deal of persuasion, he got Abou Hassan to tell him the story of his curious vow. The Caliph was amused and, really wanting to make some return for such a pleasant evening, he again asked Abou Hassan if there was really nothing that he wanted.

At last Hassan said, laughing, that perhaps there was just one thing! Quite near to his house, he said, lay a mosque to which a most disagreeable old Imam, or Moslem priest, belonged, and whenever Hassan had music at his parties this disagreeable old man made a fuss and often complained of the noise to the Walee, or judge, who then always scolded, and sometimes even fined Abou Hassan quite a large sum of money.

118

"If I, dear merchant, were the Caliph of Baghdad—
even for a day," said Abou Hassan, "I really should like to
have that interfering old Imam punished so that he
wouldn't torment his neighbours any more!"

This joking answer put quite a new idea into the
Caliph's head and, when Hassan was looking round for
another flagon of wine, he secretly slipped a sleeping-
powder into the young man's cup, so that, after a while,
Hassan fell into a deep sleep.

Then the Caliph went softly to the door that led to the
courtyard, where he knew that his own attendants were
waiting, and, very quietly, he ordered them to pick up the
sleeping Abou Hassan and put him on a mule, and when
that was done they all went back to the palace. There the
Caliph had the still soundly sleeping Hassan put into his
own splendid bed, called together all the usual attendants
and said that, on pain of his displeasure, everyone was to
treat Abou Hassan for the whole of the next day exactly as
if he had been the Caliph. Haroun Al Rashid's courtiers
and slaves were quite used to such jokes, and they all promised that they would play their parts well.

So it came about that, when Abou Hassan awoke, he not
only found, to his astonishment, that he was in a splendid
room that he had never seen before, but also that dozens
of attendants were kissing the ground before him. Soon a
beautiful slave girl was saying in her soft voice, "O
Commander of the Faithful, arise! It is now time for the
morning prayer!" Then, kneeling, the girl offered him
a delicious cup of snow-cooled sherbet.

Abou Hassan was delighted at this, but he made no
attempt to get up; indeed he just lay back on the bed
laughing because—so it seemed to him—all these people
were behaving in such an extraordinary way! Presently,

however, he thought he would see a little more and raised himself on his elbow and had a good look round.

What Abou Hassan did not see was that the Caliph was watching all this from behind a curtain; what he did see was that he was surrounded by bowing attendants and in a magnificent room. The walls were hung with embroidered silk, the roof was of blue enamel dotted with gold stars, there were silken carpets on the floor, there were lamps that gave off sweet perfumes, and among the richly dressed slaves and attendants there were many lovely girls.

After his look Abou Hassan again lay back on the bed. This time he shut his eyes and decided that either he had died and was in Paradise, or that this was the most delightful dream he had ever had.

"If it is a dream," thought he, "I had better stay asleep as long as possible."

The Caliph, Haroun Al Rashid, behind his curtain thought it would be very dull if Hassan spent the whole day in bed, so he signed to one of the attendants. This man tiptoed up to the bed and whispered in Hassan's ear in a most respectful manner:

"Is not your usual custom to lie thus in bed, O Prince of the Faithful!"

To this Abou Hassan did not answer a word. However, in order to see whether he really was dreaming, he bit his own finger to see if it hurt. He bit hard and it hurt so much that he at once sat bolt upright and, calling one of the charming slave girls, asked her who she thought he was, and where.

She answered, most sweetly and respectfully, that of course he was The Great Caliph and that he was, as usual at that time in the morning, in his royal bed.

So then Abou Hassan, still more puzzled, asked each of the more important-looking officers, one by one, "Who am I, and where am I?"

Each one, in turn, most respectfully gave him the same answer.

At last Hassan, much puzzled, began to remember his unknown guest of the night before and began to think that the man he had taken for a merchant had probably been a Jinnee or an enchanter.

All this time, behind his curtain, the Caliph was getting more and more impatient, for of course it would quite spoil his joke if Hassan just lay there puzzling his head. So, at another sign from the Caliph, one of the chief officers came bowing to Abou Hassan with a pair of gold-brocaded shoes in his hand.

"May Allah grant a happy morning to the Prince of the Faithful," said he, and with that handed him the shoes with a meaning look. But Abou Hassan, after looking at these magnificent shoes for a long time, just put them away under his pillow!

"These are shoes! Shoes to walk in, mighty Prince!"

121

said the officer in a meaning voice, and told two of the beautiful slave girls to bring the Caliph his perfumed washing water, and they poured it from a silver jug into a gold basin. More attendants brought him gorgeous robes and a splendid turban, and so at last, with a good deal of difficulty, they did in the end manage to get Abou Hassan washed and dressed—shoes and all.

Then the great officers of state all came in, looking as solemn as possible.

While they were slowly getting him dressed, Abou Hassan had been thinking that, even if this was a dream or the work of Jinns, he might as well enjoy it properly and he now decided to pretend that he, too, believed in it all.

So, trying to look like a real Caliph—very haughty—he signed to the old Walee or judge of his own district to draw near, and when this solemn, white-bearded old man had come and prostrated himself, Abou Hassan told him to go to such and such a house and to give five hundred pieces of gold to the mother of Abou Hassan with the Caliph's compliments. After that he told the Walee to go on with his guards to such and such a mosque, seize the Imam, and order the guards to set him, facing backwards, on a donkey and parade him through the streets proclaiming, to the sound of trumpets, that this was what happened to disagreeable old men who didn't like music and who annoyed their neighbours!

Finding, to his astonishment, that everyone obeyed him, Abou Hassan spent the rest of the morning just as the real Caliph did, sitting on a splendid throne and giving judgments about this and that. When he had had enough of this, he simply sent everyone away and asked for something to eat.

"To hear is to obey!" answered the chief butler.

Naturally, the dinner was magnificent. Dish upon dish of the most delicious food was set before him. Pink prawns, white almonds and green peeled grapes lay on beds of rice coloured yellow with saffron. There was chicken cooked brown in melted butter, there were gazelle-horn cakes, and sweet Indian Firnee scattered with crystallized rose-petals. The girls who waited on him and brought him the different courses were as charming as those whom he had seen that morning. He asked their names.

One told him she was called "Willow-twig."

"O lovely Willow-twig," said he, "now tell me who I am."

She answered that, of course, he was the mighty Caliph.

"I'm sure that's all lies!" he answered, looking doubt-fully from one girl to another and shaking his head. "I'm sure that all you deceitful girls are just laughing at me be-hind my back!" This, of course, was true enough, but, all the same, they just answered respectfully and he could get no more out of them. So at last Abou Hassan came to the conclusion that everyone he had seen that day—girls, guards, the Walee, and all the rest—must have all been Jinns, the palace must be the palace of Jinns, and that the man he had feasted the night before must have been the King of the Jinns, who had found this delightful way of thanking him! And so Abou Hassan passed the rest of the evening in enjoying himself.

Now by the Caliph's orders the last cup of wine that

Abou Hassan was given after his supper had sleeping-powder in it and, as soon as he was sound asleep, the Caliph had him taken back to his own house and put into his own, ordinary bed.

Some hours later, but while it was still dark, Abou Hassan began to call for various of the Caliph's attendants and especially for Willow-twig. At first, of course, nobody answered, for the whole house was asleep; but at last his mother heard him and came to him.

"What is the matter, my son? Whom are you calling?" she asked.

Abou Hassan was still not properly awake, so he answered:

"How dare you speak to the Commander of the Faithful like that?"

"Are you mad?" answered his mother. "You are not the Caliph. You are only my son, Abou Hassan!"

Very much disappointed and still not properly awake, he began to abuse her, and the poor old woman began to feel thoroughly frightened and to mutter charms over him. At last, when he seemed a little calmer, thinking to amuse and please him, she told him that the Caliph had done them a great honour that day, for he had sent her a splendid present of five hundred pieces of gold.

"And you will be pleased to hear, Son," she added, "that that hateful and interfering old Imam has been made fun of! Only think! By the Caliph's orders he was taken through the streets sitting backwards on a donkey with trumpeters and heralds who said that this was what happened to grumpy old men who didn't like music."

"What!" exclaimed Abou Hassan. "The Walee really brought you the money? And they really made fun of that awful old Imam? So it must be true after all!"

124

And then Abou Hassan, now more and more mixed in his ideas, jumped out of bed and began to shout at his poor old mother!

"I am the Caliph, you stupid old woman! I gave the order to make fun of the Imam! I sent you five hundred pieces of gold! Everybody tells me lies! Do you want to drive me mad? Stop telling me that I'm not the Caliph! Admit that I am the Commander of the Faithful, you ugly, disrespectful old thing!" And with that, still shouting, he boxed his poor old mother's ears.

They both got so wild and the old mother screamed so loudly, not only because he had hit her, but because she felt sure he must be raving, that, though it was hardly light, a crowd began to collect outside the house. They heard Abou Hassan yelling and shouting what sounded the most utter nonsense all about an Imam and gold pieces, and how he was the Commander of the Faithful, and the old woman crying out for fear, so at last the neighbours broke in and, hustling the old lady out of the way, they fetched the madhouse-keeper and took the struggling and shouting Abou Hassan off to the lunatic asylum.

Now it was the custom at that time to try to beat the madness out of those who were raving, and to chain them up in the dark and to dose them with abominable medicines. Whether those who were really mad were ever cured in this way is uncertain. What is certain is that poor Abou Hassan, who was not mad to begin with, but who knew very well it really was he who had given those orders, got madder and madder when they treated him like that! At home, his poor old mother was in despair and came to visit him as often as she was allowed.

"If only you would admit," she would repeat, wringing

her hands, "that it must have been all a dream! But till you do they are afraid to let you out!"

"But it wasn't a dream! I can remember everything! And what about the gold! And the Imam!" poor Abou Hassan would answer, wildly.

At last Abou Hassan saw that, whatever he himself believed, he had better give in. He would have to say it was a dream, or that he had been possessed by a demon. Anyhow, he really was sorry for the way he had treated his poor old mother. So at last he begged her pardon, said what they wanted him to say, seemed quite calm, and was let out.

Now during the time that Abou Hassan had been in the madhouse, the Caliph had been away in another part of his dominions. When he got back he began to wonder what had happened to the young man on whom he had played his latest joke. Disguising himself once more as a foreign merchant, he watched his time and soon saw Abou Hassan coming out of his house. Abou Hassan, when he saw him, started back, for he at once recognised his mysterious visitor the pretended merchant.

"An unfriendly welcome to you, O King of the Jinns!" he said, frowning.

"Why unfriendly? What have I done to you?" answered the disguised Caliph.

"What have you done? Only got me well beaten and chained up in a horrible madhouse, O filthiest and most ungrateful of Jinns! And that after I had taken you to my house and given you the best of my food to eat! Go away! I never want to see your ill-omened face again! He who stumbles on a stone a second time is a fool! I'll have nothing to do with you."

This answer filled the Caliph with curiosity and he

began by means of some rigmarole to persuade Abou Hassan that what had happened could not have been his fault and that he was terribly sorry to hear of all these misfortunes. Abou Hassan himself, said the pretended merchant earnestly, had probably forgotten to shut the door that night and (as everyone knew) in this way a Jinnee might easily have got in! The end of it was that Abou Hassan brought the Caliph into his house again. Once more, the two of them had supper together and, as they ate and drank, the Caliph got the whole story out of Abou Hassan. It amused Haroun Al Rashid so much that he thought there would be no harm in playing the same trick again, so, once more secretly dropping the sleeping-powder in his cup, the Caliph had Abou Hassan taken up to the palace just as before!

The Caliph now ordered all the girls, especially Willow-twig, to stand round the bed and sing and play the most delightful music, so that, this time, Abou Hassan did not sleep for long. But when the girls respectfully called him Prince and Commander of the Faithful, poor Abou Hassan was horrified instead of delighted! He at once decided that the best way to deal with these wicked Jinns was to call upon all the good powers.

"In the name of Allah!" shouted Abou Hassan. "Come to my help, O powers of good! I beg you by the Verses of the Throne, by the Chapter of Sincerity, by the inscription on the seal of Solomon to come and help me! Rid me quickly of these deceitful Jinns!"

Then the Caliph, who was hiding as before, decided that the joke had

127

gone far enough and called out:

"You have killed us all, O Abou Hassan!" and with that Haroun Al Rashid stepped out from behind the curtain. Then Abou Hassan saw that this was none other than the true Caliph, and prostrated himself before him. The Caliph raised him, and, to make up for all that poor Abou Hassan had suffered, he gave him a rich reward and a place at court.

As to what happened after that, it shall be told in the story of Abou Hassan and the beautiful Nuzet el Fuad, that is to say, "Heart's Desire".

3. Haroun Al Rashid, Abou Hassan and Heart's Desire

NOW THE GREAT CALIPH, HAROUN AL RASHID, HAD, as is well known, a lady named Zobaida as his chief Queen, and this Queen had part of his great palace for her own, and there she lived in splendour with many slaves to wait upon her. The chief of her slaves, who was also her treasurer and favourite, was a beautiful young woman called Nuzet el Fuad, that is to say "Heart's Desire". Nuzet was almost as fond of playing jokes to amuse her mistress, Queen Zobaida, as Haroun Al Rashid was of playing jokes with Abou Hassan, who—after the adventure which has just been told—had now become one of the Caliph's favourite courtiers.

At last Queen Zobaida and the Caliph decided that these two cheerful favourites of theirs had better marry each other. Abou Hassan and Nuzet thought this an excellent idea, so it was all arranged, and the two of them

SEE P. 122

Abou Hassan spent the morning giving judgments

soon began to lead a most delightful life together, living in a part of the palace that their master and mistress gave them.

But the life they led was almost too delightful, for, though Zobaida and the Caliph had given plenty of money to this young couple, and apartments of their own, it wasn't long before, with so much feasting and merry-making, so many fine clothes and jewels, all the money had gone!

Abou Hassan had often told his pretty wife Nuzet about the trick that the Caliph had once played on him, so now he asked her, laughing, if they shouldn't see if they could get some money by playing a return joke. It could easily be done if Nuzet was willing also to risk playing a trick on Queen Zobaida. Nuzet said she was quite ready to do this, so whispering together, they made up a trick between them, and for a while were busy preparing it.

So, one day while Queen Zobaida sat in her part of the palace, she heard a sound of wailing, and who should come in but her dear, pretty, charming Nuzet, with her clothes torn, dust on her head and what looked like tears on her cheeks.

"What is the matter?" asked Queen Zobaida, sorry to see her favourite in this sad state.

"O Lady! O gracious Queen! May your life be longer than the life of poor, foolish, pleasant Abou Hassan!" answered Nuzet, in a voice that seemed to be choked with sobs.

"What do you mean?" asked the Queen, surprised at this strange answer.

"Alas, Lady! Abou Hassan, my dear husband, died suddenly last night!"

Now Zobaida was not only fond of Nuzet, but she knew how fond the Caliph was of Abou Hassan, so that she was truly sorry to hear this news. She did her best to comfort Nuzet, and at last, when, still sobbing, Nuzet said she must go home to attend to the funeral, the Queen gave her a hundred pieces of gold and a splendid length of silk, so that the Caliph's favourite might be buried with honour.

While Nuzet had been taking in her mistress, Abou Hassan had been playing exactly the same trick on the

Caliph, who had been just as sorry as the Queen and just as generous about the funeral. So now the two tricksters, very much pleased with themselves and very cheerful, got home at very much the same time. So pleased were they that—as they told each other what had happened, counted the gold and admired the silk—they even danced about with glee and, after that, they sat for a long time laughing and talking and imitating their master and mistress.

Meantime the Caliph, as soon as he was able to dismiss his council of state, went at once to the Queen's part of the palace. He was very fond of Queen Zobaida and wanted to try to console her for the loss of her Nuzet! Sure enough, the Caliph found his dear Zobaida looking quite mournful. She rose, he stepped towards her and, as it happened, they began to speak almost together!

"Alas!" they both said.

The Queen went on:

"Dear husband, how sorry I am that your poor, cheerful favourite, Abou Hassan, should have died so suddenly!"

131

"Dear wife, what a pity that your beautiful favourite, Nuzet, should have died so suddenly!" said the Caliph, and then they both called out, "What?" together.

"Nuzet is dead!" answered the Caliph.

"Abou Hassan is dead!" answered the Queen.

At that the Caliph smiled pityingly and said to an old courtier who stood by:

"Even the best of women have very little sense, Mesroor! See how even my wise Zobaida gets muddled over a very simple story! As you saw, Abou Hassan was with me just now wailing and moaning, because his wife Nuzet is dead."

At this Queen Zobaida gave an impatient laugh.

"Great Caliph, this may seem very amusing to you! But don't you think we sometimes have enough of your jokes? My slave girl, Nuzet el Fuad, was with me not an hour ago with her clothes torn and ashes on her head—my old nurse here saw her. Nuzet told me herself that your Abou Hassan is dead. Also, Great Caliph, I don't like being told that I have no sense in front of old Mesroor!"

Naturally the Caliph and Queen Zobaida now each felt both puzzled and rather cross, for each was naturally quite sure that they were right. So as to settle the matter (as they thought) first the Caliph sent Mesroor, and then the Queen sent her old nurse, to find out the truth. But, as can be imagined, each brought back a different tale, for the old nurse (the Queen's messenger) found Abou Hassan laid out in his shroud with his face covered and his wife weeping over him, while Mesroor (the Caliph's messenger) found Abou Hassan pretending to weep by the side of what seemed to be the corpse of his charming wife.

Of course the messengers soon began to quarrel and each called the other names—"Liar!" "Ill-Omened Slave!" "Person with no more sense than a hen!" and every other sort of bad name, while the Caliph himself began to mutter again, saying impatiently that even the best of women had very little sense—a remark which Queen Zobaida overheard and which again made her feel very much put out. "If I am wrong, O my husband," said Queen Zobaida, "I will give you a whole room-full of

133

splendid paintings for your pleasure-garden by the river."

"And if I am wrong," answered the Caliph, "you, O Queen, shall have the whole of my mountain pleasure-garden for your own! We had better stop abusing each other! Let us set off at once and go to their apartments! There we shall, of course, easily find out the truth."

Now when great people such as Queens and Caliphs move about, even inside their own palaces, the news of it usually goes along in front of them. And so it was this time. Nuzet heard the tramping feet of the guards and, looking out of the window, saw quite a procession coming across one of the many grand courtyards. Turning pale, she called out at once to Abou Hassan:

"What are we to do now?" exclaimed she, looking rather frightened. "The two messengers came separately— it was easy to take them in! But here are our master and mistress *and* Mesroor *and* the old nurse *and* a lot of guards all coming along together!"

"There is only one thing to be done," answered Abou Hassan. "We shall both have to be dead this time!"

Now to arrange this nicely was not very easy, because, in Baghdad, the feet of a corpse should be tied together, the face should be covered, and the shroud should be neatly laid and wrapped in a special way. However, Nuzet and Hassan helped one another, as well as they could, and if the Caliph and Queen Zobaida and the others saw rather untidy corpses, they were so much surprised at seeing two that they noticed nothing!

As the two royal visitors bent over the bodies, Abou Hassan and Nuzet had to hold their breaths, so that they were thankful when the Queen and the Caliph both turned sorrowfully away and when they heard Zobaida say:

"I can see how it was! My poor Nuzet got back to

arrange the funeral and then she simply died of grief!"

"What nonsense!" exclaimed the Caliph. "If Nuzet hadn't died first, why did Hassan come to me in mourning —that is, with his clothes torn and ashes on his head? Of course it's quite clear! He loved Nuzet so much that, though, naturally, I promised him a new and better wife, he died of grief for her! So I have won and now, Zobaida, you will have to give me that roomful of beautiful paintings!"

"Not at all! It's I who get the mountain garden! It was Nuzet whose clothes were torn in sign of mourning, so it must have been Hassan who died first!"

Well, as can be imagined, neither Queen Zobaida nor the Caliph would give way, and at last the Caliph exclaimed:

"By the tomb of Mahomet! I would give a thousand pieces of gold if only we could settle this wretched question of which died first!"

Then Abou Hassan saw his chance.

"I died first, mighty Caliph!" he called out and, as he

spoke, he untied himself, sprang to his feet and then bowed politely.

"I assure you I did!" he went on, "And now I claim the thousand pieces of gold!"

At that Nuzet also rose up and, bowing before her mistress, asked pardon for both of them for the trick they had played.

Queen Zobaida seemed at first as if she was going to be cross about the whole affair, but when she saw that her husband, the Caliph, was laughing so much that he had to sit down to laugh better, she had to laugh too—indeed she admitted in the end that she was very much relieved to find that her dear, cheerful Nuzet was safe and well after all.

And so both the tricksters were forgiven. But they long remembered that, at one point in the joke, they had both felt frightened and that if they ever did such a thing again there might be serious trouble! So, ever after they behaved rather more prudently, and neither of them was ever again quite so inclined to spend every penny as soon as ever they got it.

ALADDIN
AND THE WONDERFUL LAMP

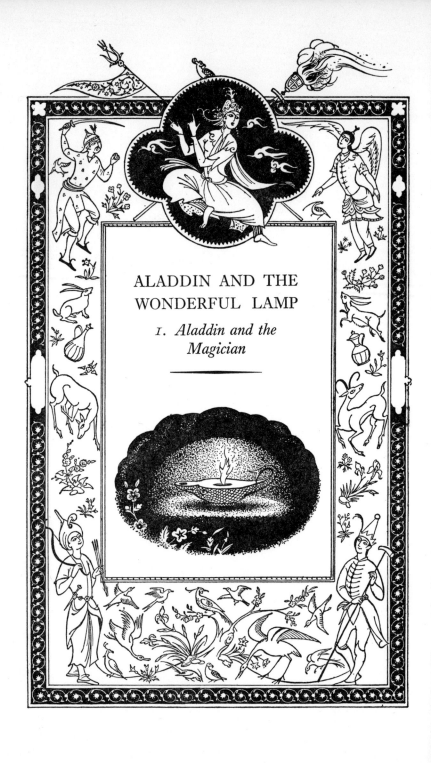

ALADDIN AND THE WONDERFUL LAMP

1. Aladdin and the Magician

IT IS SAID (BUT ALLAH KNOWS ALL) THAT IN THE mountain deserts of Morocco in the northern parts of Africa there lived, long ago, an old and powerful Magician. He, by deep study of his terrible arts, discovered that a copper lamp that he had long wanted to possess lay lost and buried in a certain cave far away in China. He knew that to whomsoever rubbed this old and battered lamp there would instantly appear a Jinnee of immense size who was known as "The Slave of the Lamp" and who would immediately bring every gift, or perform every task, that was ordered.

But, though this African Magician's arts showed him clearly enough in what cave the lamp was hidden and what must be done if it was to be got out, they showed him also that the magician himself could never get possession of it alone. He had to find someone who would be at once bold and nimble enough to fetch the lamp up out of the cave, and then simple enough to give it away again.

How was he to find anyone bold enough to go down into the earth for it and yet ready to give up the prize as soon as he had got it? Long did this magician ponder! At last he set out for China, and reached one of the largest cities of that country just at sunset.

Now the African Magician had disguised himself as a rich merchant and, as he walked slowly through the darkening streets, he saw that, as in other cities, there were many boys who played about in the streets and marketplace, and who ran in and out among the merchants, as they were shutting their stalls and shops.

Next day the Magician went again to the market, this time in a different disguise. As he watched, he spied a poorly dressed lad who seemed to be a sort of leader and

139

 whom the merchants clearly thought was a nuisance and a plague, for they kept chasing this boy away from their stalls. Calling a much younger boy to him and giving him a piece of money, the disguised Magician inquired about this young fellow. The younger boy told him that this lad's name was Aladdin, that his father had been a tailor called Mustapha, and that Aladdin himself was a wild sort of boy who had never been willing to follow a trade. "Aladdin won't do any sort of work, so he and his mother are very poor," added the boy.

Next day the Magician, this time again richly dressed, came once more to the market-place and soon again spied Aladdin.

"Child!" called out the Magician. "Is not your father Mustapha the tailor?"

"Yes, sir," replied Aladdin. "But he has been dead these three years."

"What? My poor brother dead?" exclaimed the Magician in pretended sorrow. "Dear Nephew, let me weep on your neck! You are so like your dear father that I knew you at once!" Then he gave Aladdin a handful of money, telling him to give it to his mother and to tell her that he would come and visit them the next day.

Aladdin, very much surprised, ran straight back to his mother, but, I am sorry to say, he gave her only half the money, keeping the rest for himself.

"My uncle, the rich merchant, is come!" he told her. "He sends you this money and says he will come to supper with us tomorrow."

At that his mother was very much surprised, for she

could not remember that her husband had ever spoken of having a rich brother.

However, in the morning, instead of sitting down to her spinning—by which Aladdin's mother managed to earn a little money to buy their food—she went to the market with the money and spent the rest of the day cooking a finer supper than they had had for many a long day.

In the evening, the African Magician came, as he had promised. When he had greeted them, he told Aladdin's mother, with pretended tears, how nothing had ever made him so sad as to hear that his poor, dear brother was dead, and how, in the market, he had known his nephew Aladdin directly because he was so like his poor, dear father.

Presently he began to ask what trade his nephew followed.

"Alas, sir," said the mother, "Aladdin knows no trade at all! He is an idle fellow. His father did all he could to teach him to be a tailor, but all in vain! So ever since his father died I have had to try to earn a living for us both by spinning wool. But, alas! my spinning brings in so little that we often go hungry!"

At that Aladdin hung his head.

"This is not well, Nephew!" said the pretended uncle in a solemn voice and shaking his head gravely. "Yet I will try to help you! If you will not learn to be a tailor, or a cobbler, or a weaver, I will teach you how to become a merchant like me!"

So now a fine life began for Aladdin. He went here and there with the merchant uncle, who fitted him out with good clothes, and he usually came home at night to his mother with a silver piece, or even a gold one, and always with tales of the splendid things he had seen—houses with many courtyards and carved tracery, gardens with peach trees and fountains, splendidly robed merchants who rode fine horses.

At last one day the African Magician took Aladdin out with him as usual, but, this time, they went further than they had yet ever been, out beyond the town and towards the mountains. This time, said the uncle, Aladdin was to see the finest sight of all! What this could be Aladdin could not guess, for now they were far from the city and in a part of the country that seemed little better than a dry desert, and at last they stood in a burnt up, stony valley between two mountains, with no grass and only a few spindly-looking trees.

"Go and gather sticks," said the strange uncle.

The boy was tired with the long walk and rather unwilling, and at first just stood there, but then he noticed that this dear, kind uncle of his suddenly looked rather stern and it seemed to Aladdin that, in that lonely place, it might even be dangerous to disobey. So he did as he was bid, and collected sticks. To these the Magician presently set fire and, when he threw a powder on the fire, a thick oily smoke began to rise. Then the Magician began to pronounce strange words that sounded like a spell. Suddenly, with a tearing sound, the earth opened before Aladdin's feet. There, before him, lay a great stone with a brass ring fixed in the top of it.

"Take hold of the ring and move the stone," said the Magician.

Aladdin said it was too heavy, but his pretended uncle would not help him but only told him, with an angry look, that it would move easily. So Aladdin took hold and found, to his surprise, that he could move it with one

hand. Under the stone were steep rocky steps that led
down to a door made of shining copper.

"Now listen carefully," said the Magician. "That door
will open of itself as you go down the steps. When you
have gone through it, you will find yourself in a huge
cave, and beyond that will be two more. In each of these
caves, none of which are dark, you will see great jars and
chests overflowing with all sorts of treasure. But do not
touch anything! You must even tuck up your robe, for
all is lost if even the skirts of it so much as brush against
anything. At the end of the third cave you will find a
door. Go through, and you will find yourself in a beautiful garden planted with fruit trees. Cross the garden and
you will see a wall; go to a niche in the wall and, in the
niche, you will find a small lighted lamp. Take the lamp—

though it looks old and worthless—blow out the light, pour away the oil, AND BRING THE LAMP TO ME!" So saying, the pretended uncle drew a ring off his finger and put it upon Aladdin's, telling him that the ring was a talisman which would protect him. Then he added, "Go boldly!"

But Aladdin did not feel at all bold, and indeed it was only the sternness of his uncle's looks that made him go at all.

However, go he did, the door opened just as the Magician had said, and Aladdin was so much afraid of touching anything in any of the three caves that he hardly even dared look about him, only just darting his eyes here and there at the gleaming treasure as he hurried on. Once in the garden, he saw the lamp directly, took it, blew out the light, poured away the oil and, putting the lamp in the folds of his robe, he began to come back through the garden again.

Feeling less afraid now, Aladdin went slowly and began to look about him. It seemed to him that he had never seen such a wonderful garden or fruit so fine as that which grew on the trees. The gardens of the rich merchants were nothing to this! At last, turning aside to wander among the trees, Aladdin began to pick the wonderful-looking fruits. Some were as clear as crystal, some as white as wax, some as red as blood, some as black as jet, some as yellow as the eyes of a cat, while some seemed to burn and change colour as he looked at them. He tried to take a bite here and there, but all were hard, cold and heavy. However, thinking how pretty they were, though they were certainly not good to eat, he filled two large bags with them. He found that this strange fruit made quite a heavy load.

Passing back through the caves and still being careful
to touch nothing there, with the old lamp safe, he came
at last to the bottom of the steps again—the steps that
led up to the open air. Then he called to his uncle who,

as he could now see, was waiting impatiently for him. But,
as the fruits that he had brought with him were heavy,
he asked the pretended uncle to give him a hand up.

"Give me the lamp first!" said the Magician. But he
said this in such an evil tone and with such a strange
expression on his face that the boy felt afraid and, instead
of handing it to him, shrank back.

"If I give up the lamp before I am up myself," thought
Aladdin, "I may never come out alive!" So, with Aladdin
still down out of reach, they argued, the African Magician
sometimes storming, sometimes giving his pretended
nephew sweet words.

At last the Magician lost his temper altogether. He
flew into a mighty passion.

"Son of a dog! Wretched, obstinate boy!" shouted he, stamping his foot with rage. "I will teach you what happens to disobedient boys!" With that (and quite forgetting that, in this way, he was bound to lose the lamp) the furious Magician stamped off and threw a fresh pinch of incense on the fire. Instantly there was a clap of thunder and the heavy stone immediately moved back into its place.

So now poor Aladdin found himself alone and in darkness, for at the same instant the heavy copper door, through which he had reached the treasure caves and the beautiful garden, had shut behind him.

Terribly frightened and fearing that he would never see the sky again, Aladdin began to repent his bad ways and to wish that he had been kinder to his mother, that he had followed an honest trade, not spent his time in idleness, and, above all, that he had never trusted this horrible uncle. The poor boy began to wring his hands and, as he did so, he happened to rub the ring that was on his finger! No sooner had he done this than there appeared a huge Jinnee, which glowed horribly and filled that dark place with its own light.

"I am The Slave of the Ring," said the Jinnee in a voice like roaring water. "You have summoned me! What are your commands?"

"Get me out of this dreadful place!" cried Aladdin, and, in an instant, he found himself under the sky, on the very spot where he had last stood with his pretended uncle. But now there was no sign of the fire, of the steps, or of the stone. Aladdin ran off towards home as fast as he could go and at last, out of breath, terrified and weary, he reached his mother's house and threw himself on his bed without a word.

His poor mother, who had been very much worried because her son had not come back at the usual time, was overjoyed to see him. She could tell, however, how exhausted he was and her first thought was to give him something to eat. But there was no food in that poor house, for she had been unlucky that day and had not been able to sell the wool she had spun. As she bent over him, she saw that an old copper lamp had fallen down beside the bed.

"The poor boy!" she muttered to herself. "Food he must have! I will just take this old lamp and sell it." As she picked it up she noticed that the lamp was dirty, so, thinking that if it were polished up she would get more for it, she began to clean it. No sooner had she begun to rub than the most enormous and frightful Jinnee appeared! If the first Jinnee was terrible, this one was ten times worse!

"I am The Slave of the Lamp," said this second Jinnee in a voice as terrible as thunder.

147

"You have summoned me! What are your commands?"

At that the poor woman was so frightened that, instead of answering, she ran away and hid; upon which Aladdin, whom the terrible voice had woken up, started from his bed, seized the lamp and said boldly, "Bring us something to eat!" The Jinnee immediately vanished, but, instantly reappearing, laid down a great silver tray and again disappeared, whereupon Aladdin called back his trembling mother.

The poor house now smelt of the most delicious food, for the great tray had on it twelve silver dishes, and each dish had in it some different and savoury kind of food. There was roast lamb stuffed with green pistachio nuts, there were savoury slices of meat that had been grilled on silver skewers. There was rice with saffron and there were delicious crystallized flower-petals, rose-leaf jam, and other sweet things. As they lifted the covers each dish smelt more delicious than the last. Aladdin and his mother were both very hungry, so that their mouths watered and it was not till they had eaten that Aladdin began to tell his mother all that had happened and, as he told, the poor woman wept to hear how nearly her son had lost his life.

"If he called you 'Son of a dog!'" said she when he had done, "that man was certainly not your uncle! And now," she went on, "take away that terrible lamp, for if that frightful Jinnee ever appears before me again I shall certainly die of fright!"

So Aladdin put the lamp out of sight—well hidden—and they resolved to make no more use of it.

"For," thought Aladdin, "if we keep using the magic of the lamp and if we keep making that fearful, great Jinnee appear, the Magician will somehow get to know about it!"

2. *Aladdin and the Lovely Princess*

NEXT DAY ALADDIN, WHO HAD ALREADY FORGOTTEN all about wishing he had learnt an honest trade, went out and sold one of the silver dishes. They were such poor and simple folk that he did not know how valuable it was and, the merchant to whom he sold it being a cheat, he did not get its real worth. However, he and his mother lived carefully and the good woman went on with her spinning.

So that it was not till the end of a year that all the silver dishes and the splendid tray had been sold. It was then that Aladdin remembered the fruits he had brought back from the wonderful garden. When he took the smallest one to sell he saw, by the astonishment of the jeweller and the great price he got for it, that these pretty magic fruits were not, as he had thought, simply coloured glass, but were really the finest rubies, pearls, opals and diamonds.

Now it happened that, one day, the King's only daughter, the lovely Princess Zadia, with a crowd of her attendants, went through the streets to go to the bath and, the wind happening to blow aside her veil, Aladdin, who was by now a handsome young man, caught sight of her face and was instantly smitten with love for her. "She is as elegant as a gazelle," he thought; "her face shines with loveliness as the moon shines through clouds."

She, too, noticed the handsome young fellow and saw how love overcame him, and, as she passed, she smiled.

"Mother!" said Aladdin, when he came home. "If I cannot marry the beautiful Princess Zadia I shall certainly die! When the King next sits on his throne in audience go

149

and ask him, on my behalf, for the hand of the Princess Zadia in marriage."

But at that his mother laughed and called him a foolish fellow and, when he went on coaxing her and saying that he would die if he couldn't marry the Princess, she exclaimed in horror:

"Are you mad? You will be the death of us both!"

Then Aladdin fetched out the two big leather pouches and poured out all those enormous rubies, pearls, opals and diamonds on to a large china dish, and the jewels glowed and sparkled so much that it seemed as if their

poor house was alight. His mother was even more astonished when he told her of the great price he had been given by the jeweller for one of the smallest.

So at last, although the poor woman felt sure in her own mind that her son really had run mad for love, she agreed to take the whole great dish of jewels as a present to the King, and then, if he accepted them, she was to make Aladdin's extraordinary request. So now every day, for many days, his poor old mother went to the Palace, but, though she stood there before the throne with the carefully covered dish of jewels, she was always too timid to say a word. For many days Aladdin had to wait and, as he waited, he kept thinking of the beauty of the Princess. He thought of her sparkling eyes, her cheeks like pomegranates, her lips like twin cherries, her teeth that were like pearls, and her long hair that was as black as ebony, and, above all, he remembered her bewitching smile that had, in one moment, filled his heart with longing.

Now the King, as he sat on his throne, had noticed this poor woman, who had so often stood humbly before him, and at last one day he told the Grand Vizier to send for her. Trembling, she prostrated herself, said she had brought him a present, and then, at last uncovering the great dish of jewels, the King's hall of audience was filled with their glory.

"How rich! How splendid!" exclaimed the King, who saw at once that these were finer than any of the jewels in his treasury, and who also guessed that the poor woman did not understand their worth.

He was shocked when, in a timid voice, she made the request about the marriage that Aladdin had told her to make. However, he pretended to agree, took the jewels, but told Aladdin's mother that his astrologers had just said that the time was not lucky for the Princess' wedding. He advised her to come again in three months, by which time he would have the marriage contract ready. The King then took the dish and went back to his private room to enjoy the glorious jewels.

Now the King didn't really think that this poor old woman could have been in earnest about her extraordinary request and did nothing at all about a marriage contract. So when, at the end of the three months, she again came to the foot of his throne and prostrated herself before him, he was very much surprised and not at all pleased. It was now difficult for him to draw back, for he had made

151

his promise about the marriage contract in open audience
—his whole court had heard what he had said. His Vizier,
seeing the King's dismay, now whispered in his ear that,
though he could pretend to agree, he could easily make
such difficult conditions that they would be impossible for
any mortal—still less this poor old woman or her son.

The King nodded and, out loud, told the poor woman
that Aladdin could certainly have the Princess in marriage
on certain conditions; first he must give the King, her
father, a present of forty trays each containing jewels as
splendid as those he had already given; next Aladdin must
at once build a palace as fine as that of the King himself
(which two thousand slaves had taken twenty years to
build), and finally that this new palace for the Princess
must stand alongside the Royal Palace. When she had
heard this, the poor mother went back weeping to Aladdin
and told him all that had passed.

"Ah," said Aladdin gaily, "I was afraid you had brought
bad news! Why, dear mother, do you always worry about
trifles? Just leave it all to me!"

As soon as his mother was safely out of the way, Aladdin
brought the lamp out from its hiding-place and rubbed
it. The Jinnee appeared at once and Aladdin gave his
commands.

First he ordered the trays of jewels and forty black
slaves richly dressed, who were each to carry a tray. Then
he ordered a palace, which, he told the Jinnee, must be
built in a single night and which must be far finer than
that of the King. For himself and his mother he ordered
magnificent perfumed robes of rose and amber-coloured
silk sewn with pearls. Then he ordered female slaves and
a jewelled litter in which his mother could be carried to the
palace. For himself he ordered a milk-white riding-horse,

a hundred attendants all magnificently robed and with jewels in their turbans, and a hundred large purses full of pieces of silver money.

So next day a magnificent procession filled the poor street where they lived as Aladdin and his mother, thus dressed and thus attended, set out for the palace. The black slaves went in the middle with the great trays of jewels and with armed men to guard them. Other slaves with trumpets went in front of them to clear a way through the huge crowds that soon collected. After the slaves with the jewels came the splendid litter in which his mother was carried, and on either side of the litter and of Aladdin on his prancing white Arab horse, walked the attendants with the jewelled turbans, each with a purse full of money, which they scattered among the crowds of people who had come along to watch this splendid sight.

153

Long before they got to the palace the King had already heard the noise of the trumpets and of the crowds, and had given orders that the procession was instantly to be admitted. The King was amazed when he saw Aladdin; he had had no idea that it was such a splendid young man who was asking for the hand of his daughter! So the King looked from Aladdin to the jewels and from the jewels to Aladdin. At last the King spoke:

"There is now only one condition unfulfilled, O Aladdin!" he exclaimed. "Where is the palace to which you are to take my daughter, the Princess Zadia, after you are married?"

"Deign, O mighty King, to look out of yonder window," replied Aladdin, bowing. The King turned, and saw through the window that there, upon what had been a piece of waste ground, stood a palace more magnificent than any he had ever seen. It had minarets of white marble, adorned with gold which flashed in the sun; it had steps of clear green jasper and doors of green-veined malachite. Most splendid of all was a great crystal dome in the middle, which was supported on a hundred golden pillars.

So now, since all the King's conditions had been triumphantly fulfilled, he was obliged to give his consent, and the marriage was solemnized amid great rejoicing. After that the lovely Princess Zadia and the handsome young Aladdin lived in the greatest happiness in the glorious palace. The excellent Aladdin had arranged that there should be special rooms in the palace for his old mother; nor did he ever forget that he had himself often gone hungry, so that, every day, he ordered his attendants to give money and food to all the poor people of the city.

3. Aladdin and the Magician again

FAR AWAY, THE OLD AFRICAN MAGICIAN, STILL working at his terrible arts, began to suspect that, though Aladdin, whose help he had tried to use, must surely be long since dead in the cave, someone, somewhere, somehow, had been using the mighty power of the Slave of the Lamp. So he set to work to find out more.

This time he sat himself on a mat with red circles on it and day and night made strange patterns on a tray of flattened sand. It was not long before, by these means, he found out the whole history. He discovered, to his rage, that Aladdin had not died miserably in the cave, but had escaped by using the ring which the Magician had foolishly given him, and that now he was living in royal splendour in a vast palace which, as the Magician knew, was too magnificent to have been the work of the Ring Jinnee, but could only have been built for him by the much more powerful Slave of the Lamp. When he found this out the Magician's rage knew no bounds.

"Black Dog! Gallows Bird! I will spit upon you! Cockroach! I will trample upon you!" he shrieked.

This time the evil old creature disguised himself as a poor old man, transported himself to the capital of China and, mixing among the beggars in the market-place, began to make inquiries. He asked if anyone had heard of a young man named Aladdin.

"Where do you come from, old man, if you have not heard of the famous Aladdin?" answered a blind man.

"Has he not married the King's beautiful daughter?" said an old woman.

"Does he not live in the splendid palace you see over there?" said a lame beggar.

"And," added a fourth, "best of all, this Aladdin rides out every day on a milk-white horse with attendants who scatter money among us."

The African Magician waited to hear no more. He almost ran to the street of the Coppersmiths and, pretending to be a pedlar, he bought twelve fine, new, well-polished copper lamps and a basket large enough to hold them all. Then the pretended pedlar hurried to the street nearest to Aladdin's gorgeous new palace.

He had not waited long when, sure enough, he saw Aladdin himself riding out on his milk-white horse, gorgeously dressed for hunting with his hawk on his wrist, and attended by other riders with glossy hunting-dogs on leashes. As they went, the attendants began to scatter money among the crowds of people who had run up as soon as they heard the gates open and the sound of hooves. The pedlar was indeed the only one who did not join in the scramble as the coins were thrown. He only smiled wickedly to himself and hid in the deepest shadows till the splendid and cheerful cavalcade of horsemen was well out of the way.

When they had gone, the strange-looking pedlar began to walk up and down the street and, as he walked, he called out at the top of his voice:

"New lamps for old! New lamps for old!"

It was not long before the street was again crowded, this time with people who were curious to see this queer old pedlar who seemed to want to make such bad bargains. Still the Magician cried as before:

"New lamps for old! New lamps for old!"

Soon, among shouts, jeers, laughing and noise, first one

and then another among the crowd ran home and came back with an old battered lamp and, sure enough, there was nothing to pay when they got a fine, new, shining copper lamp in exchange.

Now this curious scene had been watched by one of the ladies who attended on the lovely Princess Zadia and who had been sitting with her embroidery at an upper window. It seemed to her so odd and amusing that, after a while, she left her embroidery frame and ran to tell the Princess.

"O Madam!" cried she, "outside there is an old mad pedlar with a basket on his arm full of new copper lamps and, would you believe it, he is crying 'New lamps for old! New lamps for old!' and, Madam, the people are bringing out old battered lamps and he really is giving away his new lamps in exchange!"

The other ladies wouldn't believe her and said such a thing was impossible. At last Princess Zadia, laughing, said that they could soon settle the question. One of them must see if she couldn't get a new lamp for herself!

But where, objected another of the ladies, could they find such a thing as an old lamp in a palace so splendid that even the saucepans were all made of silver?

Then a little black page-boy spoke, saying that he had noticed that, in Prince Aladdin's own robing-room, hidden away in a corner, there lay, forgotten, an old dirty lamp.

"Yes," said the first lady, delighted. "The boy is right!

157

It's an old battered thing of no value! If the Princess
allows, we can do as she suggests and settle the argument!"

No sooner said than done, and while the little page-boy
ran off to get the lamp, the Princess and her ladies, taking
their veils, all leaned out of the palace windows to see what
would happen in the street below.

"Old man! Old pedlar! Give me a nice new lamp for
this!" called out the black boy in his shrill voice as he
opened a little low door in the great palace wall. The
crowd parted when they saw the Princess' richly dressed

158

little page. Then the Magician saw that an old dirty lamp was being held out to him by the little black hand and, when he saw it, he felt sure that this was indeed the precious thing that he had come so far to seek. Taking from his basket the last and finest of his new lamps, he almost snatched the old one out of the little boy's hand. At that the crowd shouted with laughter at the folly of the mad pedlar while, up at the window, the Princess and her ladies clapped their hands in amusement.

The moment he had got the lamp, the old Magician

dived down among the crowd and ran off. Finding a
deserted corner, he stood still and rubbed the lamp. Instantly a dark cloud covered the sun and the immense
Jinnee stood bowing before him.

"Slave," ordered the Magician breathlessly, "take me
up, as well as that palace over there—take it up, with all
who are in it, and convey us to the most distant part of
Morocco and set us down in a desert place!"

In the twinkling of an eye the thing was done, and the
place where the splendid palace had stood a moment before was once more bare and waste.

The dust of this terrible upheaval had hardly settled
before poor Aladdin rode home again on his fine white
horse.

The fury of the King, and now the grief of Aladdin,
knew no bounds. Guards had been waiting, and now they
dragged Aladdin off his horse and set him, bound, before
the throne of his furious father-in-law.

"Wretch!" cried the King, shaking with anger. "It was,
I see now, by sorcery that you built this palace, and now
again by sorcery you have robbed me of my beloved
daughter Zadia! Your head shall immediately pay for
this!"

Poor Aladdin had not a word to say, so stricken was he
with grief for the sudden loss of his dear Princess. The
guards now stripped him of his fine robes, his hands were
tied behind his back, a rope was put round his neck, and
he was immediately led off to the place of execution. But,
as he walked through the dust of the streets, all the
people wept in pity, for they had loved the handsome,
generous Aladdin. The executioner stood ready, and soon
the deadly block lay before him.

"Let me at least say my last prayers!" begged Aladdin.

"Let me raise my hands to heaven to ask mercy!"
So, in pity, they loosed his hands and, standing there
with the block before him, Aladdin chafed his fingers a
moment, for they were numb from the tightness of the
rope. As he did so, he happened to rub the ring which, in

the tumult of his grief, he had forgotten. Instantly The
Slave of the Ring (a Jinnee only less mighty than The
Slave of the Lamp) bowed before him. The bystanders
had had no time to move or say a word before Aladdin
had cried:
"Take me to the side of the Princess Zadia, wherever
she may be!"
No sooner were those words out of his mouth than,
of course, Aladdin had vanished before their eyes.

Imagine the joy of the poor Princess Zadia! For now, after her terrible adventure and when she had believed that she was alone and utterly in the power of the horrible Magician, she now, quite suddenly, found her dear husband, Aladdin, beside her once more. After they had exclaimed and embraced each other, Aladdin asked her anxiously what had become of the old lamp that used to stand in his robing-room.

Now the Princess had begun to suspect the truth, and had realized that she had been imprudent, so she told him the whole story of the pedlar and his cry of "New lamps for old!" and the joke that her ladies had made of it. She also added that the worst of it was that, now that she was in his power, the wicked old Magician was trying to force her to marry him.

"Where does he keep the lamp?" asked Aladdin, and the Princess told him that, unfortunately, the Magician took the greatest care of it, carrying it always inside his robe. They had only just had time to arrange a plan when they heard the voice of the Magician in an outer room; indeed the Princess had only time to tell Aladdin that she understood her part and to hide him behind a curtain.

The Magician had come yet again to tell the Princess that her husband was dead, to remind her that she was in his power, and to order her to marry him.

He had become very angry at what he called the Princess' obstinacy, but this time he was pleased to notice that not only did she look more beautiful than ever, but she had stopped crying and lamenting, and even seemed quite cheerful! His wicked heart was indeed overjoyed when, instead of hiding her face, Princess Zadia smiled sweetly at him and even ordered her ladies to set fruits and snow-cooled sherbet before them.

So well did the Princess play her new part that the old Magician was soon quite delighted. Calling for her lute, she sang for him, and as she sang she smiled still more sweetly and, at last, calling for a yet more delicious sherbet, she offered to change cups with him in token that she would have him for a husband. Then Aladdin, from his hiding-place, reached out a hand and slipped a sleeping potion into one of the cups, signing to the Princess which cup to take for herself. All this time the Magician had been so busy gazing at the lovely Princess that he saw nothing and, draining the drugged sherbet to the dregs, he fell into a deep sleep.

Aladdin instantly came out of his hiding-place, searched the robes of the sleeping sorcerer, drew out the lamp and told the slaves to toss the wicked old creature out of the palace window.

Then Aladdin rubbed the lamp, and gave his orders,

163

whereupon the prodigious Jinnee instantly transported the palace and everything in it back to China to the very place in which it had stood before. So gently did he do it that the Princess only felt two little shocks, one when the Jinnee took it up, and one, a moment later, when he set it down again.

And so they all lived happily ever after and, when at last the old King died, Aladdin and Princess Zadia inherited the kingdom.

POMEGRANATE OF THE SEA

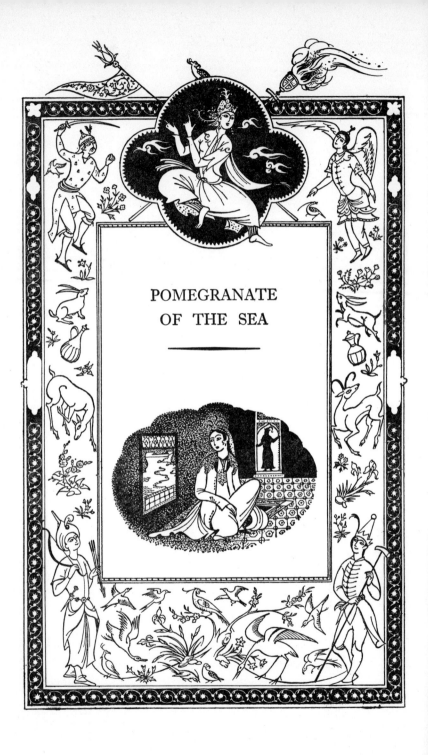

POMEGRANATE
OF THE SEA

ONCE LONG AGO, IN THE LAND OF PERSIA, there reigned a King who had no child. He lived in a beautiful palace by the sea and he had many wives, and many charming slave girls waited upon him, but he had neither son nor daughter. After a time he began to despair and to lament because now it seemed that there would never be a prince or a princess who would inherit the kingdom peacefully, as he had inherited it from his father and forefathers.

One day, as he sat in an inner court of his palace, a merchant came bringing a beautiful slave girl for sale. When he unveiled her the King saw that her face was delicately pale, her lips were red as cherries, and that she moved on small feet and as lightly as thistledown and that her great black eyes (which at first she kept obstinately cast down) had a strange expression in them. It seemed to the King that she was like a gazelle or some wild fawn that a hunter had captured. Though the King had seen many beautiful maidens, he thought that he had never seen one as lovely as this, and it seemed to him that, to him who could win her love, she would be the cure for all sickness of heart. So it was not long before the merchant departed with robes of honour and a bag of gold, leaving the beautiful girl in the palace by the sea.

The King felt sure that this could be no ordinary slave girl and he began to speak gently to her. But she answered not a word. He told the attendants that she was to be treated with honour, and gave her a beautiful room in the women's quarters, a room whose windows looked out on a wide terrace, which in turn almost overhung the sea. He ordered that the doors were to be kept locked, for he thought that the lovely silent creature might very likely try to make her escape. Then he ordered the slave girls to pre-

167

pare a perfumed bath for her and, after that, delicious food and sherbets cooled with snow, so that she might be refreshed after her journey.

In the evening the King came to visit her. Coming in, he paused for a moment and stood gazing at the lovely girl. She had not noticed him and he saw that she sat very still and was looking fixedly out over the terrace at where the first pale stars were just then rising out of the sea. When he moved and she heard him, she did no more than glance round, and again turned towards the sea, and, with her great black eyes, continued to gaze at the water. Then the King came nearer and, speaking kind words, he put his arm round her slender waist and pressed his lips gently to her cheek. To all this she made no resistance and it seemed to him that to kiss her was sweeter than to eat honey. But still, to all the loving things that he said to her she did not answer a word.

So presently the King clapped his hands for the attendants and ordered food and sweetmeats to be brought. When they came he sat by her and coaxed her and himself began to eat, but still the girl looked out to sea and still she said nothing.

"Well," thought the King, "if she will not use that beautiful mouth for speaking to me (say what I will, and although my heart is likely to break with her beauty) perhaps she will use it for eating." So he began to pop morsels of the choicest food into her mouth. These she ate, but, to all he could say, she returned never a word. Yet, though he was a great King, and was now her master, he spoke to her as though he were a young lover courting a princess.

Next day, when it was still the same, it seemed to the King that he had a right to be angry with such stubborn-

ness, for surely the girl was returning him evil for good?
But when he looked at her again the words of anger died
on his lips, so lovely did she seem to him, so that of his ill-
humour he spoke not a word and, instead, sent for scribes
to draw up a marriage contract, so that, instead of being
his slave, she was now his Queen. But even now, though
she did not repulse him and made no objection to the
marriage contract, it was only now and then that she
would even raise her beautiful black eyes to look at him,
and never once did she utter a word.

"How elegant, how lovely she is!" said the King to himself. "Surely Allah never made anything more beautiful.
If she would only speak she would be perfect!"

For a whole year things went on like this. At last, one
day the King himself took a lute, for he was skilled in
music, and, touching its strings, he sang to her:

"Far from the storms of this world there is a garden
 Whose Roses neither autumn nor winter shall ever find.
 My heart is that garden and its roses are born for you."

169

Then, laying the lute aside, the King took her hand and said, "O desire of my soul! My love for you is so great that for all this time I have been, not your master, but a faithful husband. In the name of Allah the most High, I beg you to soften your heart and speak to me! Or, if by ill fortune you are indeed dumb and unable to speak, let me know this by a sign so that I may give up hope of it! I am lonely though I am a King, and my hope was that perhaps Allah would bless us with a child, for there is no one to inherit my kingdom after me. I beg you that you will speak to me if you are able, telling me perhaps that all my love has not been in vain."

At last she raised her great black eyes and for the first time looked the King full in the face and, as she looked, she smiled, and it seemed to him that the whole room was filled with light. At last she spoke and her voice seemed to the King as soft and musical as the sound of a fountain.

"O King!" said she. "O good and magnanimous King! Your love and patience have deserved that I should break my long silence. Know that, if you had not been thus patient, I should never have spoken one word. But now you shall hear my name and my story.

"My name is Jallanar, that is 'Pomegranate Flower', and I am 'Jallanar-of-the-Sea', for I am the daughter of one of the chief Kings-of-the-Sea. My father died and I had a quarrel with my brother, the new king, and, in my anger, I swore that I would live no more in the sea, but would leave them

all—him and my mother and my sisters, and live upon the land! So, still very angry, I rose out of the water and sat upon a rock, not caring what should happen to me. The first man who passed by was struck by my beauty, just as you were, and he carried me off and wanted to force me to marry him. But I hated him and, in a struggle, I almost killed him; yet, though he was wounded, he managed to tie me with a rope and, since he now hated me as much as I hated him, he sold me to the merchant, who sold me to you.

"Know, O mighty King, that if you had not loved me and been faithful to me and had not made me your Queen, I should not have stayed with you. The locked door would not have kept me in, for at any time I could have thrown myself into the water from this terrace and, walking on the sea, as is our custom, I could have gone back to my own people.

"But your words were always gentle and your behaviour courteous, you tried in every way to please me, and so, little by little, I put off my departure and grew to love you. But still by keeping silence I resolved to see whether your love would last, or whether, because you are a great King and believed yourself to be my master, you would, in the end, treat me as a slave! But this you have never done."

When he heard her speak in this way the King was transported with delight and would have stopped her mouth with a thousand kisses, but she turned a little from him, making signs, though with great sweetness, that this was only because she had more to say.

"I have yet more to say for your delight, O most excellent King," said she. "In a short time I shall bear you the child for which you have always longed."

At this the joy of the King was complete!

171

Next day when, he sat upon his throne, all his nobles and courtiers could see that his face was full of happiness, and he soon ordered his Vizier to give a splendid thank-offering of money and food to all the poorest people in the

Kingdom. Then, going back to his Sea-Princess, he begged her to tell him if there was not anything more that she desired and that he could do.

"All my kingdom," said he, "everything that I have, is yours and I am become your slave!"

"There is still one thing that my heart desires," said she. "I long to see my brother, my mother and my sisters, and to show them our child as soon as it is born."

The King answered that he would send messengers immediately. But she smiled and said that that would not be necessary. All she wanted was that he should agree to their coming.

"We walk on the sea or we walk under it with our eyes open. Below those waves that foam down yonder are wonders and riches greater than any upon the land. Soon I will call my kinsfolk and show them that my anger is past,

172

SEE P. 177

The sea foamed once more and there was the uncle again

that I have found happiness and that my first-born child will be the child of a great king! Your part, if you consent, O King, will be to stay hidden for a while, to listen to our talk, and afterwards to welcome them."

To all this the King joyfully agreed, and not long afterwards, amid the rejoicings of his whole Kingdom, a beautiful boy child was born to them.

One calm evening Jallanar said to the King, "The time has come! Hide yourself, dear husband, where you can see and hear, and then listen patiently."

Then Jallanar went out on her terrace, and first she lit a small fire of sweet-smelling wood. Then she gave a long, low whistle and spoke magic words while the smoke began to drift out over the sea.

All at once, though the weather was calm, the sea began to fret and foam as if in a storm, and out of the foam rose a tall and handsome young man, richly dressed, and the King, in his hiding-place, marvelled, for it seemed to him that this young stranger was as handsome as his sister

173

Jallanar was lovely. Then there
rose up also a stately woman,
old and very tall, and after her
five lovely maidens, splendidly
adorned. He saw that all these
stately people had come up
from under the sea without

174

being wetted, and that now
they walked on the water and
came to the steps that led up
from the sea to the palace, and
that Jallanar made haste to meet
them and that they embraced
her with tears of joy. At last the
tall old woman said to her:

175

"O daughter, we have been now for four years without any joy or pleasure, for you had left us and we had no word whether you were alive or dead."

"Let me tell you my story, O my Mother," answered Jallanar.

So then the King saw that they all sat down, and heard that, as Jallanar told her story, they each urged her to come back to the sea with them. At this the King's heart grew cold for fear that she should leave him. But at last Jallanar answered them all:

"Dear kinsfolk, do not speak more of this! Dearly as I love you, I cannot come with you, for I fear that this King-of-the-Land would perish for grief if I left him! He has treated me with love and courtesy, so that now I have grown to love him. Moreover I have a beautiful boy-child that I cannot leave for love, nor will I take him with me, for this boy is this King's only child and heir to his Kingdom!"

When they heard this they were all glad of her happiness. Then Jallanar went quietly to the King in his hiding-place and she smiled upon him and asked if he had heard how she had praised him.

"Oh light of my eyes!" he whispered. "When I heard how they urged you to come back my heart was almost dead for fear! But now, in this good hour, I believe at last that you love me as faithfully as I love you."

"The reward of kindness is kindness!" she answered. "And the reward of love is love!" Then she led him to the Sea-King, and to her mother and sisters; they all greeted each other with courtesy and kindness, and soon the King clapped his hands, and a feast was brought, and they all ate together. After which Jallanar brought out the child so that his sea-kindred might give him their blessing.

Now this child was a lovely child—a baby not a month old. After his grandmother and Jallanar's sisters had blessed him, it was the turn of his uncle. But, as soon as the Sea-King had the baby in his arms, he began to walk along the terrace towards the steps with him, and, in another moment, he had carried off the baby and, though at first walking on the surface of the sea, he soon plunged with it beneath its surface.

The grief of the unfortunate father can be imagined, for now he was sure that he would never see his son alive again. But Jallanar consoled him.

"Do not forget that, through me, he is of the kin of the sea and that I love this little one. My brother will not let the sea harm him."

All the same, the King remained in great anxiety, pacing the terrace and wringing his hands.

But soon he saw that the sea foamed once more, and in a moment there was the uncle again, walking towards them on its surface with the little one safe in his arms. The Sea-King restored the baby to its father's arms, and the latter did not cease to bless the mercy of Allah! Then the young Sea-King asked him, smiling:

"Were you afraid for the little one, O King-of-the-Land?"

"I was afraid indeed!" answered he, holding the baby in arms that still trembled.

"What I did, O King-of-the-Land, was for his good! The child is now safe from all dangers of the sea. When this little one can walk on the land he will, like us, be able to walk safely on the water or go down to its depths. I went also to bring a trifling present for you."

With this there fell from the Sea-King's hands great chains of jewels, green emeralds, milky pearls, blue jacinths, and a hundred others, and as the chains of jewels fell they seemed to grow in length and splendour. He gathered them as if they had been pebbles and laid them courteously at the feet of the King-of-the-Land.

At last, after they had all rejoiced and feasted together for many days, the Sea-people went back to the sea; but Queen Jallanar stayed with her husband and the little one and, each year, the Sea-King and her other kindred visited them again.

As the years went by the child became a handsome boy, and learned writing, reading, history, grammar, archery and horsemanship, and when the King his father was very old and it was time for him to die, this young Prince succeeded him in peace; for all the people loved the young man for his goodness and, when he was of age to marry, his mother Jallanar and his Uncle the Sea-King found for him a beautiful Sea-Princess.

THE PICKPOCKET AND
THE THIEF

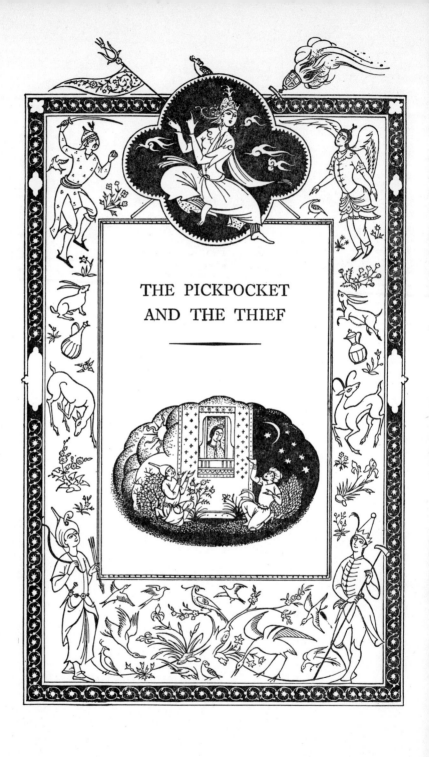

THE PICKPOCKET
AND THE THIEF

THERE WERE ONCE, IN CAIRO, TWO ROGUES, AKIL the pickpocket and Haram the thief. Each of them, unknown to the other, was courting a charming but prudent young woman who had inherited a large fortune. But, since the pickpocket stole by day, his time for singing under her window was the night, while the thief always came under this very same window to whisper and court by day, for his time for breaking into houses was the night.

As for the young woman, she very much enjoyed being courted, and so she said soft words to both. But she only sat at her window to talk with them and would never open her door or say "yes" to either. This was because neither seemed willing to tell her what he did for a living and, though she wondered very much and often asked questions, she could never get at the truth. Now such a state of things—the secret of a day-shift and a night-shift of suitors—could not last for ever. They were bound to find out that, while pretending to love only one, she was really encouraging two young men! One morning the two of them met, and discovered, to their rage, that she had been smiling at both of them, so now, under the very window at which each had spent so many hours of soft sighing and sweet whispers, they began to quarrel, to shout abuse, and to fight.

Soon, darting furiously after each other, they knocked each other down, their turbans rolled off in the dust and their clothes were almost in tatters. Still scrambling, rolling and tumbling after each other, they looked up presently and saw that a crowd was collecting. Neither of them wanted that! Such fighting in the streets was not allowed; the guards might come, or someone they had robbed recognize them, so, picking up their turbans and winding them on again and dusting themselves, they began to pretend that this had been just a friendly scrap! Putting their arms round each other in a brotherly way, but with hatred in their hearts, they walked quickly off to try to find a quieter place in which to go on fighting.

However, as they walked, each began to think that the fight had been rather an even one. Perhaps if neither seemed able to get the better of the other by fighting, they had better think of some other way of deciding which of them was to marry the young woman.

"You shall never have her! You are as clumsy as a rotten melon! But there isn't in all Cairo so clever a pickpocket as I am!" muttered Akil in Haram's ear as they still walked and pretended to be great friends.

"Rubbish, you son of a dog!" whispered back Haram. "Picking pockets is nothing! I rob houses and that is a much more daring trade than yours! You're as awkward as a cow! Your great feet could never tread softly enough for my work!"

Well, it wasn't long before they were quarrelling again, but, this time, it was about which of them was the cleverer.

They had now reached the part of the market where the money-changers had stalls, at which foreign merchants (or Cairo merchants who were going abroad) could get the right sort of coinage.

"Do you see that old man going from stall to stall with a bag of money?" said Akil boastfully. "Watch me steal his bag!"

"What? Steal it among all these people?" said Haram, who stole quietly at night, and who felt quite nervous in daylight. "You must be mad! The market guards are certain to see you!"

"Ho! Frightened, are you?" said Akil. "Just you watch! With the help of those very guards I shall make the old man give me the bag!"

Walking as lightly as a feather, Akil crept up behind the old man, undid the string that tied the bag to his belt and brought the bag of money back to Haram.

"That was certainly a smart piece of work," said Haram doubtfully. "All the same——"

"So far, that's only beginner's work," said the cunning Akil with a laugh. "I mean to get the law on my side!" So, going to a quiet corner and making Haram, who was still decidedly nervous, stand so as to hide him, Akil undid the bag and counted out five hundred gold pieces. Ten of them he took out, the rest he put back into the bag and, with them, a large copper ring, with his initials on it, out of his own pocket. Then, going back, he softly tied the bag on to the old man's belt again.

No sooner was this done than Akil rushed round in front of the unfortunate old man and began to shout and wave his arms.

"Vile scum! Wicked old man! Old thief!" he yelled. "You have done that trick once too often! Give me back my bag, or else come with me before our noble Cadi, the Judge!"

The poor old fellow was so bewildered that he came along quite meekly and didn't even struggle as Akil dragged him along by the beard till they stood before the Cadi, who, as Akil well knew, always sat in judgment on market days so as to settle all disputes immediately.

Akil, standing before the Cadi, raved with pretended indignation, declaring that the old man was a wicked pickpocket and had just stolen his bag for the third time! The poor old man kept saying in a meek voice that he had never even seen Akil before!

At last the Cadi ordered them both to be quiet.

"Whichever the bag belongs to," said he, "will know what is in it," and with that he told the old man to speak first.

"Good master, it contains exactly five hundred dinars and nothing else," said the unhappy old man.

"You lie, you thieving dog!" shouted Akil. "It contains exactly four hundred and ninety dinars and a copper ring which has my initials on it!"

And so, of course, when the guards opened the bag in front of the Cadi, that was exactly what they found in it. So Akil was given the bag and went off with it rejoicing, while the poor, innocent old man not only lost his money but was punished.

Haram, when they were alone again, had to admit that this stealing with the help of the Cadi and his guards was certainly a very neat trick!

"But," went on Haram, "clever as you are, I am cleverer! You have certainly had the laugh of the old man, and the Cadi, and all those guards. But come with me tonight and we will have the laugh of the Sultan himself!"

Now, just as Haram had felt nervous in the bright sunlight and among the crowds of the market, so, in his turn, Akil felt quite frightened when he joined Haram that evening out in the lonely street. The night was particularly dark and all the streets and narrow alleys were silent and deserted. However, he met Haram and they went together to a back lane that ran along the side of the

Sultan's garden. He was horrified when he noticed that Haram had with him a rope ladder. However, Akil was ashamed to show how frightened he was, so he helped Haram to throw the ladder till the hooks at the top of it were safely lodged on the top of the garden wall of the palace. Very quietly they both climbed up, drew up the ladder, dropped down and found themselves in the Sultan's garden. Crouching in a shadow till a watchman with a lantern, who was patrolling the garden, was out of sight, they managed to creep through a little door into the palace itself.

Inside, it was blacker than ever. As they went softly along, feeling their way down dark passages and up and down steps, Akil began to feel so frightened that he could hardly bear it; indeed, his terror made him tremble so much that his legs were almost too weak to hold him. What was his horror when, finally, Haram crept into a room in which a single perfumed lamp burned and Akil saw that this was the Sultan's own gorgeous sleeping room!

There lay the Sultan, asleep but restless, and beside him sat a young page-boy, who was gently stroking and rubbing the Sultan's legs and feet whenever he lay still enough.

"Don't be afraid!" whispered Haram. "Just hide behind this curtain and listen! You spoke to the Cadi, now I'm going to speak to the Sultan!"

Akil was too much frightened even to beg him not to!

Then Haram, moving as quietly as a moth, crept up behind the page-boy, put his hands over the boy's mouth, went on to gag and bind him—and all without a sound—

187

and then pushed him over to the wall as if he had been a parcel. Then Haram himself sat down in the boy's place and began to stroke the Sultan's feet exactly as the page had done. Presently, however, Haram began to do this less gently and indeed so hard that, after a while, the Sultan yawned and half woke. Then said Haram in an excellent imitation of the voice of a boy:

"O most splendid of Sultans! Since you cannot sleep, shall I tell you a story?"

"Certainly," said the sleepy Sultan and yawned again.

"There was once," said Haram, still in the disguised voice, "a thief named Haram and a pickpocket named Akil. Unknown to each other, they were rivals in love and, discovering this, each determined to show the other how well they knew how to steal! . . . " And then, to the listening Akil's horror, Haram went on to tell the Sultan

all about the theft of the bag and what the Cadi had said and the whole of the rest of the story. When he had explained exactly how they had got into the palace and how the little page had been got out of the way, Haram added:

"Oh most glorious Sultan, your wisdom and knowledge are so great that nothing is hidden from you. Judge then, I beg you, which was the cleverer of the two."

But the Sultan's eyes were still shut and, though he had laughed several times while Haram was telling his tale, he now only answered sleepily that it was not his custom to give judgments in the middle of the night! So then, when his snores assured the two rogues that he was safely asleep again, Haram crept back to the trembling Akil and the two of them made off as they had come.

Next morning, what was the amazement of the Sultan and his attendants to find that his little page-boy lay gagged and bound by the wall. Gradually the Sultan began to remember the odd story that had been told him in the middle of the night and, in great astonishment, ordered in his guards, telling them to search everywhere to see what the thieves had taken.

When the guards found that nothing had been stolen, the Sultan, his anger now cooled, began to remember again that it really had been a very good story, even if—as it turned out—it had been a very impudent one! At last he began to laugh so much that he had to hold his sides! Finally he sent heralds all round Cairo to blow trumpets and proclaim that not only were the two rogues forgiven, but that they would be given rewards if they came to the palace. He further ordered the Cadi to send his guards to the unfortunate old man and to give him, not five hundred, but a thousand dinars from the royal treasury!

Of course, the whole story was soon being told with

shouts of laughter in every corner of Cairo, so that it was not long before it reached the ears of the rich young woman whom both these rogues had been courting.

"So now, at last, I know what their trades are!" she exclaimed and, though she, too, laughed so much over the story that she felt quite weak, she wisely decided that she would marry neither of them!

THE MAGIC HORSE

THE MAGIC HORSE

THERE WAS ONCE, LONG AGO, A KING IN PERSIA who loved philosophy and geometry, but even more, this King loved to be astonished. Anyone who brought to his court some new magical invention was sure to get a splendid reward, so that all sorts of magicians and inventors brought him their marvels, and soon his treasure-house was full of such things as trumpets that blew themselves, mechanical peacocks that spread their tails every hour to tell the time, and many other curiosities.

Such things were always brought to the King on the first day of a certain great feast that the Persians held every year, and all the people came out on holiday to see. It was always a fine sight, for the King would be out in the main square seated on his throne, he would be dressed in magnificent robes embroidered with many colours and he would wear on his head the glittering royal diadem, crowned with a shining image of the sun.

On one day, as the King sat on this gorgeous throne with his courtiers round him, he saw the crowd part and that a strange, ugly-looking old man was coming towards him.

The old man (who was a magician) was leading the figure of a great black horse, as large as a real horse, and as they came nearer the King saw that the horse was made of ebony and splendidly caparisoned. When he had kissed the ground before the King, the old magician spoke, telling him that this horse was able to fly with its rider through the air.

Now it was the King's custom never to accept any invention or to give any reward till he had seen with his own eyes that the invention would really work.

"Mount your horse then, O sage," said the King, "and

bring me a leaf from one of the palm trees that grow at the foot of yonder mountain."

The old magician bowed, mounted the horse, the horse flew into the air and, in a few moments they were back again and the strange-looking old man had laid the palm-leaf at the King's feet.

"What reward will you take for this marvel?" asked the delighted and astonished King.

"I must have two rewards, O most magnificent King," answered the wizened old magician.

"Name them!" answered the King, looking at the magic horse with longing.

What was the horror of all who stood by, and especially of the young princes and princesses, when the hideous old magician said that he must not only have a great sum in gold, but also the hand of the King's youngest daughter in marriage!

"The first demand is easy," answered the King, frowning. "You shall have twice as much gold as you have asked for! Do not ask for the second!"

So they began to bargain, but all could soon tell that the King so much wanted the horse that he might perhaps be persuaded. However much the King's unfortunate young daughter wept, the old magician was not going to part with his horse unless he got her as well as the gold.

Now the King's son, Yusuf, the young Prince of Persia, who stood near his weeping sister, had been watching carefully and had seen that, when the magician had mounted the horse, he had put his hand to a sort of wooden peg, a turning-pin, on its neck. So, thinking that, if his precious horse was up in the sky, the horrible old man would be more likely to listen to reason, Prince Yusuf ran out from among the courtiers and guards, vaulted on to the

horse and immediately turned the pin. Whereupon the
horse soared into the air as before, so that Prince and horse
were soon out of sight.

Then a dreadful thought occurred to this bold young
man. True, he had seen what the magician did to start the
horse and to make it fly, but he had not been able to see
what he did either to turn it or to make it come down
again. Prince Yusuf pulled first one rein and then the
other, trying to turn the horse's head. But still it flew
straight on, mounting higher and higher, so that the air
grew cold and soon the Prince could no longer so much as
see the ground below him. How heartily he wished that he
had not been so hasty! However, luckily, though he was
certainly rash, he was also a sensible young man and, as
well as he could—though they were still rushing through
the air at a great speed—he began to feel about on the
horse's neck and shoulders, supposing that whatever it
was that turned the horse or made it come down must be

195

somewhere in reach of its rider. Presently he thought he felt a sort of knob on the horse's right shoulder and, putting his hand also on its left shoulder, felt that there was also another knob on that side.

So great was the speed with which the horse flew that he could hardly see out of his eyes. However, he bent down and at last saw that these knobs were neatly made in the shape of a cock's head. He thought he would try if they would turn, like the pin that made the horse fly. Turning the cock's head on the right shoulder, he found that the horse not only turned to the right but began to come down, while the same thing happened with the knob on the left.

Prince Yusuf's heart was filled with joy, for now that he had control of the flight, he was able to enjoy the wonderful sensation. He came lower now to admire the country over which they were passing. All was strange, and he saw rivers, mountains and cities that he had never seen before. About sunset he began to feel very hungry and to think that he would soon have to choose a place in which to come down.

Soon he saw below him a beautiful city, and, best of all, just near the city wall, but outside it and set in a beautiful garden, he saw a palace that seemed to be built of white marble. Coming lower, he saw that this palace had a flat roof, and on this roof the Prince decided to land.

Now though, as was said, he was exceedingly hungry and also rather a rash young man, he now wisely decided that he and the horse had better try to stay hidden on the roof till the sun had set and it was dark. So, on the palace roof and with the magic horse beside him, he sat and waited.

He had, of course, no idea what sort of people might live in this palace, but he could hear people moving about below, and soon it seemed to him that he heard the voices and laughter of girls. As soon as it was dark, he very cautiously opened a small door. This led, he found, to a little staircase and, as he hoped, down into the palace.

Everything seemed quiet, and inside it was very dark indeed, but at last, at the end of a passage, he saw a chink of light. Moving softly towards it, he saw that this faint light came from behind a curtain and, gently pulling this curtain aside, he found that he was looking into a large and beautiful room.

All round this room were divans and cushions, and on these lay, asleep, a number of beautiful girls. In the middle of the room, on a couch enriched with gold and set with pearls, lay the most beautiful of them all, and on the floor by her side dozed an old woman. The Prince was astonished by all this, and especially by the beauty of the girl on the golden couch, for it seemed to him that she was as lovely as a wild tulip. He said to himself that she must certainly be a king's daughter.

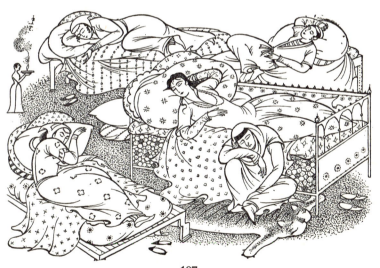

197

Quiet as the Prince tried to be, it was, of course, not long before one of the ladies in the room began to wake up, and when she woke she cried out in terror. Then they all woke and saw that, somehow, a handsome young man had got through the armed guards that always stood at the gate of this beautiful summer palace.

The Princess was the first to recover and soon her old nurse told the others to be quiet.

"For," whispered the old woman to the ladies, who had crowded behind the golden couch, "this is no doubt the young Prince of India who seeks to marry our Princess Laila! As you know, she begged her father, the King, to refuse him because she had heard that he was unbearably ugly!"

"But this young man is not ugly at all," whispered back one of the ladies.

"Of course not!" said the old nurse. "The King must have sent him here so that Princess Laila could see with her own eyes how handsome he is."

While they whispered Prince Yusuf had come nearer and had begun to talk most respectfully to the beautiful young Princess, so that any fear she might have had of him should be at an end. He told her as quickly as he could the extraordinary adventure by means of which he had got into her palace.

"If I must go in the morning," he ended, looking at her mournfully, "I shall leave my heart behind me, for your beauty has stolen it out of my breast!"

Now the old nurse, still believing that he must be the Indian prince and was there by the King's leave, had already ordered one of the slave girls to bring a tray of sweetmeats and some cups of sherbet. All the girls, and even the charming Princess Laila, laughed when they saw how extraordinarily hungry this handsome young Prince seemed to be, and they all amused themselves by bringing in more and more food. But hungry as he was, Yusuf went on telling the Princess how much he loved her, and soon, though she had begun by being afraid and had gone on by laughing at him, she began to think that she had never seen such a charming young man. All the same, she began to feel only too sure that he was not, as her nurse supposed, the Indian prince, but that the story he had told her when he first came in was nearer the truth.

"I am afraid," said the Princess, at last, "that when my father hears of all this he will be furious!"

"But will he be angry even when I tell him that I am Yusuf, Prince of Persia?"

"Yes, indeed! I am sure he will. I am ready to believe all you say. I am sure that you really are a prince, and I even believe about how you got here! But the King, my father, will not look at it as I do. You ought—he will say— if you are a real prince, to have come first to him and to have arrived with proper attendants and a letter from your father. Instead, he will say, you came like a thief! If he is half as angry as I fear, he may kill us both. Dear Prince Yusuf, though it breaks my heart to say it, I think you had better go, for he is sure to come in the morning to visit me."

At that Prince Yusuf declared that he could not bear to leave her, and the end of it was that they secretly agreed that the best thing would be for her to mount the magic horse behind him and for them both to fly back to his father's city.

"My father," added the young man, "has only to see you to be sure that you are not only a real princess, but the loveliest maiden in the world! You are like one of the wild

199

tulips that grow on our mountains, you are like one of the roses in our palace gardens. We will make sure that he receives you with all possible honour! I shall go first to him and tell him that you are willing to make me the most fortunate young prince in the world!"

As soon as it began to be light Princess Laila told her old nurse that she just wanted to go for a moment on to the roof to see a beautiful present that the Prince had brought for her, and then off they both ran, up the little staircase. The nurse was old and could only follow slowly, and no sooner were Yusuf and Laila on the roof than he quickly lifted her on to the horse, jumped up in front of her, told her to hold on tightly, and then turned the magic peg. Away they flew, leaving the poor old nurse staring after them and wringing her hands.

Now Prince Yusuf was determined, as he had already declared, to show his lovely princess the greatest possible honour, so that she should never regret having left her father and her own country. To make sure, he unfortunately decided to land with her, not at his father's palace, but at a small summer palace in a garden, rather like the white marble one where he had found her. There he left her with one or two women attendants, kissing her hands and begging her to rest after the journey, and telling her that he would go quickly to his father and tell him what had happened, and that then they would ride out to welcome her royally, and so that she could be brought to her new home with a splendid procession.

Now, while the Prince had been away, the unfortunate King of Persia had been mourning over the disappearance of his dear son Yusuf, while the magician in his turn had been mourning over the disappearance of his magic horse! Unluckily it was the magician, and not the King, who had

kept careful watch on the sky and who now saw how the
horse had suddenly reappeared again—this time with two
riders. The magician saw how it had circled, and had come
down, not in the great square of the city, but in the garden
of the summer palace.

Quickly running to the gate of this garden, the magician
asked the attendants for the news, and, peering round the
corner, saw that his magic horse stood at the palace door.

"Great news!" said the attendants. "The young Prince
has come back and brought with him a bride as lovely as a
wild tulip. The Prince has just this moment left her here
to tell his father and to get his consent to their marriage.
The King and the Prince are expected back here within the
hour to fetch the bride!"

Then the cunning magician saw a way not only to get
back his horse, but also to get his revenge on the Prince.
Making some excuse to the attendants, he went to where

the Princess was resting. Bowing respectfully before her, he said:

"Lady! Your bridegroom, Prince Yusuf of Persia, has sent me. He begs you to mount the magic horse and to ride to meet him in the great square of the city, where the King waits to honour you."

Now Princess Laila did not like the look of this hideous old man, and wondered why the Prince had sent such a strange messenger to fetch her. Guessing her thoughts, the magician added in a humble tone, "Do not wonder, oh most beautiful Princess, that he has sent me! My Prince loves you so much that he could not bear that any handsomer or younger man should come before you, for he knew that your exquisite beauty would instantly have bewitched him! He was also not sure that you know how to control the flying-horse. I am the only other person besides himself who understands it."

Now it was true that, in their hurry, the Princess had not seen how the horse was made to fly, turn and come down, so, though still with a doubtful mind, she at last consented to go with the wicked old magician.

No sooner had they mounted, and begun to fly, and saw the city under them, than she saw that the King and the Prince were that moment riding out of the palace gates with a splendid retinue and with a splendid litter carried by camels. Seeing this, the horrible old magician flew low, and the unfortunate Prince looked up. When he saw, and guessed what had happened, the Prince's heart grew cold in his breast!

As for the Princess, as soon as she felt that, instead of coming down, the horse had begun to soar into the sky again, she too saw that they had been tricked and began to lament and weep. At that the magician told her roughly to be quiet.

"Henceforth," he said, "I am your master! I made this horse and that young Prince took it from me! Now I am revenged, for I have stolen his bride and tortured his heart!"

So, in spite of her tears and pleading, on they flew and at last, when sunset was near, the magician brought the horse down and they landed in a meadow where there were trees and a river.

Now this was in a place far away from Persia, but not far from the city of a certain Greek King. It happened that this king had ridden out to hunt, and, as he was riding home, he saw in the meadow what appeared to be a beautiful black horse. He also saw that, by it, stood a hideous old man in a strange dress, and that before the old man crouched a beautiful young damsel whom he was threatening with a whip. It seemed to him that the damsel was

crying out in sorrow. So the King ordered his attendants to bring this strange pair before him and he saw that the girl was exceedingly lovely.

203

"Lady, what relation is this old man to you?" asked
he. But before she could speak the magician hurriedly
answered:

"Sir, she is my wife!"

At that the Princess cried out in indignation and told the
King that the old man was not her husband but a liar and
a rascal who had carried her off by fraud and force.

Now the King of the Greeks was very ready to believe
what she said for, though he was rather old and fat, he had
already fallen in love with her. So he immediately had the
magician carried off to prison, the beautiful ebony horse—
whose magic properties he did not, of course, understand
—was put into the king's treasury, while Princess Laila
herself was given a fine apartment in his palace.

What was her horror when, next morning, the fat Greek
King came to her and—thinking that she would be delighted—told her that he had just arranged for them to be
married the very next day.

"Look out of the window," said he. "The whole city is decorated in honour of our wedding!" In vain she protested that she did not want to marry him. He only smiled and nothing that she said would make him believe that she was not delighted with so great an honour.

Meantime the poor young Prince Yusuf, though he determined at once, in spite of his father's opposition, to set out to look for his vanished bride, was in a most unhappy state, for the fact was that he had not the slightest idea where to look! First he went back to her father's kingdom, but there they could tell him nothing, and only mourned the loss of the lovely Laila.

One day, as Yusuf sat in the bazaar in a certain city, and when he had almost given up hope, he heard a group of merchants who were talking about their travels.

"Has the Greek King married his bride yet?" asked one.

"No! How can he? She is as mad as ever!" answered another.

"And what happened to the ebony horse?" asked the first.

"I believe that it is still in his treasury," answered the second.

As soon as he heard the words "Ebony Horse", Prince Yusuf left the corner in which he had been sitting and, coming up to the merchants, began courteously to question them, and they soon told him not only about the ugly old man, the beautiful damsel and the ebony horse who had suddenly appeared, but also the name of the Greek city and where it lay.

"Unfortunately," added they, "this beautiful damsel seems to have been mad ever since she was found. The King of the Greeks has called in doctors from every country, but not one can cure her. She is certainly beautiful, but often so violently mad that, if her hands are not tied, she will pull out a man's beard or scratch out his eyes, and she gets no better. By now even the doctors are afraid to go near her."

Now, not only did the Prince, as he heard this, feel sure that this must be his Laila, but also that Laila was not really mad but had, no doubt, thought of this excellent way of putting off her marriage to the Greek King. He rejoiced greatly, for he now felt sure that she must still love him and must still hope that somehow he would find her, and this thought made him ready to sing for joy.

So, as he journeyed to the Greek city, Prince Yusuf began to think what he would do, and decided to disguise himself as a doctor. Thus disguised, he soon stood before the Greek King and, with a solemn and grave look, bowed before him.

"What is your country?" asked the King. "And what is your profession?"

"I am, O Magnificent King, a Persian," answered the Prince, "and my profession is that of a doctor. Though still young, I have become skilled in my art through deep study. I wander through many countries, curing the sick and the mad. Such, O King, is my occupation."

"Then," answered the King, "you have come to us at the very time of our need," and he began to tell his story and, though he had heard it already from the merchants, Yusuf pretended to be very much surprised.

"Alas, the lovely creature grows no better, and now it is even dangerous to go near her," added the King. "But if, O learned doctor, you can cure her, you shall have as a reward anything that you desire! She is so beautiful that my heart grows weary at the delay in making her my wife!"

Then the sham doctor pretended to ponder deeply and to ask many questions. Especially he asked about the ebony horse and, shaking his head, he soon said that the madness of the damsel was likely to have something to do with it. At last he asked to examine it, for he thought to himself that, if the horse was undamaged, it would be their best means of escape.

So the horse was brought out and, when he had had a good look at it and saw that, luckily, it still seemed as good as ever, the pretended sage said that he must next see the patient.

"I now suspect that her madness is the work of some powerful Jinnee who works by means of this ebony horse," he said gravely. "It is possible that I may be able to cure her by using the same means, but if she is as violent as this noble King has declared, I must first try to quieten her a little. Your Majesty is welcome, of course, to see what I do, but I must beg that no one should be within hearing, for I must speak secret words of power."

So the fat King took the pretended doctor to a little lattice window from which they could both see into the Princess' room and she, as soon as she heard footsteps, began to shriek and groan loudly. The King remained at the lattice where he could see, and Yusuf went into her room.

When Laila saw what she took to be yet another doctor coming in, she began to moan and throw herself down, and, in general, so violently did she pretend to be mad that for a moment or two the Prince was unable even to whisper in her ear. But when he whispered her name she knew him! But, looking up at the lattice from behind which the Greek King was watching, the clever girl only uttered a cry louder than before, and then fell down in what seemed to be a fainting fit. The pretended doctor, while every now and then he loudly called out some word that would sound to the King like a spell, bent over her. "O delight of my eyes," he whispered, "how clever has

SEE P. 200

Prince Yusuf turned the magic peg and away they flew

been your trick!" Then he called out loud, "Foul Jinnee, be silent!" Then he whispered again, "Now be patient and firm yet a little longer, beloved." Then he called aloud again: "Go back among the demons!" and then whispering again, "If we can only manage things cleverly enough, I have thought of a trick by means of which we can escape from this tyrannical king!"

"I listen, sweet Yusuf!" she whispered back, but then gave a loud groan for the King to hear. "O treasure of my heart," she whispered again, "I will do just as you tell me. OH! AH!" and again she pretended to shriek.

So, like this, they managed to agree on a plan, Yusuf all the while pretending to utter spells and Laila still pretending to cry out. They arranged that, as soon as he left her, Laila was to pretend to be rather better and was to seem weak and quiet, and was to consent to see the King. This was to make him believe in the young doctor's cleverness. Then, after that, the pretended doctor was to announce solemnly to the King that he had now discovered that the terrible madness was certainly caused by a Jinnee which worked through the ebony horse and that, for a complete cure, it would be necessary to take both her and the horse back to the original meadow and to let her sit for a while on its back while he performed certain magic rites. There were good hopes, he was to say, that he would in this way be able to get rid of the Jinnee altogether.

The Greek King was, of course, delighted when, weak though she seemed, the lovely damsel was able and willing to receive him. She spoke courteously, too, and even smiled, so, after this wonderful proof, he was anxious to do everything that the young doctor suggested.

So next day the King ordered the horse to be carried

down to the meadow. He and his bodyguard rode down, too, while Princess Laila, still pretending to be very weak, was carried down in a litter. When she arrived Prince Yusuf, still in his doctor's disguise, was already explaining to the King that it would be necessary to lift the Princess on to the horse, and he begged the King and his body-guard to stand well back so that, once more, he could see but not hear. He would be obliged, Yusuf went on, to light fires to make a smoke, and to burn magic herbs. He also would, he explained, at a certain moment, have to mount the horse in front of the damsel, when the Jinnee might make a fight of it.

"This, O Magnificent King, will very likely make the horse move in a violent way, but do not be alarmed—after that it will all be over!"

The King agreed to everything, for he supposed that what was meant by "it will all be over" was that she would be cured and he would have his bride again, safe and sound.

So then the pretended doctor lit the fires and made a great smoke all round the horse. Soon he lifted the Princess on to its back and, after a moment or two more, got up in front of her. Whispering to her to hold on tightly, he immediately turned the pin that made the horse rise, and away they flew, with the Greek King and his bodyguard looking peacefully on! Indeed it was not till he had waited half a day for their return that the fat King, beginning to feel that perhaps he had been tricked, returned sadly to his palace. However, his wise men soon consoled him, found him another bride and assured him that he was well rid of such enchantment and craftiness!

As for the happy Prince Yusuf and his lovely Laila, they flew on all that day rejoicing, and as fast as ever the ebony horse would carry them. At last they arrived at the Persian King's city and, this time, the Prince took care to land just by his father's palace.

And so they were married, amid great rejoicings, and the Princess Laila sent messages to her father telling him that she was safe and happy, and with the message Prince Yusuf, her husband, sent splendid presents, so that his father-in-law might know that it was in truth to the son of a great king that Princess Laila was now married.

As for Yusuf's own father, the King of the Persians, he decided that he had had quite enough of being astonished, and he had the turning-pin taken out of the ebony horse so that his son should not be tempted into any more dangerous adventures.

So they all lived happily ever after. Prince Yusuf and Princess Laila continued to love each other and, in due time, Yusuf reigned in his father's stead.

ALI BABA AND
THE FORTY THIEVES

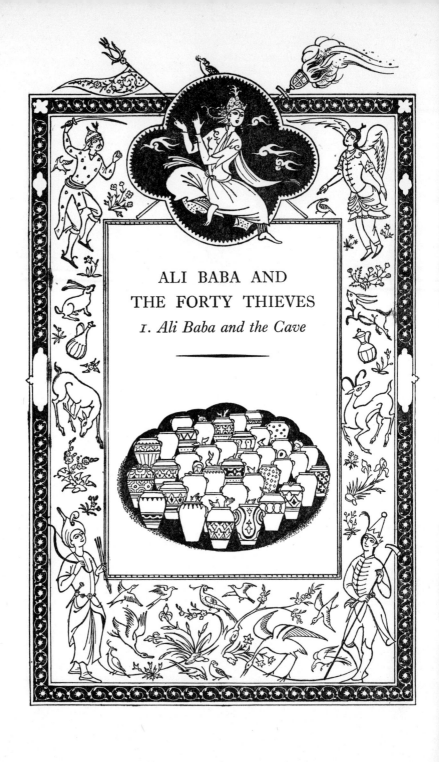

ALI BABA AND
THE FORTY THIEVES

1. Ali Baba and the Cave

LONG AGO, IN A CERTAIN CITY, THERE LIVED TWO brothers. Kassim, the elder, married a rich, disagreeable wife and, with the money she brought him, set up a shop in the market. He was a hard, shrewd, grasping fellow and got very fat, for he made a good living; but he loved himself so dearly that nobody loved him, except his younger brother Ali Baba. Luckily he and his wife had no children. So much for the fat Kassim.

Ali Baba, who earned a poor living as a woodcutter, was very different. He married a good sort of girl with no money but a kind heart. Allah blessed them with a son whom they named Ahmad, but they had no daughter, so they managed to buy a baby girl whom they named Morgiana. The good woodcutter and his wife grew to love this Morgiana and brought her up more like a daughter than a slave, though, indeed, as soon as she was big enough, she was so willing and clever that she did a great deal of work for them. Ali Baba, too, worked hard and, though at first he was so poor that he had to carry his loads of faggots on his back—all the way down from the hills and into the market—the time came when he could afford to buy a donkey and, after a time, two more.

But all this while, when even a small loan of money would have been most welcome, he got no help from his fat, selfish brother. This unbrotherly conduct of Kassim's was all the worse because they lived quite near to each other, so that Kassim and his wife knew perfectly well that, while for instance they were saving up for money to buy another donkey, Ali Baba and his family were often hard put to it to get enough to eat.

One day Ali Baba was cutting wood in a part of the forest where some great rocks marked the foot of the mountains and, while he worked, his three donkeys grazed nearby. His axe rang out loudly among the trees but, pausing for a moment, he heard, in what should have been the silence of that lonely place, another sound. Listening intently, he decided that it was the sound of galloping horses, and he was afraid, for he knew that such a sound, in such a place, boded no good either to him or to his precious donkeys. So he quickly led the beasts off and tied them up where the thick undergrowth hid them and, praying to Allah that none of them would bray and so betray their hiding-place, Ali Baba himself, who had a peaceable nature, climbed up into a tree that stood on a little knoll and gave a good view of the rocks.

Not a moment too soon! The noise of galloping grew louder and then a band of wicked-looking horsemen—each heavily armed with daggers and scimitars—swept into sight. They had dark faces, their great black beards were as coarse as the bristles of pigs and were parted in the middle, in such a way that they looked like the two wings of a carrion-crow.

Ali Baba counted thirty of them and then, nine more, and last he saw their gigantic captain, who looked more evil and ferocious than the rest. At a signal from him they all dismounted, tied up their horses, and each began to unload his heavy saddlebags. One by one they took these saddlebags to the foot of the great rock and, when they had them all piled up ready, the robber chief, standing in front of a part of the rock that was as steep as a wall, called out in a loud voice, *"Open Sesame!"*

With a noise like thunder the rock began to gape. First there was a crack and then a great split, and when the split was wide enough, each man took up his pair of saddlebags and disappeared inside. When all were in, they were followed by the robber captain. Then Ali Baba heard his voice again, "*Shut Sesame!*" and with the same noise the rock shut upon them.

"Allah grant that they don't, by their sorcery, find me in this tree!" said the terrified Ali Baba to himself, and he fixed anxious eyes on the place where he could see the branches moving as his three precious donkeys stamped at the flies and tugged at their tethers.

As he had no idea what was likely to happen next, or when the robbers might reappear, he thought it best to stay in his tree. After some time the rock opened again and the robbers all began to file out, this time carrying empty saddlebags. They went straight to their horses, and when all thirty-nine were out and had mounted again the terrible-looking robber chief came out too and called out, *"Shut Sesame!"*

As soon as the rock had shut again, he, too, mounted, when the whole black-faced, hog-bearded band of ruffians made off at a gallop.

At last, when all the sounds of shouting and horsehoofs had died away, poor, frightened Ali Baba (thanking Allah that not one of his excellent donkeys had brayed) came down from his tree. His first thought had been for his donkeys, for it was on them that he and his family depended for a living.

But now Ali Baba was overcome with curiosity and, going up to the rock, he examined it carefully. He looked, he felt with his finger, but the rock showed no sign of the split he had seen, indeed there seemed not to be even a crack into which he could have got the point of a needle.

"This place is certainly guarded with a spell," said he to himself, "and yet, all I heard them say was the name of a harmless grain—sesame, the grain that my wife buys sometimes to make cakes. I wonder if that is really enough?" And then, in a trembling voice, Ali Baba, turning again to the rock, said softly, *"Open Sesame!"*

To his amazement the rock at once obeyed and, with a noise like thunder, the great split appeared in its smooth face, and then, once more, the forest was still.

Ali Baba was almost too frightened to look inside, but at last, plucking up his courage, he took a step forward and then he stared with all his eyes. What he had expected to see will never be known, but what is certain is that this was not a dreadful cavern dripping with horror. On the contrary, a dry, level gallery led to a large hall hollowed out of the mountain and cunningly but rather dimly lit by slits contrived in the roof. Ali Baba turned back to the opening and, saying the words which shut the rock (for he feared that if one of the robbers came back he might be seen), he walked boldly on and, in a few steps, found himself in the great cavern.

As his eyes got used to the light he saw that all along the walls, piled up to the roof, were bales of silks, bars of silver and gold, and great chests which were so full of treasure that their contents spilled out on to the floor. Ali Baba could hardly put down a foot without treading or tripping on something precious!

Looking more closely, he saw that some of the gold cups and necklaces and bracelets were of ancient workmanship, and some were new, so that it seemed to him as if this cavern must have been, for hundreds of years, the secret store-place of many generations of robbers.

"Allah be praised!" said Ali Baba. "For he, who loves to reward the simple, has made me, a poor woodcutter, master of the fruit of terrible crimes. Now, instead of being used by those ruffians, the treasure will be put to the innocent use of a poor family!"

Then Ali Baba began to think once more of his three donkeys, and sat down to consider how much treasure each could carry without being overloaded. He calculated that each must also carry a small load of light faggots so that no one should guess his secret.

He decided to take only coined gold, for, if a poor woodcutter were to try to sell even one of these emeralds and

diamonds, or a single gold cup or bracelet, then who knows what questions and trouble might follow. So, with modest good sense, Ali Baba only gathered up what it seemed prudent to take—that is, what the robbers would not be likely to miss immediately and what his precious donkeys could easily carry.

Safely Ali Baba once more opened and then closed the rock, safely he brought up his three donkeys, safely he put on to the back of each two small bags of gold nicely hidden with faggots. As they all four walked down the mountain to the city, Ali Baba found himself speaking quite softly and respectfully to his donkeys instead of shouting at them. He told them that they had eyes like dark pools of water—which was true. He called them "Grey Pearl", "Silken Ears" and "Nightingale", instead of "Obstinate Pig", or "Stumbler", or "Daughter of Evil", as he often did (just to make them mind their work). For now he kept remembering that on their humble grey backs they carried enough gold to make a dowry for a princess. So the donkeys—for such is the nature of donkeys—loitered and stopped often to snatch a nice-looking mouthful of grass and, in short, took double their usual time to get back home.

Once safe in his own courtyard, Ali Baba threw down the faggots and began to take the six small but heavy bags of gold into the house. Now these were bags from the cave and, since they were poor, his wife knew every bag and basket that they had, so she was surprised to see six strange bags, and still more surprised when—to help him —she lifted one of them and found how heavy it was. So she began to ask where they came from.

"These bags are from Allah, good wife! Help me to carry them, and don't torment me with questions!"

"Money!" said the good woman to herself as she heard the clinking, and she supposed that they must be full of copper coins. But six bags even of copper coins seemed to her a great treasure and she began to be frightened, thinking that in some way her good, honest, timid Ali had been up to no good. She even began to beg him to take them away in case they brought bad luck, so, before letting her see what the bags really held, Ali Baba swore her to secrecy, and when, after locking the door, he had poured the flashing gold out on to the floor, she became so frightened that he thought it best to tell her the whole story.

When she heard it, and knew that Ali Baba had been able to bring it all safely and secretly to the house, the poor woman's joy was as great as her terror had been.

2. *Ali Baba and Kassim*

"HELP ME NOW, WIFE!" SAID ALI BABA WHEN HE HAD finished the tale of the robbers and the treasure-cave. "We will only keep out a few coins at present and we will dig a trench under the floor of the kitchen and hide the rest of the money."

"But we must count it first!" said his wife.

Ali Baba laughed. "Poor, foolish woman!" said he. "You could never count all that!"

She said she could, he said it would take too long. She began, but after an hour she gave it up.

"But surely, husband, we must at least weigh or measure it? I will do the measuring while you dig under the floor," she went on. "Like this we shall know how much our dear son will inherit from us."

"But we have no measuring bowl or scoop, for we have never been able to buy enough grain or flour at a time to measure anything," he answered.

"That is true," said his wife. "But I will just step round and borrow a measuring scoop from our sister-in-law— Kassim's wife."

"Be sure you don't say a word about the treasure!" said Ali Baba and his wife, agreeing, promised not to say a word.

Now, though Kassim's wife was so mean that she had never given her nephew Ahmad or the girl Morgiana so much as a sugared chick-pea—the very cheapest kind of sweet—while they were children, she could not very well refuse the loan of a wooden measure for a few minutes. All the same, she was curious to know what sort of grain these poor people had in such quantity that a measure was needed.

"Will you have the small measure or the large one?" she asked.

"The small one, O my mistress, if you please," answered Ali Baba's wife humbly.

As she was fetching the measure, Kassim's wife thought how interesting it would be just to know what it was wanted for.

"My poor, silly sister-in-law," said she to herself, "is sure to put the measure down on the grain, so if I rub a nice, thick bit of suet on to the underside a little of whatever she is measuring is sure to stick, and then I shall know."

Sure enough, when Ali Baba's wife got home the first thing she did was to put the borrowed measure down on the top of the pile of gold and, just as Kassim's wife had intended, the suet stuck to what it had been put on, so that a single gold coin remained on the under side and, in this way, Ali Baba's wife—poor creature—was the innocent means of giving away their great secret!

No sooner was the measuring done and the gold buried, than back she ran in a great hurry to her sister-in-law's house and, thanking her for her kindness, gave her back the measure.

Hardly was her back turned when Kassim's wife turned the measure upside down, and what was her amazement to see, sticking to the under side, a shining golden dinar!

Kassim's wife at once felt furiously jealous! The thought that, in her sister-in-law's house, they had so much gold that they measured instead of counting it, was poison to her. However, she just had enough sense not to go shouting to the neighbours about this strange affair. But as soon as her husband came back, she showed him the gold and told him what had happened.

Instead of rejoicing at his kind brother's good luck, Kassim grew yellow with envy and he felt that he could never rest till he not only knew the secret but got some of the gold for himself. So, without waiting a moment, he rushed round to his brother's house.

He found Ali Baba in the kitchen, still with the pickaxe in his hand and, without a word of greeting, and speaking low between clenched teeth, Kassim hissed in Ali Baba's ear:

"O ill-omened brother! How dare you be so secretive! Tell me immediately how it is that you—dirty, starved-looking creature that you are—have so much gold that you measure instead of counting it?"

Poor Ali Baba was dumbfounded, and when his horrible brother shook the gold dinar under his nose and threatened to tell the rulers of the town that Ali Baba was a robber and to have his donkeys killed and the whole house pulled about his ears, he at last told Kassim the story, but without telling him the magic words which opened the rock.

"The words! The words that open the cave!" said Kassim, looking furious. "Don't dare to hide anything!"

"Dear brother," answered Ali Baba gently, "we are the children of one father and one mother! I will willingly share the treasure with you, good brother! But don't ask me the words! To prove that I am in earnest you can have half of all that I brought home to-day."

SEE P. 216

" *Open Sesame!* "

"No!" answered the black-souled Kassim. "The words! I must know the words! I want to be able to go there myself! Tell me directly or I will tell everyone that you stole the gold."

So, though he feared that evil would come of it, Ali Baba was obliged to tell his brother both the way to the rock and the words which opened the treasure-cave.

Now Allah contrives many ways in which to bring the wicked and heartless to destruction, and it was through his own selfish greed that Kassim met with his just reward.

The very next morning, as soon as it was light, Kassim, who had refused Ali Baba's offer to act as guide, stole off secretly with ten mules each carrying empty sacks. He found his way to the place, tethered the mules, stood before the smooth face of the rock and cried with all his might, *"Open Sesame!"*

When the rock opened he rushed into the cavern and, almost stunned by the sight before him, had hardly breath to give the order that closed the rock again. He saw gleaming silks, cups made of chased gold of exquisite workmanship, jewels fit for the turban of a Sultan, anklets, necklaces, bracelets, earrings, bars of gold, minted money! All this was piled in great heaps right up to the top of the cavern or was littered and scattered about. The sight quite dazzled Kassim and he began to mutter:

"Ten mules? Pooh! Not enough! Twenty mules? Pshaw, only a beginning! Not all the camels of all the merchants that visit our city at the great fair will be enough to carry away all this splendour!"

Talking out loud to himself and rushing from one side of the cavern to the other, fat Kassim began to beat his forehead and scratch his head, trying to think how he would ever be able to contrive to get it all for himself. Soon he began to collect "just a little" (as he called it to himself) into the sacks that he had brought. But he was so greedy that he was always unpacking a sack in order to put in something still more valuable that had just caught his eye and, being very fat, he was soon quite breathless and exhausted. At last, still thinking how he could get yet more, he began to drag his heavy sacks to the end of the gallery and to pile them up. It was not till he was nearly fainting with his effort and his wild excitement that he decided to go.

And now it was that Allah turned Kassim's shocking greed against him, for, in his excitement, and thinking only of his wild plans to keep all the treasure to himself, he found that, when he needed to speak it, he had forgotten the word! He stood thinking! It was the name of a grain —he knew that much—but which grain?

"Open Barley!" he cried. *"Open Millet!"* *"Open Wheat!"* But all in vain; the rock remained shut. He began to be afraid.
"Open Rice!"
"Open Rye!"

Still it was of no use. There he stood, speechless now, and growing more and more terrified and confused. At last he heard a noise like thunder and a crack of light began to appear. It was the robbers! They had come back, had seen the mules, had leapt from their horses, had looked everywhere for the mules' owner, and now their chief, pointing his drawn sword at the rock, had spoken the magic words, *"Open Sesame!"*

Kassim, guessing the terrible truth, made a wild rush for freedom as the rock split, only, at the very entrance, to be cut into six pieces by the swords of the furious robbers. The thieves laughed loudly, wiped their swords, tossed the wretched fragments inside, emptied out the sacks of treasure that Kassim had piled up, and then had a look to see if anything else seemed to have gone. But so great was the mass of treasure that they never missed the six small bags of gold that the careful Ali Baba had gathered from here and there.

And now the forty robbers sat in a circle discussing (as well they might) how this greasy citizen, who had not looked the sort of man who ever came to the forest, could have discovered their secret. They got angry, so that, if it seemed that one of them had accidentally betrayed it on a visit to the town, the others were soon quite ready to cut off his head and to leave him to keep company with Kassim.

Unable, talk as they would, to guess how this strange and awkward event had happened, they decided to leave Kassim's body in the gallery, where, said the robber chief, it would be a warning if anyone else, by ill fortune, had also discovered the way to the cave.

Now all that day, Kassim's wife, who alone knew where he had gone, waited in vain for him, and so it was that, when night fell, she went wailing to Ali Baba's house to beg his help. But it was now pitch dark, so, till morning came, all that Ali Baba and his wife could do was to try to comfort the weeping woman, She, to tell the truth, was quite as much crying and wailing because the treasure might be lost, as for fear of what might have happened to her fat husband.

As for Ali Baba, he was truly troubled about his brother; he had forgotten all Kassim's heartlessness and only remembered how they had played together as boys. So the dawn was scarcely grey in the sky before the good Ali Baba and his three donkeys once more set out for the forest.

First he hunted about for his brother's mules, but the robbers had taken them all, and when he did not see them Ali Baba grew terribly afraid. When, at the threshold of the rock, he saw a stain of blood he shuddered for pity, so that it was in a trembling voice that he cried once more, *"Open Sesame!"*

Alas! What a sight met his eyes! His knees knocked together with terror when he saw the six pieces into which the robbers had hacked Kassim, and cruel and heartless as the dead man had been to him, Ali Baba wept.

"The only thing I can do for you now, my brother, is to give you decent burial, so that your poor ghost shall find rest," said he to himself and, though he very well understood the danger of what he was doing (for it would mean that the robbers would know that this dead man was not the only one who knew their secret) he found sacks and divided the new load in such a way that it could be put on the backs of his three donkeys and hidden, as the gold had been, with faggots and branches. Then, when all was finished, closing the rock once more, Ali Baba set out sadly on his journey home.

3. Ali Baba and Morgiana

WHEN ALI BABA GOT BACK WITH KASSIM'S BODY IT so happened that it was not his wife, but their adopted daughter—the slave-girl Morgiana—who came out to meet him and to help him to tie up the donkeys. Ali Baba was glad to see who it was, for he was rather superstitious. Indeed, as he had walked back sadly from the forest with the donkeys, he had been thinking that, perhaps, as it had been through his wife, who had insisted on measuring the gold, that his brother and sister-in-law had discovered their secret, the less the good woman had to do with it all, the better. Though innocent, she might, he thought, bring them all back bad luck again. So he was pleased that it happened to be young Morgiana who helped him to unload, and it was to her that he first told what had happened.

"Morgiana, my pretty one," he ended, "we shall need all your wit and cleverness over this! While I go with your adopted mother to break this terrible news to my sister-in-law, you try to think of some way in which we can manage to have a proper funeral. We don't want questions! Somehow the neighbours had better be made to believe that poor Kassim died of a natural illness. But I can't think how it's to be managed!"

With that Ali Baba left her and went into the house and, telling his wife briefly what had happened, they both went off to try to break the news to Kassim's widow in such a way that she would not let out the secret. She really must be persuaded not to do too much loud crying and wailing or else the neighbours would guess that there had been a death.

229

So young Morgiana sat down and thought, and, being a very clever girl, she soon hit upon an excellent plan. She went off to a certain neighbouring druggist who she knew was a great gossip. When she got to his shop she told him, with a very long face and in a tone as though she were rather frightened, that she had been sent by her master to buy a certain very expensive mixture that was well known to be good against a fever called the Red Evil. "My master's brother," she added, "Kassim the merchant, has suddenly fallen very ill."

Some hours later she went again.

"Alas," said she, "the merchant Kassim grows no better! We fear it may indeed be the Red Evil! His face is yellow, he cannot speak, and seems blind! Allah help him! He hardly moves or breathes! Our only hope is now in your skill, oh most learned druggist!" (Here she seemed ready to burst into tears.) "Let cost not be thought of! Mix us something so powerful that it will bring my master's poor kinsman back from the very edge of the grave!"

On each walk to this gossiping druggist, as she came and went, Morgiana had taken care to chat with everyone she knew about the sad illness of her master's brother. She told them, moreover, that Kassim had been moved to Ali Baba's house for better care.

The consequence was that, next morning, the neighbours were not surprised to hear piercing cries and lamentations and to be told the news that Kassim the merchant was dead.

Now Kassim, as has been told, had been chopped into six pieces, and it was the custom in that city not to have the dead put into coffins, but to bury them well wrapped in costly shawls.

"We shall have succeeded in nothing, Master, if we cannot manage to make him seem to be all in one piece!" said Morgiana thoughtfully to Ali Baba when he praised her for what she had already done. Ali Baba dolefully agreed, but could think of no way of managing this.

Now there was a poor old cobbler who lived in the district, and what did the excellent Morgiana do but hurry off to him. Slipping one of the gold dinars from the treasure into the old man's hand, she said to him:

"Oh most excellent of cobblers, we have need of your best skill! Also," and here Morgiana dropped her voice to a whisper, "we have two more of these gold dinars."

"If it is anything lawful that you ask me to do, oh excellent and charming one, I will do it!" answered the delighted old cobbler, whose work very seldom brought him one, let alone three, gold pieces.

"It is indeed lawful! In fact it is only a little sewing! But also it is a secret," replied she. "So my master has told me that, unless, when you come with me, you will consent

231

to be blindfolded, I am to take the two other gold dinars elsewhere!"

The end of it was that, that night, Morgiana came to fetch him, and the old cobbler agreed to have his eyes bandaged, and Morgiana, taking an extra turn or two for safety, led him round about to a cellar under Ali Baba's house.

When the old cobbler's first surprise and dismay were over, he finally did his work very neatly and was taken back just as he had come.

Thus it came about that Kassim was, once more, all in one piece, and neatly wrapped in thick shawls and tidily arranged on a carrying litter. When the Imam (who was the priest of the nearby mosque) and all the neighbours assembled for the funeral, no one could possibly guess that it had been the swords of forty furious thieves, and not the Red Evil, that had brought the greedy merchant to his end.

And now, for almost a whole month, peace descended upon the two households. Ahmad, Ali Baba's son, who was a pleasant, handsome young man, took over the shop of his dead uncle, and the customers found him so much more agreeable and so much more honest, that the shop prospered more than ever. Ali Baba's wife, who, though perhaps rather a silly, fussy woman, had a very kind heart and a forgiving nature, went to be with her sister-in-law during the time of her widow's mourning. Then, as otherwise Morgiana would now have had all the work of their house on her hands, Ali Baba bought a strong, cheerful young black slave named Abdullah so that, after all that the clever girl had done for them, his dear Morgiana's work should be light.

Morgiana, who truly loved her master and mistress (who were indeed the only father and mother she had ever known), would hardly accept the pretty bracelets, anklets, earrings, and other small presents that the grateful Ali Baba gave her. As for Ali Baba himself, he knew that he had secrets to keep and that he had many inquisitive neighbours, so he was careful not to alter his way of life and so draw attention to himself. So he used very little of the gold under the kitchen floor, but went on, just as before, cutting faggots and selling them. Indeed, except the buying of the young black man, the only change in Ali Baba's way of life, and that of his three donkeys, was that never, never did he turn their grey noses down any path that led anywhere near the rock of the robbers, but cut his faggots as far away from it as he could.

Now the reason why, for nearly a whole month, all had been so peaceful was that the thirty-nine thieves and their captain had ridden off, far out into the desert, to attack a caravan, and it was only after this long journey that they came back to their cave. As soon as the captain had said the magic words and they began to go in with their booty, the very first man saw at once that Kassim's body had disappeared. They were all now much alarmed, for they realized (as Ali Baba had been sure they would) that this meant that some living man knew their secret!

Again they searched the cave, this time more thoroughly. Still they did not miss the small amount of treasure that Ali Baba had taken. Finding that only the dead body had vanished, their surprise was all the greater and they began to quarrel violently with each other, and each man accused another of having, in some way, betrayed the secret.

At last the ferocious robber-captain clapped his hands for silence. Then and there he told them that one of his followers would have to venture, disguised, into the city as a spy and try to find news of a man who had been cut into six pieces.

"Know, before anyone offers himself for this task, that if he fails, or in any way betrays our secret, I shall myself strike off his head with my scimitar!"

In spite of this, one of the thieves at once agreed to go. So, next morning, before it was light, this thief disguised himself carefully as a wandering dervish or holy-man, and went down to the market.

Now when he got there it was still so early that it was scarcely light and most of the shops were still shut, but seeing an old cobbler already in his shop and busy threading a needle, the pretended dervish greeted him politely and remarked what excellent eyesight he must have.

"Yes (thanks be to Allah!) my eyes are good," answered the cobbler, pleased at the compliment. "Indeed I can do even better than that! Why, not long ago I even sewed together the six parts of a dead body in a cellar that had less light than we have now."

The pretended dervish, who had already made out that he came from far away, said that he was surprised to hear that sewing up the dead was one of the customs of the city.

"Nay, it's no custom here! This was done secretly!" answered the cobbler.

"How very interesting!" answered the pretended dervish. "I should dearly like to see the house!" And with that he offered the cobbler a piece of money if he would show him.

"How can I show the house to you, O holy man? I was blindfolded and led there by a young slave-girl who took me there and back with many turns and twists!"

The end of it was that, partly by bribery and partly by flattery, the pretended dervish persuaded the old cobbler that he was sure to be clever enough to find the place if he were again blindfolded and allowed to grope his way there.

Alas for Ali Baba and all in his house! The cobbler did, in the end, succeed in leading the disguised robber to the very door.

Now the street was a long one with many doors and courtyards, all rather like those of Ali Baba. Determined that there should be no mistake when he brought along the others, the robber at once pulled a piece of white chalk out of his girdle and marked the door with it and then, having paid and thanked the old cobbler for his trouble, he hurried back to the forest, and there he boasted to the robber-captain about how well and quickly he had done his errand.

Now it so happened that hardly had the cobbler and the pretended dervish left the street, than Morgiana—on her way to the market—came out of the house. Ever since the strange events of nearly a month ago the clever girl had been on the alert and more than ever quick in noticing every little thing, for she felt only too sure that they would not be left in peace for ever. So now, as she left the house, she turned back for a moment, upon which her eye fell on the white chalk mark.

"This did not write itself!" thought Morgiana. "Some enemy has marked us out for misfortune," and, slipping back into the house, she got another piece of white chalk, and quickly marked every door and gateway on both sides of the street. Then, well pleased, but still a little uneasy, she went off to do her marketing.

Early next morning, on their captain's orders, the robbers began to come two by two into the city. Not wanting to attract attention, each pair chose a different road. What was their bewilderment, when they met in the street which the first thief had described, to find that not only one, but more than a dozen houses were each marked with the white chalk which was to have been the signal! There was nothing for it but to go back to the forest, where, in his rage, the robber-captain cut off the head of his first unsuccessful spy. The robbers were now more uneasy than ever, for it seemed to them that their enemy must be very much alive, and also exceedingly clever.

There seemed nothing for it but to send another thief to bribe the old cobbler once more. This time, with no difference except that the second robber dressed himself up as a foreign merchant, the same thing was done. This time the pretended foreign merchant made a very small red mark instead of a large white one. But Morgiana was on the look-out now, found the red mark almost as soon as it was made, and, when the robbers crept two by two into the city again, it was to find small red marks on all the doors for half a mile around! When they all got dolefully back to the forest, the second thief met his end.

Then it was that the robber-captain decided that he would go himself. The old cobbler (who was growing quite rich and had decided that sewing corpses paid much better than sewing shoes) told his curious story again to someone who seemed to be a peddler and led this third inquisitive stranger to the house. But the Captain—wiser than his followers—only looked and remembered, and made no mark which could tell Morgiana to be on her guard. As soon as he was back in the forest he quickly ordered his followers—there were now thirty-seven of them—to go disguised to the market and there to buy thirty-eight large oil-jars with wide necks. Each was to be large enough for a man to crouch in. Thirty-seven were to be empty and one was to be full of the very best olive oil.

"I know the house now and the fate of all who live in it shall be terrible!" added he and, as they got ready, they all sharpened their daggers and scimitars.

Next evening, the unsuspecting Ali Baba, who was tired from his day's work of cutting faggots, was sitting at his door to enjoy the cool air, and, as he sat, he saw a string of laden horses coming up the street. There seemed to be only one man with them, and as he came opposite the house this man greeted him politely.

"O Master," said the traveller, "I am an oil-merchant and my horses have come far to-day. I am a stranger here and, as I have fodder for the horses, I venture to ask you, of your kindness, to allow me to tie my horses in your yard and also to give me shelter for the night. If you consent, Allah will bless you for your hospitality."

Now one of the things that delighted the good Ali Baba was that, now he was no longer so poor, and now that his son Ahmad was an independent shopkeeper, he was usually able to give just such help to strangers. So, answering joyfully, he rose immediately, opened the gates of his yard, and, calling to Morgiana and to the black slave, he told them that they had an honoured guest and that an excellent supper was to be prepared. He himself

238

bustled about, helping the supposed oil-merchant to set
down the heavy oil-jars and tether the horses.

Later, as they ate together at supper, he found the
traveller a most interesting companion, for he seemed to
have been in many strange lands and had many interesting
tales to tell.

At last it grew late and the oil-merchant said that before
going to bed he would just like to see that all was well with
his horses, so, while Ali Baba and Morgiana went to bring
out pillows and mattresses to make him a comfortable bed,
the robber-captain—for it was none other—began to talk
loudly to his horses in the yard.

239

"Stop that stamping and fidgeting, White Star!" he would call, and then, when he was near one of the jars, he whispered under his breath:

"When I throw a pebble out of my bedroom window!"

Then aloud he said again, "Steady, mare! Daughter of a fidgety fiend! If your hoof isn't over your picket rope!" and then, whispering again, "When I throw a pebble out of my window!" And so he went on, speaking in turn to each robber hidden in each of the thirty-seven jars and telling him the signal at which he was to come out and help in the slaughter.

To the last jar he did not speak, for that one really did contain oil.

When Morgiana had finished helping her master with the bed, and when the supposed oil-merchant was comfortably lying in it, there were still the supper-dishes to wash. As she worked in the kitchen at the washing-up, what should happen but that her lamp should run out of oil. She was put out and called the news to the black slave Abdullah, saying how silly she had been to forget to get in enough oil.

"By Allah!" answered Abdullah, laughing. "How can you say, O my foolish sister, that we are out of oil when, to-night, there are thirty-eight jars of the very best oil just outside in our yard!"

Morgiana hadn't thought of that, but now, taking a ladle, out she went in the moonlight and, taking out the fibre stopper from the first jar she came to, she put in her ladle, which, as luck would have it, hit one of the hidden robbers bang on the head!

"Pebble, Captain?" said a deep, hoarse voice from the jar. "That was more like a rock! But we are ready!" And with that the jar began to rock as the crouching robber began to raise himself.

SEE P. 246

Morgiana began to dance as lightly as a happy bird

Anyone but the excellent Morgiana would now surely have screamed with fright; but, though her mouth was dry and she felt her heart pounding, she managed to whisper, "Be quiet! Not yet! Not yet!"

As she put back the fibre stopper, she began to realize what the plot must be and, though her knees shook, her lips trembled, and her long black hair almost stood up with fright, she went steadily from one jar to another, tapping on each, and when the deep voice of a robber answered, she repeated again her, "Not yet! Not yet!"

At last she came to a jar from which there was no answer. Then once more she took out the fibre stopper, put in her ladle, filled it with excellent oil and, returning to the kitchen, at last relighted her lamp.

What was she to do? This had taken some time. All the three men were now asleep—the black slave Abdullah, her master Ali Baba, and the man whom she now knew to be the dreadful captain of the robbers. Then Morgiana thought of a fresh plan.

First she lit a great fire in the kitchen fireplace, and over it she hung the largest cauldron in the house—one which was generally used for boiling clothes. Backwards and forwards went Morgiana with ladle and bucket to the real oil-jar, until she had filled the cauldron. As soon as the oil was boiling she filled their largest bucket with it and, going softly to the first jar, she relentlessly poured into it a great dollop of the boiling oil, which killed the first robber directly. She went in this way from jar to jar, till at last her work was done. Then she went back to the kitchen, put out the fire and her lamp, and hid herself.

Silently she waited and, at last, she heard that, upstairs, a window was being opened. The robber-captain cautiously put out his head and, seeing all the house in darkness, he supposed that all his intended victims were safely asleep. Then he took up the pebbles that he had ready prepared, and began to throw them one by one at the jars. Though the moon was down and it was very dark, he could tell by the sound, as they struck the jars, that his pebbles were reaching their marks. But there was no answer! No stirring! No rush of armed men!

"The dogs!" he said to himself in a fury. "They have all gone to sleep!" Then, creeping downstairs, he went to the jars. To his horror, each jar felt as hot as an oven and, opening each of them in turn, he realized that they now contained only lifeless corpses! With that the robber-captain took one leap on to the top of the courtyard wall, let himself down into the road, ran for his life down the empty street, and did not stop running till he had reached the safety of his cave.

Morgiana, though she could not see, had heard it all and, realizing with thankfulness that they were now safe, waited till the first light of the morning before she waked her master.

4. Ali Baba and the Invited Guest

NOT UNTIL IT WAS LIGHT DID MORGIANA WAKE ALI
Baba. Then, asking him to come down to the courtyard,
she begged him to lift the cover of the first jar.

Ali Baba started back in horror at what he saw, but
when Morgiana had told him the whole story of the night,
he wept tears of joy.

"O daughter of good fortune! O moon of excellence!"
he cried. "Surely the bread that you have eaten in our
house is a little thing compared to this! Henceforward,
dear Morgiana, you shall be our eldest child and the head
of the house!"

So he and his slave Abdullah spent the rest of the day in
digging a great pit in the garden and there, when it was
dark, they buried the thirty-seven robbers. It only remained to dispose of the horses, and these they sold one by
one, so that the curiosity of the neighbours should not be
aroused.

And now, once more, they lived peacefully for a while;
but Morgiana was still watchful, for she could not believe
that they had heard the last of the terrible captain of the
robbers.

It happened that one day Ali Baba's son, Ahmad, who,
as was told, had inherited his uncle Kassim's shop, mentioned that a new merchant, who called himself Hussein,
had set up a shop near his own. Soon Ahmad began to tell
them more about this Hussein. He said he was a venerable
man with a long silvery beard and very pious. He said he
was a most excellent and hospitable neighbour and was
continually doing him some little service or other. At last
Ahmad said to his father:

"Five times have I shared the midday meal of this excellent old man. Do you not think, O my Father, that we should return his hospitality?"

Ali Baba agreed at once, so it was arranged that the white-bearded merchant who called himself Hussein should be asked to supper the very next Friday—the day of rest. Hussein, after making a few polite excuses, agreed to come. All day Morgiana, Abdullah the black slave, and a woman (who now did most of the cooking) worked to make a really splendid supper. Hussein was duly welcomed and, while he, Ali Baba, and his son Ahmad ate, Morgiana waited on them.

Now it certainly seemed—as young Ahmad had said— that their venerable visitor had a particularly splendid, long, silvery beard and, as she passed the dishes, Morgiana looked rather closely at this beard. She also noticed that this Hussein had in his girdle a particularly long dagger, and it presently seemed to Morgiana that she had somewhere seen this dagger before. However, she said nothing and, when the last dish had been served, she retired to her own room, leaving the three men to their wine.

What was Ali Baba's surprise, when a few minutes later, he saw Morgiana entering the room again, dressed, not in her usual clothes, but as a dancing-girl. She seemed to have put on every trinket that he had ever given her! On her forehead were glittering sequins, on her ankles and wrists were clinking silver bracelets and anklets, each set with little rows of tinkling bells, at her neck

hung a long string of amber beads, at her waist was a golden belt, and from the belt hung a jade-hilted dagger. This was an ornament such as dancers often wear so that the dagger, in its long decorated sheath, will swing

245

out in time to nimble dancing feet and clinking anklets.

Young Ahmad gasped at the sight. He had no idea that Morgiana—a girl whom he saw every day busy with the work of the house—could look so lovely! Her eyes, which to-night were darkened with kohl, seemed to glitter with a feverish light, her slender hands and feet were adorned with henna, her long, shining hair swung down to her slim gold-circled waist.

When they could take their eyes off her they saw that Morgiana was followed by Abdullah the black slave, who beat softly upon a tambourine. First bowing low to the honoured and venerable guest Hussein, Morgiana began to dance as lightly as a happy bird and, as she danced, the rhythm of the tambourine grew louder and stranger for, like most of those of his race, the young Abdullah was a master of rhythm. First Morgiana danced the kerchief dance, then she danced a Persian dance, and all the while the pace of the beat of the tambourine and the clink of her dancing feet grew swifter and swifter. At last signalling to Abdullah, she broke into the slow, swaying dagger-dance; slowly she drew the jade-hilted blade from its silver sheath, and then once more the pace quickened and she began to sway and leap with blazing eyes, pointing her dagger now here, now there, striking the air like a warrior surrounded by enemies.

Now the rhythm quickened to fever pace, faster and faster she whirled, closer and closer she came to the men as they sat as if under an enchantment, and then at last, with a sudden movement, she plunged her dagger into the heart of Hussein!

In horror at such a deed, Ali Baba and his son started up, but there she stood before them, panting and wiping the dripping blade of her dagger.

"Look!" said she, and shuddered as she fixed her eyes on the lifeless body. Then they saw that the long, venerable silver beard had slipped aside and revealed black, hoggish bristles and a cruel face that was by now only too well known to Ali Baba!

"The oil-merchant! The robber-captain!" he cried. Then he took Morgiana to his breast and, kissing her between the eyes, he exclaimed, "Blessed child! Light of my eyes! Be my daughter in very truth! Marry this handsome son of mine!"

Now Morgiana had long secretly loved Ahmad, her master's son, and it seemed to Ahmad, now that he had seen Morgiana in her sudden blaze of beauty and courage, that no fate could be more fortunate than to marry such a wonderful girl.

And so, not long after, Ahmad and Morgiana were married, but not before Ali Baba had buried the robber-chief in the grave which hid the rest of his cruel band.

For a long time Morgiana, who had saved them and who was slow to forget the dangers that they had all survived, begged her young husband and Ali Baba not to visit the treasure-cave again. Ali Baba had told her that there had once been forty thieves and, not knowing that two had been beheaded by the captain's own hand, she begged them both to consider that there might very likely still be danger.

But time passed and, at last, Ali Baba and his son persuaded the prudent Morgiana to come with them to the cave. As they went, she saw for herself that the path had become quite overgrown, not only with grasses, but with woody shrubs, and that now, long creepers hung down in front of what had once been the split in the rock. Then even the careful Morgiana agreed that no one could have passed that way for a very long time and that Allah, in his mercy, had somehow ended their danger.

So now, once more, Ali Baba—this time with his son and Morgiana—stood before the rock. Once more he called out in a firm voice, *"Open Sesame!"*

And then, for the first time, the two young people went in and saw the vastness of the treasure which was to be their inheritance.

"Glory be to Allah who gives abundance beyond counting to the humble!" exclaimed Ali Baba once more, and once more he took only a few sacks of gold and precious stones.

And so they all lived for many years in peace and happiness, taking care not to excite the envy of the neighbours by too sudden prosperity, but, instead, earning blessings by their kindness to the poor and their hospitality to strangers.

MAAROOF

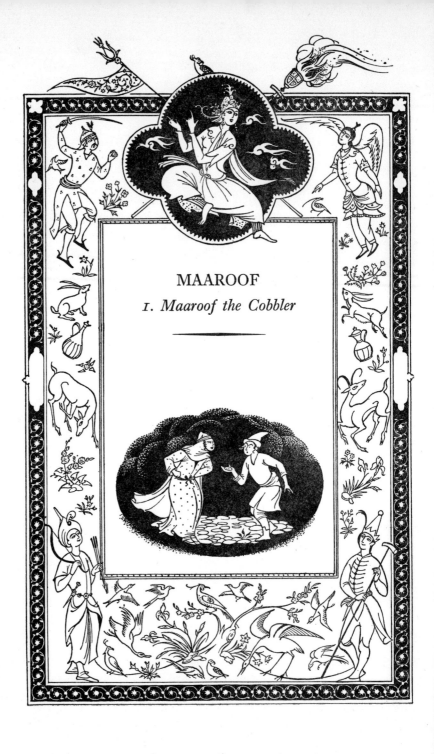

MAAROOF

1. Maaroof the Cobbler

THERE LIVED ONCE IN THE GREAT CITY OF CAIRO
—chief city of Egypt—a poor cobbler named
Maaroof. He was honest and, in spite of being
poor, he would have been the most cheerful as well as
the kindest young fellow in the world, if he had not had
such a plague of a wife. But she couldn't forgive him for
being poor and, as she did not care in the least what the
neighbours or the customers thought of them, she would
often come to his cobbler's shop and abuse him or else
shout and make scenes in the street where they lived.
Maaroof liked a quiet life and to be friends with everyone,
so that he hated this.

"Oh, please don't shout like that, Wife!" he would say
gently. "What will our neighbours the pastry-cook and
that excellent Ahmed the perfume-seller, and all the
others, think of us?"

At which she would only scream at him the more.

So, by making scenes and shaming him, this horrible,
spiteful woman always got her own way. When, by working hard, sewing and hammering at shoes all day, poor
Maaroof managed to earn a little money, she was sure to
get it away from him—usually by making such a scene
that he would buy her whatever she wanted, just to keep
her quiet. He himself had to dress in rags and got little
enough to eat. But the more he gave in to her the worse
she got.

"See that you bring me some kunafah cake this evening!" she shouted out to him one morning. Now this is an
expensive kind of cake made of pastry, and poor Maaroof
sighed, wondering if the day's work would bring in enough
to buy it, but when she added, "And let it be dripping
with melted butter and the best honey!" why then his
heart sank.

"If Allah sends me good custom you shall have some," he answered peaceably. "But this morning I haven't got a single copper piece! However, the mercy of Allah is great!"

"A fig for the mercy of Allah! If you don't bring me some of that cake I can easily think of a new way to make the night black for you!"

Poor Maaroof! He sat in his shop finishing off the work of the day before, but not a single customer came all that long day, either to pay him for finished work, or to bring in new. However, in the evening, home he had to go and, as he passed the shop of the pastry-cook, which was near his own, he stopped and looked longingly in, for he could see that, inside, was a great slab of splendid kunafah cake.

"Why so sad, young Maaroof?" called out the pastry-cook, who was a jolly fellow. "Come in and tell me your troubles!" So Maaroof, who was friendly with everyone, came in and told him. The pastry-cook laughed and said,

"How much kunafah cake will content her?"

"Ten ounces would be enough, I should think," answered Maaroof, looking hopeful.

"You shall have it!" said the pastry-cook. "You can pay me some other time. But I'm afraid I haven't any honey to-day. But I'll put some of my best syrup on it."

So the pastry-cook weighed out a big slice of the cake, put it in a dish, and then poured melted butter and syrup all over it.

"There now!" said the pastry-cook, holding out the dish to Maaroof, "that kunafah cake is fit for a Sultan!"

Maaroof salaamed before him and thanked him, took the dish with the cake and, calling down the blessings of

Allah on the pastry-cook's head, went home to his wife.

But no sooner had that horrible woman tasted the first morsel of cake than she rushed at Maaroof in a fury, just because there was syrup instead of honey on it! She said Maaroof had done it on purpose to spite her, and at last she threw cake, dish, syrup and all at him. As he put out his arm, trying to defend himself from the hard dish and the soft mess, his hand happened to hit her. Without a word she rushed out of the house. Poor Maaroof!

It was too much to hope that she had gone for good, and indeed she had done nothing of the sort. She had gone straight to the Cadi, the judge of the district in which they lived, and, with her clothes torn and with blood running down from a scratch she had made on purpose, she told the Cadi that her cruel husband had attacked her and had beaten her unmercifully. The Cadi, who was new to the district, unfortunately believed her, so he sent his guards, who dragged Maaroof before him and with poor Maaroof's wicked wife and the guards listening, the Cadi gave him a regular lecture on the proper treatment of wives. It was in vain that Maaroof tried to explain, for every time he opened his mouth his wife pretended to begin to cry and sob so pitifully that she drowned his words. However, the Cadi only lectured and did not actually punish Maaroof, and all might have been well if, after they had left the court, the guards had not demanded money.

"We came a long way on purpose to arrest you! Now you must pay us for our trouble!"

"But I have no money in the world!" said poor Maaroof.

"We'll soon see about that!" said the horrible chief of the guard. "Woman! Where is this man's shop?"

The spiteful wife was, of course, delighted to lead them

253

to it, and, then and there, with poor Maaroof looking on
helplessly, the guards broke open the shop and took out of
it everything on which they could lay their hands—tools,
bench, and even the mended shoes that were waiting for
their owners to fetch them.

"I haven't done with you yet!" muttered the horrible
wife gleefully to Maaroof as she watched the guards at
their plundering. "This isn't the last you'll see of guards
and Cadis!"

When he heard this poor Maaroof took to his heels without another word. On and on he ran, and at last came to a
distant part of the city, where he thought he might be safe
at least for a little time. Putting his hand in his pocket, he
found that all he had left in the world was his cobbler's
knife, the one with which he pared down the soles of shoes.

"What use is my knife to me now?" he thought, looking
at it sadly. "All the rest of my tools are gone! And then the
shoes that the customers had left in my charge! How can I

ever either return them or pay for them? I am utterly ruined!"

So he determined that he would at least have a piece of bread to eat and, going into a baker's shop whose owner was a cheat, he offered his knife and was only given a single loaf of bread for it.

Now it hardly ever rains in Cairo; yet, as the unlucky Maaroof came out of the shop, heavy rain began to fall. Soon he was wet to the skin, but (afraid to rest or shelter) on he trudged. At last, as it began to grow dark and he found that he had reached the outskirts of the city, he began to look about him and, among rubbish-heaps and filth, he saw a ruined hovel without a door. He thought that perhaps his wife would not find him there and crept in to get out of the rain. At least he could now eat his loaf of bread in peace! But he found that he was too miserable to eat and, instead, began to wail and to lament:

"Who will save me from this fiend of a woman and from these robbers of guards?" he said. "Alas! Why am I not in some far-off land where they would never find me?"

All at once the wall of the hovel opened and, to Maaroof's terror, an enormous Jinnee appeared.

"O man!" said the Jinnee in a voice as deep as thunder. "I have lived in this ruin for two hundred years, but, in all that time, I have never heard anyone who wailed and lamented like you!"

Then poor Maaroof, frightened though he was, began to tell the Jinnee his miserable story and how he was utterly ruined, and, as he told it, the Jinnee kept shaking his head in sympathy.

"My heart is moved with pity for you, O unfortunate young man," said the Jinnee at last. "Mount on my back and I will take you so far that neither that dreadful wife of yours nor those rascally guards will ever be able to follow you!"

What was poor Maaroof to do! He decided at last that this Jinnee, though he was frightened of him, was not really as terrible as his wife and the guards; so, trembling a little, he thanked the Jinnee and climbed up on to his back, upon which the Jinnee immediately soared into the sky.

On and on they flew all that night, until, when the light of dawn began to redden the sky, the Jinnee dropped gently down to the top of a high mountain. Showing Maaroof the city that lay below and telling him the best way to get down the mountain, the Jinnee took his leave, wished him "better fortune", and flew off again.

As Maaroof got nearer he saw that this strange city, though not as splendid as Cairo, was well walled and seemed to have merchants' houses and a palace inside it. The gate had just been opened for the day and when, at last, he walked through it he saw that the Jinnee must have flown very far with him, for the people here were dressed in quite another fashion from those of Cairo.

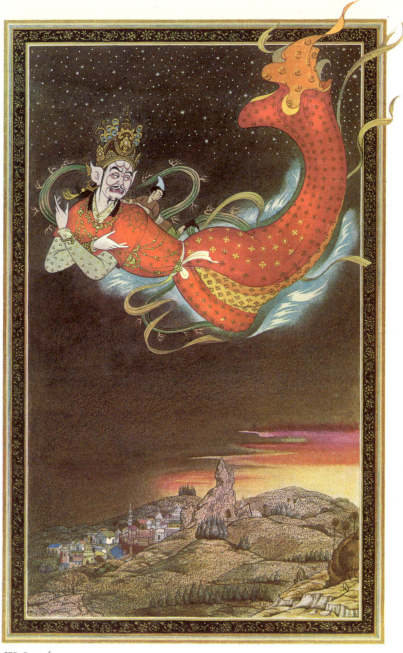

SEE P. 256

On and on they flew all night until the dawn came

"Where do you come from, stranger?" called out one of the crowd.

"From Cairo," answered the truthful Maaroof.

"Cairo? But that's in Egypt—a very far-off land! When did you leave it?"

"Last night," answered Maaroof.

By this time quite a crowd had collected to stare at him, and everybody laughed at his answer.

"What a liar!" said someone in the crowd. "Don't you know that Cairo is a year's journey from here?"

"I don't know about that," answered Maaroof. "But do you know what sort of bread they make in Cairo?"

"Yes," said another man, "I know! I was there once."

"Then look at this!" answered Maaroof, and he pulled the loaf, which was still fresh, out of his pocket. By now there was a large crowd and more came running. Everybody wanted to feel the bread, everybody laughed and pulled and pushed, so that poor Maaroof was nearly knocked down.

Now all this time a merchant, mounted on a fine mule and with a slave beside him, had been watching.

"You ought all to be ashamed of making fun of this stranger!" called out the merchant and, telling his slaves to clear the way, he pushed his mule close to Maaroof, signed to him to follow, and told him that no harm should befall him. So Maaroof followed.

Presently they came to a fine house and went in and, when Maaroof had eaten, the merchant sat down beside him. "Pray tell me, brother," said he, "are you really from Egypt, as you told the people in that crowd and as you seem to be from your dress?"

"Yes, master! From Cairo," answered Maaroof.

"What is your trade?"

"I am a cobbler."

"Where did you live in Cairo?"

"My house is in Red Lane, near the North gate."

"Who are your neighbours there?"

So Maaroof, who knew everyone who lived near, told him a whole list of names and ended up, "And lastly there is Ahmed the perfume-seller."

"Is Ahmed well?" asked the merchant.

"Yes, Master, he is well," answered Maaroof. "And so are his two sons; one is also a perfume-seller and the other teaches in the school at the nearby mosque. But, alas! the third, whom I loved dearly and with whom I used to play as a boy, my special friend, Alee, has disappeared. It seems years since we or his father have had news of him."

Then the merchant rose up and embraced Maaroof.

"I am Alee! Praise be to Allah! For now I know that you are indeed my dear playmate Maaroof!" And they rejoiced together.

Now Alee the merchant had very much wondered how Maaroof had really got to this far off kingdom (which was called Sohatan) and it was not long before Maaroof had told him the whole sad story. But now the merchant began to shake his head, just as the Jinnee had done.

"You are altogether too simple and too truthful, dear Maaroof! It's lucky that I suspected who you were just now and stopped you from telling everyone in the crowd that you are only a poor cobbler and that you are running away from a spiteful wife, and that you were brought here on the back of a Jinnee! You know the saying, 'Be careful that your tongue doesn't cut your throat!' Tell that tale and you will either be the laughing-stock of the whole place, or else people will be afraid of you because you

258

admit that you have a Jinnee for a friend! Besides, everyone knows that I come from Cairo and many people saw
that I befriended you to-day, so that my reputation will
suffer as well! Don't you know the other proverb which
says, 'Where Truth will bring disaster it is better to use
cunning'?"

"But what am I to say then?" asked Maaroof.

"Rest now," answered the merchant. "To-morrow you
must do and say what I did when I also first came to this
city as a poor man!"

"What did you do and say?" asked Maaroof.

"Wait until to-morrow," answered Alee.

2. Maaroof the Merchant

NEXT MORNING HIS FRIEND ALEE GAVE MAAROOF A
fine robe and turban and a purse of a thousand pieces of
gold, and told him that, in an hour's time, he was to
mount the best mule and, with a slave behind him, to
ride to the market-place.

"Now that you are properly dressed, you really look
very fine, my dear Maaroof! I am sure we shall succeed!
You will find me sitting among the best merchants in this
city. As you get near, I shall whisper to them that you are
one of the richest merchants in Egypt. I shall greet you
with great respect and shall ask you questions, and so, of
course, will the others. Now it is quite usual here for a
merchant to travel across the desert faster than his camels
and all the rest of his caravan and, when he gets here, to
wait for them. That is what I am going to make them
believe that you have done. So you must answer every
question as if you soon expected an immense train of pack

animals laden with goods. If I say, 'Master, are you expecting any yellow silk?' you must say, 'Plenty! Plenty!' and so on. The money in that purse you will really lay out in goods that you can buy here and you will trade with them, pretending that this is just so as to have something to do. When this famous caravan doesn't arrive, we shall give out that robbers have seized it! But by then this will not matter, for you will already be a merchant and can gradually pay me back from the profits of trading—I will teach you how to buy and sell. As you can see, all this pretence will harm nobody. But mind! Not a word about being a cobbler! Not a word about kunafah cakes and spiteful wives and—especially—not one word about Jinns!"

Everything went off splendidly that morning. Alee had whispered to all the other merchants that Maaroof was one of the richest men in Egypt, and when Alee asked him if the mules and camels of his caravan would be carrying any bales of yellow silk or fine white cloth, Maaroof answered, as he had been told, "Plenty! Plenty!" and seemed to be thoroughly enjoying himself.

There was only one thing that slightly worried Alee. When one or two beggars came, and when the other merchants each gave them a few copper or silver coins, Maaroof pulled out gold coins from the purse that Alee had given him. Of course, the other beggars soon got to hear of this and there was soon a crowd of them, and each got a gold coin from Maaroof. Though this made the other merchants all the more sure that he must be very rich, Alee, who had given this money to Maaroof for trading, was not quite pleased.

Things went on like this for several days, and then Alee found, to his horror, that not only had Maaroof bought all sorts of useless things, not only had he flung away all the

money he had given him, but that he had also begun to borrow quite large sums from the other merchants.

"But this is hopeless!" said Alee, when they were alone. "How will you ever pay back this money?"

"How? When my caravan comes in, of course! Then if they want gold, they can have gold! If they want goods, they can have goods!" answered Maaroof gravely.

"But you haven't got a caravan!" cried the horrified Alee.

"How do you know?" said Maaroof, looking important.

The fact was that, what with the Jinnee, what with the pleasant life he had been leading, and what with repeating the same story so often, Maaroof by now had almost begun to believe that he really was a rich Egyptian merchant. It was anyhow much pleasanter to believe it. After all, hadn't it been his friend Alee himself, his old playmate, who had done so well for himself, who had told him, on the very first day, that where the truth would give people mistaken ideas it was better to use a little imagination?

As for Alee, he felt terribly upset at an answer like that and at the way Maaroof was going on. Maaroof had not only borrowed at least sixty thousand pieces of gold from various merchants, he had not only failed to buy goods with any of it, or made the least attempt at trading or at any other work, but, worst of all, the foolish creature now seemed to have begun to believe his own lies.

"You are a fool, Maaroof! Have you taken leave of your senses?" Alee kept saying, and at last he added, "If you go on like this, I shall have to tell the merchants that you're really a poor cobbler and a shocking liar!"

"Oh, you'd better not do that, dear friend!" said Maaroof, laughing. "Remember, it was you who told them that my wonderful treasure was on the way. Besides, how do you know that it isn't true?"

At this answer Alee rushed away in a fury!

Now the King of Sohatan, which was the name of that country, was a greedy old man who loved money and, like many such people, he was so anxious to get richer that he was quite often taken in, because he would believe all sorts of stupid tales. Sometimes he was tricked by a tale of buried treasure, sometimes it was an alchemist's tale about turning lead to gold.

Now this old King had heard about the rich merchant from Egypt, and about how a splendid caravan of laden baggage-camels and mules was expected, and how, after talking with him, all the merchants in the bazaar quite despised everyday goods and talked of nothing but trading in silks, jewels, perfumes and spices.

He thought he had better call this splendid Egyptian before him and found that, after the usual respectful salutations, Maaroof really did begin to talk about pearls and emeralds as if they were as cheap as grains of rice or green coffee-beans. Bales of yellow silk, blue and crimson velvet, and embroidered robes he spoke of as if they were common sacking, and to all the King's questions about the goods that were on the way Maaroof answered, "Plenty! Plenty!"

After he had gone, the King called his Vizier for a secret talk.

"We must certainly see that this splendid young man doesn't let those wolves of merchants get all the treasure when that glorious caravan of his arrives," whispered the King. "They're all quite rich enough already."

The Vizier only bowed respectfully.

"I might even give him my daughter Jasmeen as a wife. Then I should be sure of getting a share of all these splendid things."

Now the Vizier didn't like that suggestion at all. He had a son and had hoped that this son might be the one that the King would choose as a husband for the Princess.

"But are we sure, O excellent King, that this Egyptian merchant is telling the truth?" said the Vizier.

"I know why you say that!" answered the old King, with a cunning look. "You want my daughter for that good-for-nothing son of yours!"

However, as the Vizier had now put a doubt in his mind, the King did send for Maaroof again and showed him a

263

very fine pearl from the royal treasury just to see if he knew its worth. Maaroof passed this test very well, for he had learnt quite a lot since he had been in Sohatan. And still he talked about his splendid merchandise, till the King's excitement and greed became unbearable. The Vizier got more and more irritated as he saw how the old King smiled and rubbed his hands.

"At least, O mighty King," he whispered, "wait till the goods are here!"

"Treacherous dog!" whispered back the King. "You don't give a thought to what an excellent husband this handsome and generous young man will make for my Jasmeen! And if I wait till his caravan comes, it's those wolves of merchants, to whom he owes money, who will get all the profit!"

The end of it was that a wedding was arranged between Jasmeen and Maaroof, for not only did no one except Alee know that he had a wife already, but every True Believer has a right to have four, so Maaroof thought it quite unnecessary to raise the subject. And so it was that a poor cobbler, who had not a penny in the world, found himself made a Prince and married to a young and charming Princess.

However, as shall be told in the next story, this was not the end of Maaroof's adventures.

3. Maaroof the Prince

NOW BEGAN A FINE TIME! MAAROOF'S FIRST WIFE had been a spiteful, greedy vixen, and as ugly as she was cruel; but Princess Jasmeen was the very opposite of all this. She was not only as graceful as a gazelle and as slender and light as a willow-branch, she was not only cheerful and merry, but she was altogether so charming and sweet-voiced that the girls who waited on her did not praise her too much when they called her "Queen of every silky thing".

She and Maaroof liked each other very much and would often spend the whole day feasting, telling stories and singing. First Jasmeen would sing for him and then she would sit and laugh at the stories he told her till the tears came into her eyes. In short, for a while, the newly married couple felt that they must already be living in Paradise.

But in the bazaar, among the merchants there was dismay! Now that he was the King's son-in-law, the merchants were afraid to press Maaroof to pay back the money he owed. As for Alee, who had spoken so highly of Maaroof, he was now both frightened and ashamed, and found it convenient to start on a journey, for he saw to his horror that the King himself was pouring out money from his treasury, all to please a son-in-law whom he still believed to be the richest man in Egypt.

"How is all this to end?" said Alee to himself. "Allah have mercy on us all!" and he left the city.

More than a month passed, and still Maaroof boasted, and still there was no sign of mules and camels and dromedaries, bales of silk, boxes of jewels, flasks of perfume and bundles of rare gum and spices. At last the King began to feel anxious, visited his treasure house, and saw that Maaroof's extravagance had almost emptied it, and he was still more worried when he found that the merchants, who were just as anxious, had never heard of a caravan being so long delayed.

"What shall we do?" said the old King to the Vizier.

"Allah prolong your days, O my master!" answered the Vizier with a satisfied smile. "I still say that this man is a liar! I doubt if he ever had a caravan, or merchandise, or jewels, or wealth of any kind. But really, Master, I don't see what you can do, for, mark my words, not even the plague will come to rid you honourably of this sham and make a widow of the Princess!"

"If I thought he was a liar and had deceived me," said the King, "I should soon order up my executioner! How shall we find out?"

"Who knows a man's secrets better than his wife?" answered the Vizier. "Ask your daughter, the Princess Jasmeen, to come with you to the little lattice window. I will stand outside and question her cunningly!"

So the King sent for the Princess and told her to speak to the Vizier through the lattice.

266

Now the Princess, as she came, had been wondering what the Vizier wanted.

"Honoured lady," he began, "the Royal treasury is almost empty because of the extravagance of the stranger to whom your mighty Father gave you in marriage, while the merchants tear their beards and wail in the market-place because this Maaroof has borrowed such great sums of money. And still his caravan does not come. We desire, therefore, that you should tell us all you know about your husband."

Now all this was not exactly news to the Princess, for the gossip of the bazaars reaches even the most respectable and noble ladies. Princess Jasmeen thought a moment and then she answered:

"O servant of my Father! I know little! My husband is always promising me jewels, delicate veils, and exquisite perfumes. But as yet I have seen nothing."

"Lady," said the Vizier, "if that is so, question him to-night!"

"Promise him," added the King, "that, if he tells you the truth, you will keep his secret. But afterwards you must come and tell us everything."

So the Princess Jasmeen bowed respectfully to her father and retired.

That night, when they were alone, the Princess spoke to her husband with such sweetness and cunning, and told him so many times that she loved him and would help him whatever the truth, that at last Maaroof came out with the whole story. He told it so amusingly, especially the part about the honey for the kunafah cake, and all the wicked cunning of his first wife, and the villainy of the guards, that the Princess Jasmeen laughed and laughed.

"O husband, you have played a wonderful trick upon

us all! You are indeed a fearful liar! Please admit that you have behaved extremely badly!"

"Yes indeed!" said Maaroof penitently. "In fact, now that I have told you, my life is in your hands. O Queen of every silky thing, have mercy! For if your Father were to know all this, he would certainly put me to death."

"It was he," answered the Princess, "who ordered me to make you confess!" But then she added, "But if he kills you, dear husband, I shall die of grief," and she put her arms round Maaroof and comforted him.

"What is to be done?" said poor Maaroof at last.

"Take these fifty dinars," said she, "put on the dress of one of the royal messengers, take a fast horse from the stable and leave the city immediately."

Now Maaroof was as unwilling to leave the lovely Jasmeen as she was to part with him, for, if he went, it seemed uncertain if they would ever see one another again.

"And besides," said he, "what will the King and the Vizier do to you to-morrow morning, my lovely Jasmeen, when they find I have gone? They are sure to guess that you have warned me!"

"Leave that to me!" answered Jasmeen, who already had a cunning plan. "But when you are safe, do not forget me and send me word!"

And so they parted.

Next day the King sent for his daughter and, once more, the Vizier stood behind the lattice.

"Tell us everything, O my daughter!" said the King eagerly.

"May Allah blacken the face of your Vizier, O my Father!" answered Jasmeen in a voice of pretended anger. "Fortunately I said nothing to my dear husband of that evil man's stupid suspicions! Listen, O mighty King, and

SEE P. 276

No one had ever seen so wonderful a caravan

hear what happened. Last night a messenger came to Prince Maaroof with a letter, and when he had read it he came back to me.

" 'Ten guards stand under the palace walls, dear wife,' said he, 'and they and this letter bring news! The Arabs of the desert have attacked my caravan; there was a terrible battle, in which a hundred camels with two hundred loads of merchandise and fifty of the guards were all lost! However, do not grieve, dear Jasmeen! That is but a little thing compared with the riches that are left! Only one thing distresses me! I shall have to leave you for a few days in order to see to the re-forming of the caravan!'

"Then, O mighty King, my dear husband left me with many words of tenderness, and I looked down from my window and there stood the guards! Truly, O my Father, there is not a man in this court so richly dressed as the least of them or who has a horse as splendid as Maaroof's. How fortunate, O my Father, that this happened before I had time to question him, as your evil Vizier suggested! If I had, he would have hated and despised me for even suspecting him!"

The Vizier, who had, of course, heard all this, immediately slunk away; as for the King, he believed every word, and Jasmeen retired, feeling that she was now almost as good a liar as Maaroof!

As for Maaroof, he was now riding on and on through the desert. Poor Maaroof! He was afflicted with despair! He did not know where to go, he did not know what to do next, he had no idea whether his lovely Jasmeen could have been clever enough to explain things to her tyrannical father! Indeed, he feared that she might at this moment be in prison.

Riding in this miserable fashion, about noon, when the

heat had become almost unbearable, Maaroof found himself near a small and wretched-looking village, and just outside it he saw a poor old man who was ploughing with a yoke of oxen.

Remembering that he had some money in his pocket and feeling both hungry and thirsty, Maaroof greeted the ploughman in the name of Allah, and asked him if there was anywhere where he and his horse could get something to eat and drink.

"I see by your dress, Master," said the ploughman, "that you are one of the King's servants. Alight now off your horse and eat and drink with me."

"Your wishes are hospitable, O my brother!" said Maaroof, who could see that the man was very poor. "But it is better for me to buy something in the village."

"It is such a poor place, Master, that you will get nothing! Rest! I will go and fetch dinner for us both and fodder for your horse."

Pleased at the poor man's kindness, Maaroof agreed to this and, getting off his horse, sat down to rest in the scanty shade of a small tree.

As he sat, Maaroof began to remember what it was like to be poor and only just to earn a bare living by hard work; after a while he said to himself:

"Because of me, this poor feeble old man is losing his time! The night will be upon him before he has finished ploughing his poor little patch of ground." So now Maaroof rose and set his hand to the plough, for as a boy he had often done such work. He called to the oxen to go on; and so they did and for a while—up one furrow and down the next—Maaroof ploughed the patch of field for the good old man.

All of a sudden the oxen came to a stop. Maaroof shouted at them, and they strained again at the yoke, but strain as they might, the plough would not budge. Maaroof, supposing that the ploughshare had stuck on a hidden stone, stooped and cleared away the soil with his hands. What was his astonishment to see that it had caught in a large golden ring. Scraping away a little more, he saw that this ring was fixed in a large slab of alabaster. Disentangling the ploughshare from the ring, he made the oxen move on a step or two, and then, after scraping the whole big slab clear, he managed to lift it and saw that it had concealed a flight of steps. Commending his soul to Allah, Maaroof ran quickly down and found himself standing in a great hall, out of which led four smaller halls, each of which was packed from floor to ceiling either with gold or with jewels, so that rubies, turquoises and diamonds, all as big as hazelnuts or even walnuts, glittered and sparkled in the light that fell from the stairway. Right in front of him, at the far end of the chief hall, was a large chest that seemed to be made of a single flawless crystal and on the top of this chest, stood a little gold box, no bigger than a lemon. Splendid as the jewels were, Maaroof

271

felt such a longing to know what could be in the little gold box that, without waiting a moment, he went forward and opened it.

Inside was a single gold ring, and on the ring—in writing so fine that it seemed to have been made by the creeping of ants—were written what seemed unknown words. Maaroof slipped the ring on to his finger and, as he did so, a voice began to speak.

"At your service! At your service, Master!" said the voice.

Maaroof looked round, but could see no one.

"What commands have you for your servant?" went on the voice. "Do you want to build a town, or to ruin a great city, or to kill a king? Or do you want to have a new bed dug for a river? Anything of that kind I can perform!"

"Let me see you!" answered Maaroof, and at once perceived that a huge Jinnee was bowing respectfully before him.

"Who are you?" asked Maaroof.

"I am the slave of whoever rubs the ring, Master! But I am also the lord over seventy-two tribes each of a thousand Jinns. Each Jinnee rules over a thousand giants, each giant rules over a thousand goblins, each goblin over a thousand demons, and each demon rules over a thousand imps. Everything that you command shall be done. Only I beg you to take care not to rub the ring twice in one day. The charms that are written on it are so powerful that, if you do, they will burn me up and you will lose me!"

"Can you transport all this treasure out of this treasure-house?" asked Maaroof.

"That is an easy task, Master!" answered the Jinnee.

"Then perform it immediately!" ordered Maaroof.

Then the Jinnee made a sign with his hand, the earth

above the treasure house seemed to be thrown back, next the stone roof itself rolled away, and Maaroof saw that a number of beautiful young lads with baskets on their heads had begun quickly to move out all the treasure.

"Who are these?" asked Maaroof.

"These are merely my children! For such a light task it was not necessary to summon a powerful band of Jinns," answered the Jinnee. "And now what else do you want, my Master?"

"A caravan of camels and mules with pack-saddles and chests to carry these things to the principal city of Sohatan."

No sooner had he spoken than the pack animals appeared with mule drivers and camel drivers to conduct them, and the treasure was soon loaded.

"And now a few hundred loads of precious stuffs," ordered Maaroof.

"Will you have Syrian damask, or Persian velvet, or Roman silk, or Egyptian muslins?"

"A hundred loads of each!" said Maaroof.

"My Jinns shall be sent to these distant lands immediately. To-morrow morning they will all be here."

"If there is to be a delay, bring me a tent and a dinner that I may wait in comfort," said Maaroof.

No sooner had the tent and the dinner appeared than Maaroof saw the ploughman, who was walking along with

a big wooden bowl of lentil porridge in his hands and with a bag of fodder for the horse on his back. When the old man saw the tent and the mules and all the slaves and guards he was so much afraid that he would have run off, but Maaroof sent for him and spoke kindly, telling him that he was the King's son-in-law.

"We had a quarrel!" added Maaroof. "But now we are reconciled, so the King has sent all these attendants to take me back to the city."

The old ploughman prostrated himself.

"As for your bowl of lentils," said Maaroof, raising him, "I like it better than all this splendid dinner, for the lentil porridge was offered with kindness to me when I seemed only a poor messenger."

So he made the ploughman eat the wonderful dinner that the Jinnee had brought. It was food such as the poor old man had never even imagined. There was meat stewed with hibiscus, there was hot pilaf with rice and butter, there was a cool salad of cucumber and perfumed sweet-meats dusted with sugar, honey-melon, pale red pome-granate seeds, and fresh honey-coloured dates. As for Maaroof, he ate only the lentil porridge. When the wooden bowl was empty Maaroof filled it with gold and gave it to the ploughman, telling him to take it home and that, whenever he was in want, he should come to him in the King's palace. So the old man took his oxen and his plough and went joyfully home, praising Allah.

All that night, in his fine tent, Maaroof dreamed of his great caravan of camels, mules and merchandise; but when the morning broke he found that the reality was even more splendid than the dream, and indeed, if possible, even more glorious than the lies he had told!

The Jinnee was now disguised as a caravan leader and he had forgotten nothing, having even brought splendid robes for Maaroof to wear and a magnificent litter in which he could be carried. Maaroof put the robes on and got into the gilded litter.

"Only one more thing is needed," said Maaroof as the great string of pack animals, horsemen and guards began to wind slowly along. "Transform yourself, O Jinnee, into the likeness of a messenger and ride swiftly before us to the city to announce our coming!"

The disguised Jinnee soon reached the city and, when he had given his news to the King and merchants, the whole place was in a ferment! The merchants were astonished, the Vizier hung his head, the King was gleeful, and as for the Princess Jasmeen and his old friend Alee (who had returned from his journey) they alone did not know what to make of such news, and, indeed, each half feared that it might be yet another of Maaroof's tricks.

So now the King, and behind him half the citizens, rode out of the gates of the city to meet Maaroof, and when they saw the splendid caravan winding its way across the desert they were astonished. No one had ever seen so many camels, mules and guards, or so grand a litter or such splendid robes as those of Maaroof. The old greedy King,

leaving his horse, now came the rest of the way home, sitting at Maaroof's side in the litter, and, to those who watched, the King now seemed no grander than a beggar. Long after the King and Maaroof were already in the palace the interminable train of laden pack animals was still winding along the city streets and far out into the desert.

In the palace, as the first bales were undone, it can be imagined what splendid presents Maaroof set aside for his dear Jasmeen, with what glee the merchants each received twice as much as whatever Maaroof had borrowed, and with what satisfaction the King saw how his treasury was once more full, and with jewels far more splendid than he had ever seen before. As the King and Maaroof sat on two

thrones watching these things, his old friend Alee came near and spoke in Maaroof's ear.

"What a fearful trickster you are! But really you almost deserve your good luck!"

At that Maaroof only laughed and stuffed a handful of jewels into Alee's sleeve.

That night, when they had kissed and rejoiced, wondered and exclaimed, Jasmeen said to her husband:

"Was it just one of your jokes when you told me that long story about only being a poor cobbler?"

"Yes, O Queen of every silky thing!" answered Maaroof, smiling, "I was afraid that you might love me only for my great riches! But now I know that you love me truly, for you risked your father's anger and the malice of that horrible old Vizier for my sake."

And so they all lived in happiness and splendour, and, when the old King died, Maaroof and the Princess Jasmeen inherited the kingdom.

BIRD AND BIRD-CATCHER

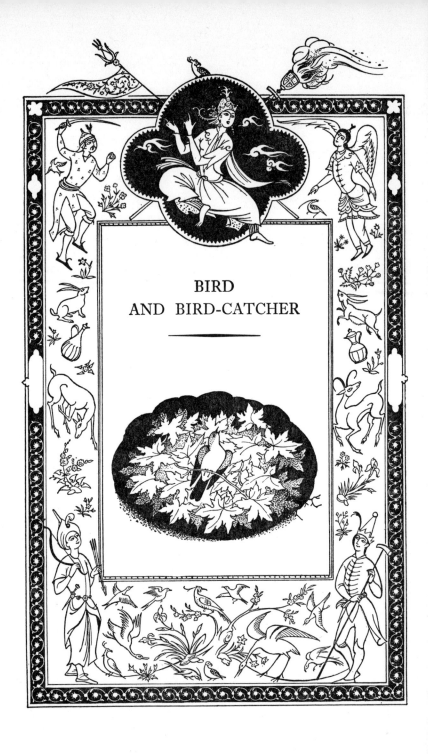

BIRD
AND BIRD-CATCHER

NOT FAR FROM THE CITY OF BAGHDAD, DOWN among some trees near the shores of the huge river Tigris, a small cock bird lived with his wife and fledgelings. He was not much bigger than a sparrow, but he was bold and merry.

Hopping down to the ground one day, in a place where he could usually find a good meal of insects, he saw something strange. It was a bird-trap, but, as he had never seen one before, he wondered very much what it could be. However, he thought it best not to come too near and flew up into a nearby bush. Perching safely in it, he spoke most politely to the trap, begging it to tell him its name.

"My name," answered the trap, "is Hold-Fast, and I am the son of the mighty Bind-Fast and, if you would only come nearer, dear little brother, I would be your true friend!"

"Hold-Fast sounds a noble name," answered the bird, still perching safe in his bush. "And I feel sure that you must belong to a splendid tribe! I wonder why you sit here on the ground so far from any of your noble relations?"

"It is because I have a very religious nature!" answered the trap. "And so I come here alone to pray!"

"Could you also kindly tell me why you have that cord round your middle?" asked the bird.

"So that I can pull it tight and then I don't feel so sleepy when I pray in the night!"

"Excuse my asking yet another question, but you seem to be propped up by a stick?" went on the bird.

"I fast and pray so much that I get weak and so have to lean on that stick," answered the trap.

Then the bird noticed something else.

"I wonder why all this delicious-looking grain is scattered round you?" he asked.

"Rich men and merchants bring this grain," answered the trap, "so that I can give it away in charity to those who are hungry!"

"As it happens, I'm hungry myself," said the bird, cocking his head on one side and with his little black eyes shining. "Do you think that I might have some?"

"Certainly! Certainly! Come near and eat, little brother! For are you not my dear companion? To whom should I give it if not to you?" answered the trap.

At these words the bird at last flew down out of his bush and, after picking up many delicious grains of corn, at last, coming too near, he was, as can be guessed, caught by the trap!

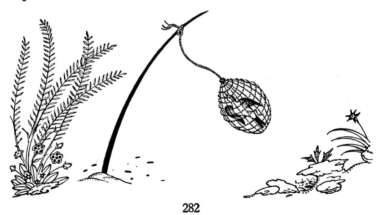

"Zik Zik! Mic Mic! Let me go!" cried the bird. "Let me go!"

"It's your own greed as well as my deceitful words that caught you!" said the trap, delighted. And at that—for it was partly true—the little bird stopped struggling. Just then the bird-catcher and his boy came out from where they had been hiding and the man picked up the bird.

"In the name of Allah! Be merciful, and let me go!" begged the bird. "I'm so small and so thin that I'm not really worth eating!"

"Oh yes, you are!" said the bird-catcher and, handing him over to his son, he went on, "My child! Take this bird home and kill it and then . . . let me see . . . ! We might make a mushroom stew with part of him, and some we might cook with lemon juice, and another part we might serve with pomegranate seeds, and yet another part with vermicelli, and the tenderest part we had better just fry. Let me think again! Yes—with another bit of the meat we could make that excellent dish with the six leaves! Of course, child, you must be sure to save the sinews for stringing bows! Oh, and then his gullet would be handy

283

for a rain-water spout from our roof. His skin would make a very nice tray-cloth too! Be certain not to waste the feathers, for we shall be able to stuff plenty of cushions and pillows with them."

The little bird had been nearly crying with fright, but when he heard the bird-catcher's ridiculous words he began to laugh instead.

"Where have your wits gone to, O stupid bird-catcher?" he said. "Are you Jinn-mad or half-asleep? Even if I were nearly as big as a Roc or as a fattened camel, or even as a nice plump buffalo, you couldn't make all those dishes and bow-strings and tray-cloths and rain-water pipes out of me!"

"Do you really think not?" asked the bird-catcher, scratching his head.

"Only look how small I am!" answered the bird. "Your little boy holds me easily in one hand! But if you were to order him to let me go, I could tell you things that would be as good as a fortune to you and your whole family!"

"What could you tell me?" asked the bird-catcher.

"Well, for instance, you don't seem to know that there are two splendid grey Falcons who live in those trees and who are great friends of mine. You could sell those two birds for a great deal of money as hunting-falcons. If I were free, I could help you to trap them. And then there is a spell that I know. . . ." And so the little bird went on chattering, and the long and the short of it was that, after a while, the bird-catcher told his boy to let the little creature go, whereupon, shaking his feathers, he flew up into a high tree, and when he got there the bird sat and laughed so much that he nearly fell off his perch.

The bird-catcher, in amazement, began to call after him: "But I thought you were going to help me to catch those two splendid friends of yours—the grey falcons?"

"You must be the silliest fellow in Baghdad!" answered the bird. "Did you ever see a little bird like me that was friendly with even one falcon, let alone two? I haven't got any falcon-friends! I should hope not!"

Then the bird-catcher began to curse the bird and his own folly, but the more he swore the more the

little bird went on teasing him, and at last he told the bird-catcher that he had missed a fortune by not killing him.

"How's that?" asked the bird-catcher, stopping his swearing for a moment.

"I swallowed a splendid jewel this morning," answered the teasing bird. "It weighed an ounce—it's still in my crop! If you'd only slit my throat you'd have had it!"

At this the bird-catcher was so disappointed that he tore his clothes and threw dust on his head, and at last the foolish fellow even began to try to coax the bird down from his tree, telling him that if he would only trust him he should have a most delightful life and live on sugar and

285

pine kernels! At this the little bird began to laugh more than ever.

"You really are the stupidest creature I ever saw!" said the bird. "Jewel indeed! What I told you was so silly that even you ought to have seen through it! I don't weigh much more than an ounce myself, so how could I have flown about all day with a great jewel like that in my crop?"

"Oh I see," said the bird-catcher in a sad voice. "But won't you at least tell me the spell as you promised?"

The bird laughed again.

"Very well then, and much good may it do you!" Then he sang these words in a loud, chirruping voice,

> "Do not mourn for what is past
> Nor at the future rejoice too fast
> Nor believe aught save that
> Whereon thy glance is cast."

Then, without another word, he flew away to his nest. There he made a fine tale of it, so that the hen bird and their nestlings fairly gaped to hear of the terrible adventures which had befallen their splendid cock.

PRINCE KAMARELZIMAN

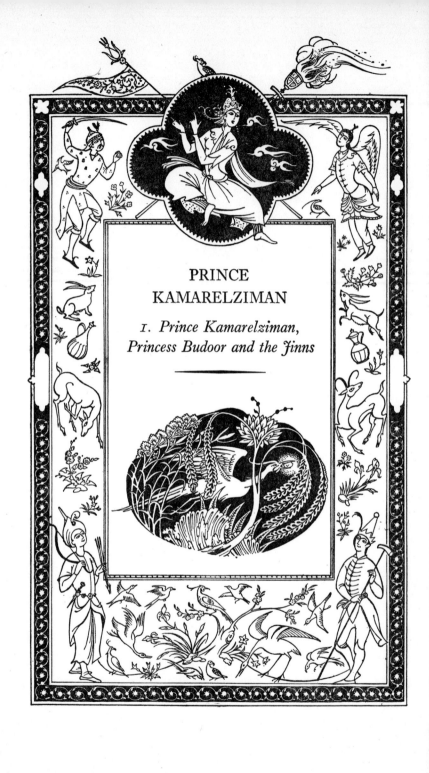

PRINCE
KAMARELZIMAN

1. Prince Kamarelziman,
Princess Budoor and the Jinns

THERE LIVED ONCE LONG AGO AMONG THE islands of Khalidan, not far from Persia, a Sultan who had one son.

He was old, and though his son Prince Kamarelziman was still little more than a boy, the Sultan, wishing the succession to the throne to be made sure, told the young Prince that it was time for him to take a wife.

To his surprise, the charming young Prince only hung his head and said:

"O my Father, do not order me to marry! It is true that I owe you obedience, but I have read so much of the wickedness of women that I cannot endure the idea. Women, as is well known, are the cause of all calamities and misfortunes!"

The Sultan was not pleased with this answer, but his Vizier advised that, as the Prince was so young, he should be given time.

After some months the Sultan called Kamarelziman again, and again he told him that it was time for him to marry.

"But I have read," the young Prince pleaded, "that women are so cunning that, though a man should build a thousand castles of iron and lead, all this will be of no use! With their fingers dyed with henna, and their hair arranged in plaits, with their painted eyelids and their false smiles, I am sure that they bring nothing but misfortune!"

Again the Vizier advised the angry Sultan to have patience.

"See, O mighty Sultan, how every day the young Prince grows more and more charming! Time, with the blessing of Allah, will also make him grow more obedient and sensible."

The third time, instead of speaking privately as before, the Sultan called Kamarelziman before the throne and spoke in front of all the Emirs and grave counsellors and impetuous warriors.

"Before this great assembly," said the Sultan, "I command you to do your duty and to marry a daughter of some neighbouring King, so that the royal line shall not die out! Otherwise the succession to my throne will not be safe and peaceful!"

But the young Prince only looked wildly about him and, flushing hotly, in the foolishness of his youth exclaimed before them all:

"O my Father, your words are foolish and I will not obey you! I have already declared this! No! I will not marry even if you make me drink the cup of perdition!"

At that the Sultan was very angry, for he felt that his son had not only defied him in front of all the grave counsellors, mighty lords and impetuous soldiers, but had spoken most rudely. So he shouted out loudly in his wrath:

"Do not dare to answer me with such insolence, O disobedient son! Hitherto you have never known punishment nor anger! Now learn what it is to disobey a Sultan and a Father!" With that the guards were ordered to seize Kamarelziman and lock him into a dark room without windows at the top of a high tower of the royal castle. The Sultan ordered them to give him only a couch, a coverlet, a lantern and a pillow, and to post a guard at the door.

"How wretched am I," thought the young Prince when the door had been shut upon him. "A curse on marriage and girls and deceitful women! It is because of women that I have brought shame upon myself."

So there he sat alone all day, repenting of having spoken so rudely. He tried to pass the long day in reciting chapters

of the Koran aloud—the chapter called "The Cow", and another called "The Compassionate".

At last, when night came, some food was brought him and, having eaten, but still with a heavy heart, the young Prince fell asleep.

Now this castle tower was very old and had not been used for many years and in its foundations was a well that had been dug in the time of the ancient Romans. It chanced that, in this well, lived a Jinneeyeh—a female Jinnee—named Meymooneh, who was a great one of her tribe, for she was no less than the daughter of one of the Kings of the Jinns. She had heard the recitation of the Koran and now, in the night, when all was quiet, she came up from her well and was surprised to see light in the room at the top of the tower.

She found that the door of the old deserted room was shut and that a guard slept on the threshold. Naturally such things as guards and shut doors meant nothing to

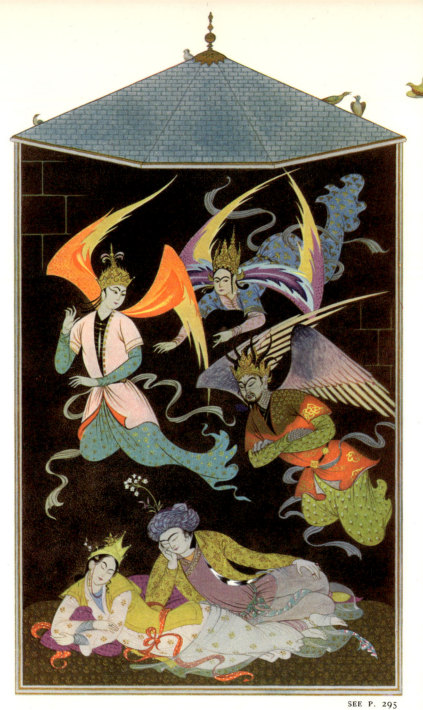

SEE P. 295

Kashkash declared solemnly that they were alike in beauty

of the Koran aloud—the chapter called "The Cow", and another called "The Compassionate".

At last, when night came, some food was brought him and, having eaten, but still with a heavy heart, the young Prince fell asleep.

Now this castle tower was very old and had not been used for many years and in its foundations was a well that had been dug in the time of the ancient Romans. It chanced that, in this well, lived a Jinneeyeh—a female Jinnee—named Meymooneh, who was a great one of her tribe, for she was no less than the daughter of one of the Kings of the Jinns. She had heard the recitation of the Koran and now, in the night, when all was quiet, she came up from her well and was surprised to see light in the room at the top of the tower.

She found that the door of the old deserted room was shut and that a guard slept on the threshold. Naturally such things as guards and shut doors meant nothing to

Meymooneh and, entering the room, she saw a charming young man asleep on a couch.

She took up the lantern to see him better and was amazed at his beauty. She saw that his clothes and the covers on his bed were of silk, and felt that it must have been his voice that had recited the Koran so melodiously.

"By Allah!" said she to herself (for she was one of the Believing Jinns). "This is the most beautiful young man that I have ever seen! His voice was as charming as his looks! How could his family have left him deserted in this lonely place? I am sure that there is not his like in the world!"

She bent down and heard that Kamarelziman was muttering in his sleep, "Do not force me to marry, O my Father! Do not punish me!"

"So he will not marry! Alas that womankind should be

292

SEE P. 295

Kashkash declared solemnly that they were alike in beauty

deprived of him!" said the Jinneeyeh to herself, and she stood with her great wings folded, gazing at him. At last, setting down the lantern, after giving him a farewell kiss between the eyes, she flew through the roof of the tower. Spreading her great wings and rising high into the air, she soon heard near her the beating of other wings and, flying near, saw that this other pair belonged to a certain less powerful Jinnee.

"Hurt me not, mighty Princess!" called he, seeing her poised above him like an eagle about to strike. "It is only Dahnesh!"

Hearing him speak so respectfully, she flew lower.

"Where do you come from, Dahnesh?" she called.

"I come, O powerful Lady, from the islands that border China," he answered.

"What did you see there?"

"The exquisite Budoor, daughter of the King of the Seven Palaces. Alas, her Father is offended with her and has imprisoned her. Yet Allah never created a human being so beautiful!"

"A fig for your princess, O stupid Dahnesh!" she called back. "Come down here! I will show you a young man much better than she can be. It is he, not she, who is the most beautiful of all human beings."

With that both Jinns came flying down and entered the tower. There they stood, one on each side of Kamarelziman's bed.

"See now!" said Meymooneh. "His eyelashes are like silk!"

"Her eyelashes are like the wings of moths!" answered Dahnesh.

"His hair is as dark as the wing of a raven and his forehead as white as a pearl."

"Budoor's hair is as black as clouds at midnight and her forehead is like the moon!"

"His lips are like coral."

"Hers are like rubies."

"His wrists are as delicate as lily stems and as strong as whipcord."

"Budoor's little feet are so small that it is a wonder! Yet she walks more gracefully on them than a fawn."

And so they went on.

"She must have a most disagreeable disposition," said the Jinneeyeh at last, "or her father would certainly not have shut her up, as you say."

"That is only because she refuses to marry, O powerful Lady! She has no liking for men, but says that they are the cause of all the evil in the world, and so her father declares that she is mad. I go every night to gaze upon her while she sleeps!"

"If she is asleep now, you had better fetch her here immediately!" said the Jinneeyeh. "We will put them side by side on this very couch and compare them. Then you will soon see that I am right."

At that Dahnesh spread his wings and flew away, and was soon back carrying the sleeping princess and, when the two Jinns had laid them side by side, they saw that they were both exquisitely lovely and so much alike that it seemed impossible to decide which was the more elegant and charming! So still one Jinnee praised Kamarelziman and the other praised Budoor. Though Dahnesh hated to give in, he was secretly afraid of Meymooneh, so he said:

"Let us, O Lady, call up Kashkash, the oldest of all Jinns, to decide."

So Meymooneh stamped her foot, and at once Kash-

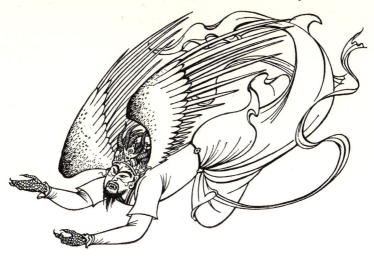

kash, oldest of all Jinns, appeared. Meymooneh and Dahnesh were comely and their wings were like those of rare
birds, but Kashkash was hideous with age. He had seven
horns on his head, slit eyes, and a skin like a crocodile's.

"Judge, O Kashkash!" said Meymooneh. "Look carefully at these two young sleepers and say which of them is
the most beautiful!"

For a long time Kashkash looked out of his slit eyes and
declared solemnly that this prince and princess were equal
in beauty and together were the wonder of the world.

"But you are here to decide, O Kashkash," objected
Meymooneh, frowning.

"Then wake them in turn, powerful Lady!" he
answered. "We shall then see which will behave the most
discreetly and lovingly."

Knowing that Budoor hated men and Kamarelziman
hated women, neither of the two Jinns much liked this
suggestion. However, there was no help, for they had
agreed to abide by Kashkash's judgment.

295

So (the other two making themselves invisible) Dahnesh at once transformed himself into a flea and bit Prince Kamarelziman in a soft place on his neck, so that he woke with a cry.

What was the Prince's surprise to find that, though he was still in prison, a lovely girl was sleeping by his side. Rising on his elbow, he gazed at her and all his ideas of the vileness of women began to fly away and to dissolve like black clouds before the sun, and soon he began to think that this girl was surely the most exquisite thing that Allah had ever made.

"Speak to me, O most beautiful!" said he. But, say what he would, implore her as he might, he could not rouse her from her enchanted sleep and he was filled with despair. At last, fearing that, in the morning, he would believe that all this had only been a dream, he decided that he would try to find something that would prove that it had been real.

Catching sight of a curious ring on one of her fingers, he took it off and slipped it on to his own. No sooner had he done this than Meymooneh touched him with one of her wings and the young Prince fell at once into an enchanted sleep.

Now it was Budoor's turn. Dahnesh, still in the likeness of a flea, bit her as hard as he was able. When she opened her eyes and sat up, she saw to her astonishment that she was in a strange place and that a young man was sleeping by her side. But, though at first she felt frightened, as the young man neither spoke nor stirred, she soon plucked up courage and began to look closely at him.

Now this charming Princess had always lived secluded in one of her father's seven palaces and, except her father and an older foster-brother of hers, she had never seen a man close to. But now, there beside her, lay the most elegant of young princes fast asleep. Long she looked and, as she looked, she began to doubt if men could really be as strange and odious as she had always declared that they were. This was not a long-bearded tyrant, but someone who seemed as young and innocent as herself. Soon she had fallen deep in love with him.

"O beloved of my heart!" she said softly. "Wake from your sleep! O jewel among Princes, let me hear your voice."

But, of course, all her coaxing was no use, for the Jinns had cast him into an enchanted sleep. At last Budoor decided, just as Kamarelziman had done, that (in case later on she should believe that this had all been a dream) she would take something from him that would be a proof that it had been real, so, in her turn, she took a ring from his finger and put it on her own. As she did so, what was her amazement to notice that, on his other hand, was her own ring! But Dahnesh did not give her another instant in which to think what this might mean, but immediately put her to sleep again.

By now the night was almost gone, so Kashkash declared that there was no longer time to make a judgment on such a difficult case!

"These young creatures have now, it is clear, given up their foolish ideas, and each has been equally loving to the other. I will myself carry the Princess back," went on the old Jinnee, "for no harm must come to these two beautiful works of Allah. And do you two," added he to Meymooneh and Dahnesh, "cease to quarrel and wrangle! One of them is a boy and therefore preferred by you, O powerful Lady! One is a girl and therefore preferred by Dahnesh! Allah made each lovely, but which of us can compare male and female? They are made for one another."

2. Kamarelziman, Budoor and
the Search

NOW WHETHER IT WAS BECAUSE THEY HAD OTHER
business high in the air, or because, in his wisdom, Allah
forbade them to meddle any further in such affairs, or
because they were neither of them pleased with the judgment given by old Kashkash, what is certain is that
neither Jinnee nor Jinneeyeh came any more either to the
Prince or the Princess.

So now, therefore, since the Princess had been carried
back to her home on the islands that border China, the
distance which separated the lovers was so great that
neither could get any news of the other.

In his castle the Sultan of Khalidan soon felt more
worried than ever about his son because, though, indeed, Kamarelziman was perfectly willing to marry, he
now declared that he would only marry the exquisite girl
who had slept by his side on the night of his imprison-
ment.

"But it was a dream, my son!" the Sultan would assure
him. "The guard at your door heard and saw nothing!
There is no window, so there can have been no beautiful
girl!"

At that Prince Kamarelziman would only shake his head
and point to the strange ring which was still on his finger.
Soon he began to refuse food and to waste away because
no one could find his beloved.

As for Princess Budoor, when she began to tell her
father that she had changed her mind about the evil nature
of men and was quite willing to marry, but then when she
refused one King's son after another, he felt surer than

ever that his unfortunate daughter was mad! Indeed, to prevent the fury of her suitors whom he had to refuse, he made a public proclamation that she was mad and therefore could marry no one. And so things might have gone on—the Prince growing more and more love-sick, and the Princess—far away—shut up for mad by her father.

Fortunately, however, the Princess's older foster-brother was very fond of her. Coming back from a journey, he heard the King's proclamation which said that the Princess Budoor was mad and, not believing it, he hurried to the palace and soon persuaded their old nurse to smuggle him in disguise into the women's apartments.

"O my sister!" he said, horrified and throwing off his disguise. "It grieves my heart to see you chained as if you were a madwoman!"

"It is not madness, dear brother," said she, "unless it is madness to love the most beautiful young prince in the world!" So, then and there, she told him the whole story,

299

described the room in which she had found herself, told him that, for a moment, she had seen her own ring on the young prince's finger, and then showed him the ring she had taken and that it bore the writing of a distant land. "Since then my heart has been breaking for the sight of this Prince!" added she sadly.

"I agree with you that this was not a dream!" said her foster-brother, examining the ring. "And I am also sure there is no other cure for you, dear sister, than for you to be reunited to your young prince. Do not despair! I was about to set out on my travels again, and now I shall do so immediately and inquire in every city for this princely young man."

True to his word, he set out and, for a month, he journeyed, but could hear no word or clue that might lead him to a country whose inhabitants wrote such characters as those on the ring, or whose garments, or the furnishings of whose rooms, were such as Budoor had described.

At last, in a distant city, he heard that, among the islands of Khalidan, lived a Sultan whose only son was dying for love of an unknown lady and that a ring was the only token he had of her.

Setting sail, he had almost reached the shores of Khalidan when a terrible wind began to blow. This wind, and the great waves that it soon roused, carried away his sail, and finally broke the ship's mast, whose fall swamped the ship.

Now it so happened that the Sultan had taken his almost dying son to a certain palace close to the sea-shore in the hope that the cool air might make him better. Looking out of the palace window, one of the attendants saw the shipwreck and then a man struggling in the water, and begged leave of the Sultan, who sat by his son's bedside,

to go down and help this poor stranger to the shore.

It was by this means that, when he had recovered a little and the Sultan sending for him, Budoor's foster-brother found himself face to face with a beautiful young man who seemed indeed to be a young prince and who, pale and wan, lay upon a couch on a terrace above the sea. Now it happened that the hand of the sick young man lay upon the embroidered coverlet of the couch and on one of the fingers was a curious ring that Budoor's foster-brother thought he recognized.

However, he was too prudent to show his surprise, for by the side of the bed sat the old Sultan, who looked sternly at him.

"Who are you, stranger?" asked the old Sultan. "And what is your profession? And why do you come uninvited to our palace?"

Bowing low, the foster-brother answered that he was a

poet, but had also, in his travels, learned some skill in curing those who were sick.

"Allow me, oh mighty Sultan," added he, "to while away the time by reciting a few verses, for, as is said, the words of poets are sometimes the healers of souls."

Now the Sultan was tired of all the doctors and magicians who kept coming to the palace without number, for none had been able to do anything for his son. However, he thought that a poem could do no harm.

"Speak then!" said the Sultan.

The foster-brother began to consider. He thought that perhaps, through a poem, he might give a riddling message which would only be understood if this was indeed the young Prince who was loved by Budoor, so he began:

"Alas for the Prince who is wounded by love,
His wound is one hard to heal.
Of her eyes the arrows pierced as deep
As those shot from a bow of steel.
But the bow of steel in sleep
Wounded her who now mourns like a dove
Who knows no more of her love
Than the circle of a ring
Till the circle of love be done
And he and she find healing
In giving kisses and sealing
A faith that can make them one."

Neither the Sultan nor those who stood by could make anything of these odd verses, but they all noticed that a new light seemed to have come into the eyes of the young Prince, who, almost too weak to speak, made a sign to the Sultan that the stranger should be allowed to come nearer. Unfortunately the Sultan, though he was overjoyed to see that his son seemed to have enjoyed the verses, remained sitting with them, and so for a long time neither the Prince nor Budoor's foster-brother thought it prudent to speak of what was in their hearts. All the Prince could do was to keep playing with the Princess' ring in such a way that the stranger could get a good look at it. But now the Prince spoke for the first time for many days and asked for a little food, saying that he would eat with this excellent poet.

Still the Sultan stayed, glad to see that his son had at last eaten a little rice and fish.

At last Kamarelziman pretended that he wanted to sleep, but asked that the strange poet might remain beside him so that, if he woke, he might be able to soothe him to sleep again with more verses. So at last the Sultan left them and, the attendants taking up the couch, the Prince and the stranger retired to Kamarelziman's room.

As soon as they were alone, Kamarelziman sat up and, with his eyes shining, asked the meaning of the riddling verses about "rings" and "sleep" and "love". As he heard the story, the Prince felt more and more sure that his own mysterious lady really must be this exquisite Budoor, daughter of The King of the Seven Palaces and foster-sister of the man before him. What excited him most was to learn that all that he himself had suffered from love had also been felt by the lovely girl. Kamarelziman's terrible weakness gradually began to leave him and he rose from his bed and began to pace about the room.

"There is no longer any doubt in my mind," said the stranger when Kamarelziman had described his own ring, "that you, O Prince, are my foster-sister's lost love and that Budoor is your lady!"

So then they began to discuss what was to be done, for Kamarelziman felt sure that the Sultan, his father, would be most unwilling to allow his only son to go on a long and dangerous journey. They decided that in the morning the Prince was still to seem to be weak and weary, but to seem to recover gradually but only to feel better when the stranger was near, and that they should both pretend that this was not only in consequence of the reciting of poems, but also of spells or herbs.

So, after a few days of this, and when the Prince had let it seem that he was almost strong again, he asked leave of the Sultan to go hunting in the desert and to take the stranger with him.

"Go then," answered the Sultan, "but stay away no more than one night, for I shall miss you sorely and also I cannot believe that you are more than partly recovered."

Under pretence of needing much food and water and a tent, they loaded a camel with necessities for a long journey, and the two of them mounted the best horses in the Sultan's stable. Unfortunately the Sultan ordered six of his mounted guards to go with them.

However, during the hunt, they made pretence of chasing a particular gazelle and managed, taking the baggage-camel, to get away from the guards. Then, as soon as they were out of sight, they abandoned the hunt and made off as quickly as they could in the direction of the kingdom of The King of the Seven Palaces.

Long did they travel, over both land and sea, and many times, when some new city came in sight, did Kamarel-

ziman ask, "Is it this?" But each time Budoor's foster-brother would shake his head. At last there came a time when he answered:

"It lies before us, O Prince!"

Now, as her foster-brother already knew, Princess Budoor was kept shut away in the women's part of the palace, and to these apartments her father would certainly not have admitted any young man who seemed in the least like a suitor.

They had spoken often of this difficulty as they travelled and decided that the only way in which the young Prince could hope to see Budoor was to disguise himself as a doctor, but that it would be best first to smuggle in a letter which would prepare Budoor. The letter would explain that, though the doctor was not a doctor, yet this was not some new trick planned by the King her father to coax her into marriage.

So now, in the city, they lodged in the Khan or rest-house of the merchants, and there Prince Kamarelziman wrote his letter.

"This letter," he began, "is from the tormented heart of the distracted, the distressed, the passionate, the perplexed Kamarelziman, son of the Sultan of Khalidan, who has not ceased to be the captive and slave of the incomparable Princess Budoor. I send you, lovely lady, your ring which has been my only consolation since I took it in exchange when we were together. O lady more lovely than the dawn, send me back mine in token of your kindness!"

This letter, some elegant and loving verses, and the ring, they managed to get smuggled into the women's apartments in which Budoor sat chained and, as they had planned, the letter reached her just in time for her to have read it at the moment when the pretended doctor had been allowed to stand outside her room. No sooner had she seen that it was indeed her own ring and finished reading the letter than, with a mighty effort, she broke the silver chains that bound her, pushed aside the curtain and, holding out his ring, stood before the dazzled Kamarelziman in all her radiant joy.

The happiness of the lovers can be imagined, and indeed they were so joyful that they almost forgot that they still had The King of the Seven Palaces to reckon with. Fortunately Budoor's foster-brother had remembered this and had been busy telling the King about his journey, and had taken care to say how splendid was the Court of the Sultan of Khalidan, and about how a certain young prince, of incomparable beauty, was the heir to the kingdom.

So, when the Prince and Princess prostrated themselves before the King, and when he had heard the whole story, he forgave them for Kamarelziman's deception in getting to see Budoor by pretending to be a doctor. The marriage was celebrated immediately and, for a whole month, there was nothing but feasting and rejoicing in The Kingdom of the Seven Palaces.

What befell after that happy time shall be told in the Story of Kamarelziman, Budoor and the Ebony Islands.

3. *Kamarelziman, Budoor and the Ebony Islands*

Now THE SULTAN OF KHALIDAN HAD LOVED HIS ONLY son, and the Prince had, as yet, found no means of letting him know of his happiness and good fortune, and so it happened that, after a while, Kamarelziman began to be troubled every night with dreams in which it seemed to him that he saw the unhappiness of his father and indeed that the whole kingdom of Khalidan was plunged in mourning.

Budoor, noticing his trouble, asked him the cause of it and, when she heard it, they agreed that she should go to her father, the King, and ask leave for Kamarelziman to go and pay the old Sultan a visit. The King was not very willing, but at last he consented. What was far harder was to get him to let Budoor go, too. But she pleaded with him so prettily, and declared so sadly that, if they were once again separated, she would probably die, that, at last, he gave in.

So the Prince and Princess set out on the long journey. The King provided them with a train of camels, mules and horses loaded with tents and all they would need, with a splendid mule-litter for the Princess in which she could lie shaded by curtains if she felt tired, and, of course, with splendid presents for the Sultan of Khalidan.

For a whole month they travelled, through deserts and across mountains, camping each night.

One evening, their tents were pitched in a pleasant meadow, and here, since they had spent many days and nights in desert places, they were glad to rest under the shade of cool trees and with the sound of water and of the song of birds in their ears. There was grass for the animals and wood to cook their evening meal, and Kamarelziman and Budoor were weary after a whole month of journeying.

In the morning, very early, before anyone else in the camp was astir, Prince Kamarelziman woke, but the Princess and all the attendants still slept. Standing by the Princess as she lay, Kamarelziman noticed that, near her hand, tied into the band of the muslin trousers that she wore, was a red jewel that he had not noticed before. He did not doubt that this must be some talisman or lucky stone that she valued. There seemed to be writing on the jewel, but it was rather dark in the tent, so, curious to see if he could read the inscription, he took it outside to look at more closely. No sooner had he come out of the tent than a large bird swooped down and snatched the jewel out of his hand.

Feeling sure that the stone must be precious to his dear Budoor, Kamarelziman was after the bird in a moment, for it had not flown right away, but had alighted again on the ground. The bird did not take wing but only fluttered and hopped, fluttered and hopped, in front of him, so that Kamarelziman felt sure that he would soon be able to

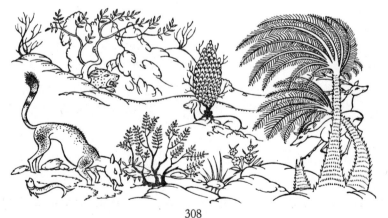

SEE P. 308

The creature fluttered just out of Kamarelziman's reach

catch it. But now, the faster he ran, the faster went the bird. Up hill and down dale went the thievish bird with the Prince after it, till at last, just as the sun was setting, the wretched thief suddenly flew up to the top of a high tree far out of reach. Looking round him, Kamarelziman remembered with horror that he had left the camp without a word to anyone and had spent the whole day chasing the bird. Now he saw that, worse still, he was now completely lost and had no idea in which direction he must go to find Budoor again. It was now too dark to see to walk at all or to see what had become of the bird, so, hungry, thirsty, and bitterly repenting his foolish conduct, poor Kamarelziman lay down under the tree.

Meantime, of course, Budoor had long been awake and was not only surprised but very much grieved and alarmed at finding her husband gone. She wondered what she should do. It seemed to her that she was indeed in great danger.

"If I go and tell the guards that the Prince has gone, they might easily decide to take all our treasure and even carry me off to sell as a slave."

Now she remembered that they still had the curtained

litter with them in which, if the Princess was weary, she could rest and be carried by the mules in a kind of curtained bed. So now she told one of her slave girls that, during the next part of the journey, she herself would ride and that the girl could take her place in the curtained litter.

That done, she put on some of Kamarelziman's clothes and, as men often do in the desert to keep the dust out of their mouths and nostrils, she wound a second scarf round one of his turbans in such a way that it hid part of her face. Then, imitating Kamarelziman's way of speaking, she told the attendants and guards that they had decided to stay one more day in that pleasant place in order to rest the animals. What she hoped was, of course, that, if they did not move off at once the Prince would find them more easily. All that day and the next night she waited. But at last, with a heavy heart, she disguised herself again, called out the guards and muleteers and, as Kamarelziman had done on other days, gave her orders as to how the loads were to be distributed. She was an excellent rider and she had disguised her voice so that, as they rode slowly on their way, no one suspected that this was not the real Kamarelziman and that the lady in the curtained litter was not Budoor. It can be imagined that they now travelled slowly and that, in case he should somehow come up with them, Budoor was careful to leave word in every village through which they went and with every horseman they chanced to meet that it was the caravan of the Prince Kamarelziman and the Princess Budoor that had passed that way. But in truth poor Budoor knew not whether it

310

would be best to go forward or back, so that her heart was heavy.

At last they came in sight of the sea and of a great city. This was the capital of the Islands of Ebony, which lay on a tongue of the mainland. She knew that this city was on the way to Khalidan and, because of that, she decided to make a stay there if she could, so, not far from the city, she ordered their camp to be pitched. This would, she thought, be a place in which Prince Kamarelziman would be likely to inquire for her.

Now the King of that country was a courteous old man and, when he saw their encampment, he sent a messenger to invite the young Prince, who seemed to be the leader, to come to his palace. Princess Budoor, still in her man's dress and still giving herself out to be Prince Kamarelziman, came, and was graciously received. Indeed her reception was altogether too gracious. In fact, it was not long before the old King, taking a sudden fancy to this charming young man, invited her to marry his daughter and to become King in his stead!

What was Budoor to do? She was afraid that if she confessed that she had deceived him, the old King of the Ebony Isles might well feel foolish, and that, if he felt foolish, he would very likely also feel angry and then, if she tried to get back to her camp and then push on towards Khalidan, he might possibly send an army after them and kill them all.

It seemed to her that the least dangerous plan might be to pretend to agree and then, when they were alone together, throw herself on the mercy of this daughter of his, a girl whom she had never seen.

"If she will so much as consent to hear my story, surely any girl might pity me?"

311

But, as can be guessed, it was with a heavy heart that poor Budoor attended the wedding rejoicings and took her seat on the throne of the Ebony Isles.

At last, as soon as she was alone with Amina en Nufoos —for that was the name of the King's daughter—Budoor, to the girl's amazement, threw herself at her feet, weeping and begging her help! Amina could not imagine what help was needed by this charming young man, and her wonder increased as Budoor told her the story.

"O my sister," ended Budoor, "turn the eye of mercy and kindness on me! In the name of Allah I beg you to keep my secret!"

Upon that Amina put her arms round Budoor and comforted her, and so, alone together, they passed the time in kindness as if they had indeed been sisters.

And now every day Budoor sat upon the throne and did justice and levied or remitted taxes and settled the affairs of the army and the merchants. But of all those who lived in that whole city only Princess Amina knew Budoor's secret, and with her alone Budoor could rest from her long pretence.

Now, as has been said, both Kamarelziman and Budoor, though they had lost each other, still both knew one thing. This was that this kingdom of the Ebony Isles was on the way to Khalidan. So the lost Kamarelziman was trying to find his way there, just as the forsaken Budoor had planned to wait there, for that seemed to each the best hope.

It happened that, as he travelled, Kamarelziman came to a certain city of the Magians—the Fire and Sun worshippers—which was ruled by a violent King who hated True Believers. Indeed, if it had not been for a good old man who was a gardener, and who lived just outside the

312

place, it might have gone hard with Kamarelziman, for he was a pious young man and every day he repeated the morning, noon-day and evening prayers that are pleasing to Allah, and so he would soon, without thinking, have revealed his faith. Indeed the old gardener, who was himself a secret Moslem, recognized him at once as a True Believer.

"Why do you come to this dangerous city, O my son?" asked the old gardener as soon as he had Kamarelziman hidden safe in his house. Then, little by little, Kamarelziman told his story and how now the only hope he had of finding his lost Princess was to get to the Ebony Islands.

"We have all heard of the Ebony Isles," said the gardener. "But alas, there is only one ship in every year that trades there, and that ship has just sailed. So you must now wait for many months. Allah will grant you patience, my son!"

Now Kamarelziman was a prince who had had power over treasures and slaves, so that his first thought was to get a special ship for himself. Then he remembered that he was now poor, in fact utterly without money, and, very humbly, the Prince begged the old man to let him work for him in the garden just for food and shelter till the ship sailed. To this the good old gardener agreed with pleasure, for it was long since he had had one of his own faith to talk to.

And so the Prince stayed in the garden, working with hoe and basket, or opening or shutting off the rills that watered the fruit trees. He helped with all the old man's concerns, cultivating the ground and gathering the crops whether of melons or of other fruits. But, though this garden was a pleasant place, his heart was heavy with sorrow at this long separation from his beloved Budoor.

One morning, when the old gardener was away selling the produce in the market, Kamarelziman, looking up, saw three strange birds who were fighting. They soared high into the air and he saw that two were attacking the third bird, and that presently, still on the wing, they killed it, ripping up its body. As the dead bird fell to the ground Kamarelziman saw something that shone, lying among the scattered feathers and the sprinkled blood. Going up to see what it was, he found to his astonishment that it was none other than the jewel that had been the cause of his absence from the camp and of the separation from Budoor. He recognized it at once and his heart was lightened.

"This is surely a good omen!" said he to himself. "This is a sign that the time of our misfortune is drawing to an end."

And so, indeed, it proved, for, no sooner had he begun his work again, loosening the ground round the roots of a tree which bore the long, sweet, black pods of the locust-bean, than he noticed that the blow of his hoe gave out an unusual hollow sound. Surprised at this, he scratched away the earth, found under it a trap-door and under that a treasure of gold stored in ancient leather jars. No sooner had he put back the trap-door and earth than he heard the old gardener's returning footsteps.

"Good news, my son!" called out the old man in a joyful tone. "There is a ship now in the harbour which will sail in three days to the Islands of Ebony."

Kamarelziman, delighted, embraced the old gardener and kissed his hand, and said that he also had good news, and told him how he had found a great treasure. The old gardener marvelled, for he, and his father before him, had cultivated that garden for eighty years and had found nothing.

"The treasure is yours, my son!" said he.

Nothing that Kamarelziman could say could persuade the kind old man to take more than a few of the gold pieces.

So, at last, Kamarelziman set sail with his treasure, having first, on the advice of the old gardener, hidden the gold by putting at the top of each jar a layer of fine ripe olives. Then, after a prosperous journey, they reached the chief city of the Ebony Isles where Budoor reigned as King.

Now it was Budoor's custom to question all the merchants whose ships put into the port, for she hoped in this way to get news of Kamarelziman. So, as usual, the master of the ship was brought before the throne.

"What merchandise have you on your ship?" asked she.

"I have spices, O mighty King, and sweet gums for incense, and medicinal herbs, aloe wood, and costly stuffs and tamarinds, and there is a merchant with me who has jars of splendid olives such as grow only in the country of the Fire Worshippers."

Budoor decided to buy the olives and asked to which of the merchants in the ship they belonged. Kamarelziman himself was brought before the throne. She recognized him at once, but, as she sat in her dress as a King and high on a throne, he did not know her. Naturally Budoor longed for her beloved, but she said to herself that, in all this time, perhaps Kamarelziman's heart might have changed towards her. Besides, she knew she must be prudent, for she herself had deceived the old King of the Ebony Islands. If she acted hastily, she feared for the safety not only of herself and for Kamarelziman, but also for the kind Princess Amina. She owed her life to Amina, for she alone knew her secret and, for all these

SEE P. 315

The blow of Kamarelziman's hoe made a hollow sound

months, she had kept it well. Indeed, this Princess had now become dearer to Budoor than a sister.

So Budoor merely bargained for the olives, bought them, and gave out that she had taken a fancy to this charming and accomplished young merchant. Soon she began to show him every sort of honour, introducing him to the old King and keeping him constantly at her side.

All this greatly surprised Kamarelziman, who could not imagine why this young King should almost overwhelm him with kindness. At last he said to Budoor:

"O mighty King! You have bestowed on me favours innumerable, yet I have one favour left to ask you."

"What is it?" asked the pretended king.

"Take back, noble young King, all that you have given me and let me go to my own country!"

"Foolish and ungrateful young man!" cried she, in pretended anger. "Why do you want to rush headlong into all the dangers of travel, when, at my court, you have all that your heart could desire?"

"Alas!" cried he. "My heart desires only one thing! Though you are like a Sun of goodness to me, my heart cannot know peace, for I have lost my only real treasure, my lovely and dear Princess Budoor. There is nothing in the world that can bring me pleasure or happiness except to find her again. It is for this reason only that I beg you to allow me to return to my own country, for it was to that place that we journeyed when I lost her and it may be that she is there."

At that Budoor rejoiced greatly, for now at last she was sure that his heart was as true as her own. So, taking him by the hand, she led him to an apartment where they could be alone, and then all that day and the night that followed were not enough for their joy and for telling the history of what had happened to each of them. He told of the good old gardener and Budoor praised the kindness of Princess Amina, her pretended wife.

At last the time came when the whole tale must also be told to the old King, so Budoor, dressed once more as a Princess, and with Kamarelziman at her side, told it all. The old King was amazed, and as for Budoor her joy was only diminished when she told him that she supposed that now she would have to part with her dear loyal friend, Princess Amina.

"Need that be?" said the old Sultan at last. "Does not the prophet allow four wives to the Faithful? Why, therefore, cannot this Prince have two?"

At this Budoor's heart was lightened and delight filled her, and, Kamarelziman and Princess Amina consenting gladly, the thing was done.

And this is the end of this strange tale.

The wisdom of Allah had now, as has been seen, decreed that Kamarelziman, the young Prince who had refused to marry because he said that all women were evil, should gladly marry two wives, who loved both him, and each other, tenderly, and who had both performed good and eminent deeds, while Budoor, the young Princess, who had said that all men were evil, had for long not only loved a young man better than her life, but had herself taken the part of a man and a king. Kashkash, the old Jinnee, had indeed declared truly when he said that men and women are made for one another.

QUEEN SHAHRAZAD

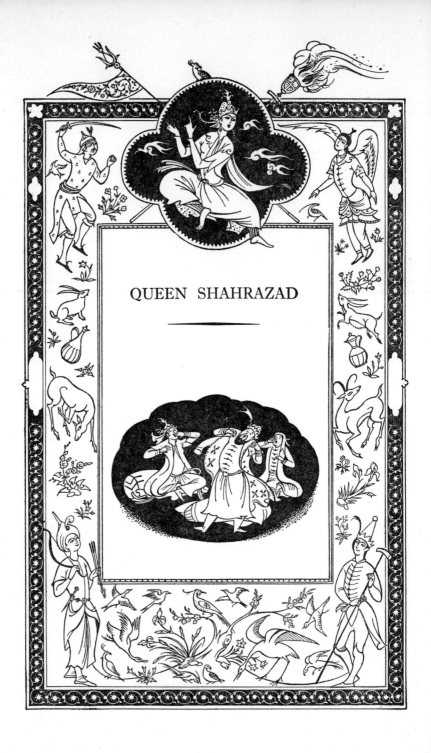

QUEEN SHAHRAZAD

SUCH, OR SO SAY THE STORY-TELLERS OF ANCIENT times (but Allah knows all), were the tales which Queen Shahrazad, daughter of the Grand Vizier, told to the King her husband, and to her sister Dunyazad. As well as those that are related here she is said to have told many others.

One was a tale of a magic bird, another a tale of the wife of a woodcutter who was so ugly and disagreeable that she frightened an unfortunate Jinnee out of his well. There was a tale of a man who became a dog and made his master's fortune because he could always tell false money from good. She told a tale of how Haroun Al Rashid was angry when he saw a young man ill-treating a beautiful white mare, and also one about how he saw a beggar who refused a purseful of money, and how the Caliph could not rest till he knew the reasons for their conduct. She told a cheerful story of a poet who was pulled up in a basket, she told a story of wicked ghouls who robbed a burying-ground, and one about sea-people who mocked a man-of-the-land because he had no tail. She told stories of kings and thieves and dervishes, tales from Persia and China, tales of birds and animals, stories of the sea and of the land—so many that it would be too long even to tell their names!

All these, Queen Shahrazad told in the early morning and she always took care that, when the sun rose, she had just come to the most exciting part, so that, each time, her husband, the King, anxious to hear what happened next, put off fulfilling his terrible vow. For he had vowed that, because he had once been shamefully deceived, any wife of his must have her head cut off on the very day after their marriage.

And so, for a thousand nights Shahrazad told these tales,

and always when the sun rose she either stopped in the middle, or had already just begun a new and marvellous story.

On the thousand and first night, however, the Queen did something that she had never done before. She finished one of her stories just as the sun rose, without leaving herself time to begin another. At this her young sister, Dunyazad, who had come as usual to listen (bringing the cups of sherbet cooled with snow), was amazed and alarmed. Seeing, however, that her sister was looking at the King with a smiling face, she said nothing, though up till now, it had always been her task to ask questions and to beg for yet another story.

"For a thousand nights, O King," Shahrazad now said after a short silence, "I have whiled away the hour before the dawn with some tale of adventure or pleasure, ransacking the treasures of the Arabs, the Jews and the Persians and of the men of many other lands for your amusement. Have I yet—have I, in all this time—found favour in the eyes of the King? Can I now ask for a reward?"

At her words the King hung down his head in shame, for he remembered that, even to the least of his subjects who tried to please or amuse him, it was his custom to give splendid rewards and, in all this long time, this loving Queen, this most excellent of story-tellers, had asked for nothing! When he seemed troubled and did not reply, Shahrazad went on gently:

"Allah does not demand from his servants the fulfilment of an evil vow, O King!"

At that the repentant King let fall a tear, and then he rose and embraced Shahrazad, saying:

"O most beloved of Queens, it has long been impos-

sible for me to fulfil that evil vow! For in truth I have long
known that you are the most excellent of women, the best
of wives, and the light of my eyes! I have long bitterly re-
gretted my former cruelty and wickedness towards the
daughters of the Moslems and all by reason of your excellence! How can I reward you?"

But his Queen answered him in a gentle voice, saying
that she wanted no reward except to hear such excellent
words from his lips, and also that perhaps he would assure

323

her good old father, the Grand Vizier, of the same thing, so that he might, at last, be certain that she was in no danger and that, instead, she and her dear sister Dunyazad had the King's love and protection.

So that morning with joy and gladness, speaking from his high throne for all to hear, the King proclaimed that he had abandoned his evil vow. Then he heaped honours on his old, faithful Grand Vizier. And after his repentance Queen Shahrazad and King Shahriyar lived a long and happy life.

THE END

WARNING TO CHILDREN

Next come notes for grown-up people. They are horribly dull and written in long words and small print. No child could possibly enjoy reading them, and no sensible child would even try.

You have been warned!

GENERAL NOTE

One of the few things that seem certain about our familiar "Arabian Nights"—loved by many generations of British children—is that their alternative title, "The Thousand and One Nights", has a solid foundation. No less than two hundred separate stories (most of them so long and involved that they must, in any company, occupy a number of sittings) together with many shorter anecdotes, really were written down in Arabic.

They were thus written—not composed—in places as far apart as Cairo and Calcutta, mostly during the years between 1200 and 1550.

The bulk of the tales that we know first appeared in Europe in French, when twelve volumes of them, translated by Antoine Galland, were published in Paris between 1704 and 1712. The stories became so popular that they were soon being translated from Galland's French into the leading European languages.

Later (in the early nineteenth century) there followed a period of "romantic" Eastern travels, such as those of the fabulous Lady Hester Stanhope and of Lord Byron. The writings of "poetic" travellers began to familiarize English and other European readers with the details of Moslem traditions and customs. It was soon realized that Galland (French and eighteenth century) had adapted much, as well as translated much in his *Mille et Une Nuits*, while Sir Walter Scott's excursions into folk traditions, such as those of the Border legends, had by then created a taste for the "genuine".

So in 1839 E. W. Lane, a notable Arabic scholar, long resident in Cairo, began to produce a new translation of a selection of the Arabian Nights and to "authenticate" each tale with copious notes. This translation of Lane's Mr. Dawood (a native of Baghdad and the latest selector and translator) unkindly, but not unjustly, calls "a bowdlerized selection intended for the drawing-room". Lane's version—with this reservation—is admitted to be "admirably accurate", and I have made much use of it.

Sir Richard Burton was next, in the eighteen-eighties, with a new, unexpurgated, "complete" re-translation in sixteen large volumes with notes as copious as those of Lane. There are, in English, further important editions by John Payne (13 volumes, 1882 to 1889) and a later one—very free and without notes—by a French and an English translator working together, Madrus and Powys Mathers, in several volumes.

Now anyone who has any knowledge of modern views on Folk Lore and anthropology, while admiring the care, scholarship and thoroughness of these editors, is almost sure to be exasperated by one recurrent feature of the vast notes that bulk out the already immense nine-teenth-century editions. Lane and Burton, particularly, seriously be-lieve that it must be possible first to find a "correct", "only true" version of each tale, and even of each incident, and that it ought to be equally possible to give, in most cases at least, approximate dates and places, and they become deeply shocked at each other's failures to do this. They call up the ghosts of learned German scholars, and everybody accuses everyone else of "inaccuracy".

Wiser now, we have become aware that, by and large, it is usually im-possible either to give a date or a place to any legend or traditional tale, and that all written texts are "corrupt" for the excellent reason that story-tellers (and these are "told" stories) always use their imaginations and "ad lib" as they tell, while those who write stories down are practi-cally always late comers and often draw from one local informant. So—as for an "only true" version of the Arabian Nights, such a thing never could exist.

As for the inevitable difficulty which confronts a scholar bent on history and dating, I am tempted to give an example from another body of folk-lore. There is a "Cornish story" (that is a story which comes down to us via the Cornish "Droll" tellers) which purports to relate the story of three generations, "Tom" who killed "Giant Denbrass" in the correct single combat, "Jack the Tinkard", and then Jack's family. In the course of this, it tells, very well, the history of Cornish tin-mining and hunting over many centuries, from the Stone Age via the Phoeni-cians to the late Iron Age. Just to add to this extreme compression, and confusion, wagon wheels and trouser pockets come in right at the beginning—at which the head of any student of artifacts and of the history of costume is likely to reel, for these useful things were certainly not amenities of the Stone Age.

Lane, trying rather delightfully to date stories by the known time of the introduction of coffee, and also Burton, when he mocks Lane on some other count, can both be compared with two men each trying to make an accurate measurement of a cloud, who then fall to abusing each other because their figures don't tally. However, this curious and even frantic pursuit of unobtainable "correctness" need not make us despise them and their admirable scholarship. They are only following an almost universal nineteenth-century tradition and, incidentally, justifying the French proverb which says that, however great a man may be, he always belongs to his epoch.

II

The fact that we thus belong to our respective epochs is an answer that I should like to put forward should the reader question the need for yet another re-telling and yet another selection of already familiar stories. A little boy, one of the children to whom I read the present tales, put the doubt plainly. "But why did you have to type it all out again?"

I believe that, if these, and indeed any traditional, stories are to be vivid to the children of yet further centuries, re-tellings and re-selections will always be necessary from time to time. Children's tastes may not change as quickly as those of adults, but, all the same, they do change. Since, as we have seen, the version that we may have loved when we were children is not, and cannot be (as we then most fervently believed) the "only true" version, it seems perfectly proper to meet— from the immense store-house of the "Thousand and One Nights" —these changed tastes.

Most current re-tellings for children have become so blurred as to be rather lifeless, because they have, in the main, been based on neither Lane, Burton, nor Galland, but on nineteenth-century adaptations for children. Thus they read as (what they too often are) "the copy of a copy of a copy".

Of course children want the old favourites, of course the stories, in the main, remain the same; but to go back, as I have done, to Lane, Burton and the rest and to adapt afresh, is, I believe, to find fresh delights. It may have been desirable to find a new description of the beauty of some heroine, not because the original description was poor, but because, repeated in story after story, the standard points of an Arabian "lovely" pall. Or a fresh instance of the tricks of some rogue may be discoverable, or, maybe, a swifter way of getting to the point of some exciting drama. The new element may merely be the use of more characteristic verbs. It is better that Sindbad's sea-captains should hoist their sails and pull up their anchors than that they should "depart".

As for merely adopting one or other "correct" or "authentic" version, that, for children, is practically ruled out. The chief and insuperable difficulty is almost always that of holding on to the thread in these labyrinths of tales within tales. Besides, children could stand neither Burton's almost intolerable archaisms and repetitions nor Lane's romantic tediums.

III

Perhaps a further and fundamental point should be discussed. "Why bother with such stories at all?" a reader may ask, to which the short answer is, "Because children will enjoy them." The long answer can only have a rapid summary in a note such as this.

Its first point is that experience suggests that to hear the traditional legends and stories that have survived the test of time makes children able—later—to enjoy more kinds of adult imaginative literature—*i.e.* Good fairy tales, taken early, help to form a literary taste.

A second point is that such tales help to make many historical points real. Taken as a whole, *The Arabian Nights* bring out remarkably clearly that, for long, ordinary men apprehended the world as a series of islands of civilisation which existed in a sea of the unknown. There are no charts, no maps, no chronometers, and yet, arriving blind (so to say), you may find a highly sophisticated civilization which has existed almost in isolation time out of mind. A little trade in spices, jewels, silks and tall stories, alone links these islands of culture. The ship sails only once a year to trade with the Ebony Isles. Sohatan has heard of Cairo, but dangerous deserts stretch interminably in between. Such is just the picture that modern archaeological and historical research helps to draw for us.

A third reason why children should have access to fairy tales is that such stories, though often apparently alarming, appear to produce much the same sort of psychological effect as the "Play Therapy" which is used by child psychiatrists for children who are in difficulties. Here the principle that seems to be at work is that the child's own imaginary fears are rather like the legendary dangers in the stories. (Traditions that do not have this quality have not survived "trial by nursery".) In such stories the characters with whom the child sympathizes ("identifies" is the psychologist's shorthand) invariably get the better of surrounding dangers either by courage, cunning, a good deed, or the help of friendly powers. The "hero" may be, and often is, a rogue, and in this case the psychological effect seems to be that the laughter engendered produces the consolatory feeling that, however bad the child believes itself to be, it has never been as bad as all that! I have found this sensible and true view to prove helpful to children. Such tales do not, as more realistic stories are said to do, lead to imitation in the real world, because the child is well aware that you are not Haroun Al Rashid and that friendly Jinns are as rare as Rocs.

The modern Western child will not believe in a ring that can call up a Jinnee, in magic fish, or sea-kings who rise dripping with jacinths, pearls and diamonds, yet it finds it pleasant to entertain such ideas because the magical and irrelevant have a real congruity with its own day-dreaming. It is, to the child, as it still is to the peoples of many other cultures, our Western, non-magical world, our view of cause and effect, which is the more unexpected. Like the partly Westernized "primitive", the nine-year-old among us still has a foot in each camp.

So, of course, have these Eastern stories, for they often reflect a deep knowledge of character and human affairs. Again and again a situation or a character rings true, so that, besides their magical content, these tales, like all good imaginative literature, provide vicarious experience, and such experience is one of the things which all intelligent children seek. Far be it from me to suggest that children should read *The Arabian Nights* because they will later understand better the reasons why Pakistan separated from the rest of India, or what members of the

332

Moslem brotherhood feel about the dominance of "Unbelievers". Yet, all the same, when they are grown, children who have had access to them will, half-consciously, have a better grasp of what will still, no doubt, be "current affairs". Should they chance to hear a class of little Moslem boys chanting a chapter of the Koran in unison, they may understand such an activity better because they remember Prince Kamarelziman in his prison or Zobaida's pious young husband. Perhaps also ("But Allah alone knows all") having vicariously experienced the power of a variety of absolute and highly unreliable Eastern monarchs, they may, later, be more tolerant of the lesser inconveniences of democracy.

IV

Lovers of the poems of Hafiz and Omar Khayyam will regret the absence from these pages of verses of merit. I hesitated a long while before deciding that it would be impossible to smuggle in any such thing. They seem so often to have an elegiac note which makes them profoundly unsuitable. Even the less-known poets are apt to have the same cadence. Hear this from *The Diwan of Shams-i-Tabriz*:

"O lovers, O lovers, it is time to abandon the world,
The drum of departure reaches my ear from heaven.
Behold, the driver has risen and made ready the files of camels
And begged us to acquit him of blame; why, O travellers, are you
    asleep?
These sounds, before and behind, are the din of departure and of the
    camel-bells;
With each moment a soul and a spirit is setting off into the void."

I turned to another source—Joan Penelope Cope's charming prose translations of Arabic poems written in the eleventh century during the Moors' occupation of Spain. They are warlike and there are no wars in these tales, but in Spain, too, the lovers must part.

"On the morning of departure we said
farewell to each other—full of sadness
at the thought of coming absence.
Upon the camels' humps I saw the palanquins
in which they went, beautiful as moons
covered by thin golden veils.
Below, the veils—locks of hair, like scorpions
coiled themselves against her fragrant cheek.
They are scorpions which do no hurt to the
cheek on which they play—instead, they
stab the sad lover's heart."

333

NOTES

It seemed impossible that there should be nothing to be found in Omar Khayyam but all seemed exquisitely unsuitable.

No! These present tales belong to a less reflective, less exquisite, but far more vigorous and more humorous company. Not till they reach their teens or early twenties will our present-day nine-year-olds feel the slightest sympathy with the mood of such poets or seek to enjoy Fitz-Gerald's genius. For the present, let them enjoy the tales.

PRACTICAL NOTES

Pronunciation of Arabic.

I have been asked to add a note on how best to pronounce the proper names which occur. I can really only advise the reader not to worry. There are complications that make "correctness" practically unattainable.

In writing Arabic the vowels are omitted, their place being usually marked by an apostrophe, while the consonants do not correspond to ours. Those conversant with spoken Arabic whom I have consulted give many instances of "true gutturals", as in German. Further, spoken Arabic varies much from, say, Saudi Arabia to Cairo, the differences—in pronouncing words with the same root—being often as great as those between, say, French, Italian and Portuguese.

Thus the spellings of proper names in different translations vary so much as to make an old friend—say Aladdin—almost unrecognizable. He may well be "Al a Dinn". Different translators have all been obliged to transliterate, that is, attempt to convey by means of the English alphabet pronunciations based on (say) a speaker from Calcutta or on another from Mecca. What I have done here is to try to give each name a spelling that (pronounced in a way natural to someone reading aloud in English) will sound easy and euphonious, and that will not (from over-attempts at phonetics) stand out like an unscalable rock to a child reading to itself. Names which seemed incapable of such adaptation I have often boldly changed to others—culled either from the poets or from current Arabic usage.

Dressing-up.

Children often like to use a favourite story as an excuse for dressing-up, and possibly acting. An approximation to the dress of the characters in these tales can be achieved with hardly any buying or cutting up of the parental wardrobe.

Boys: Turbans, as the Sindbad story shows, are wound from a straight length of fairly narrow stuff (say a long scarf), either direct on the head, or, when the wearer already has on a "tarboush" (high red Turkish or Egyptian head-dress) or a skull-cap, round it so that the top shows. Length of stuff about the wearer's height. For India or Ceylon secure with gaudy brooches and small plumes to taste. The loose trousers are really fairly elaborate in cut, but a large square piece of stuff folded with a leg hole left at each corner does capitally. To secure the waist, a narrowish scarf in a contrasting colour makes a "cummerbund". Still more simple is a "sarong" (Far East) or a "dhoti" (India). The sarong is a straight bit of stuff, its top selvedge rolled round the wearer's waist in the bath-towel

A suggested costume for a boy

A simple example of a girl's costume

manner and ankle-length. The dhoti is a loose over-size nappie. Both can be patterned and gorgeous in colour. Beards can be "Father Christmas" beards dyed, say, fox-red or almost blue. (Fun, but hot.) A white blouse and a bolero jacket (borrowed from mother) can make the foundation for the upper part, over which cloaks, dressing-gowns and straight or shawl-shaped draperies can be arranged.

Girls: In Morocco and Algiers, in the street, an all-enveloping bed-sheet wound round in the manner of an Indian sari is quite general wear. Under the part drawn over the head a thin white handkerchief is tied at the back of the head and falls to the breast, so that only mysterious eyes show. Little girls are not veiled and, in some Mahomedan tribes (Berbers are one example) grown women do not veil either. For a little girl with short hair, long artificial plaits of black or brown knitting silk with brilliant tinsel ribbons plaited in can be attached to a jewelled head-band under a light coquettish scarf. Necklaces, anklets, bracelets and earrings are all appropriate. Separate small sequins stuck to the forehead (with dabs of nail varnish?) should be a feature of Morgiana's dancing-girl outfit.

Footwear for both sexes would be heelless slippers or sandals. Paint an old pair with gold or aluminium paint and stick on sequins while the paint is wet. Bare feet are a proper alternative.

Make-up is fun. Girls can have very red lips and heavy eye-shadows. Many Easterns are as fair as we are, but cocoa (messy) or the sort of brown leg make-up guaranteed not to come off, adds enchantment. Don't forget arms and legs. Socks are not permissible.

Food and Drink.

In case the dressing-up leads on, not to a drama, but to an "Arabian Nights" children's party (the suggestion of a young mother who remarked on the comparative ease of this sort of fancy-dress) see the feasts detailed on pages 62, 123, and 275.

Colour rice, or noodles (spaghetti or flat macaroni) with cochineal and the green commonly used for icing cakes. "Dhal" is the same as "lentil porridge" eaten by Maaroof (page 275). Indian Firnee (see page 123) is made of semolina boiled in milk, and can be decorated with "hundreds and thousands". Serve in little saucers or glasses. "Tender meat on skewers" can be mutton, liver, kidney and slices of liver sausage. To cook, skewer the pieces and lay the laden skewer flat in a deep frying pan with plenty of fat.

Meat is usually served with rice, noodles, raisins, dried prunes, cut-up tomatoes, oranges and so forth (not all together but "to taste"). Few children like curries.

Sweet dishes take second place, and are almost replaced by cakes and sweetmeats. "Turkish Delight" is easily got. "Kunafah Cake" (see page 251) is often prepared as small cakes, the basis being sweet spiced pastry rolled into a flattish sausage dipped in honey and then rolled up (as with a Chelsea Bun) before baking. To avoid undue mess it can, like Turkish Delight, be rolled in icing sugar.

All kinds of almond sweets, moulded and coloured marzipan, macaroons (including those which we call "Maids of Honour") are eaten. "Gazelle Horns" (see page 123) are made of a thin pastry shaped as its name implies, and filled with a spiced and sweetened mixture of milk semolina and almond paste.

"Delicious Sherbet" could be either sherbet powder from a sweet-shop, or, a home-brew made with tinned pineapple juice, any other fruit juice (from tins or home bottles) iced and diluted with fizzy or plain lemonade. (True, pineapples were first brought from America by Sir Walter Raleigh but this is no time to be pedantic.)

For mint tea (page 62) make China tea in a large pot, but only half fill the pot with water. Infuse, then fill up the pot with fresh mint leaves and quite a lot of sugar. On this pour more boiling water. Put more fresh mint into each tumbler. No milk. Delicious and most refreshing on a hot day.

Coffee (if liked) could appropriately be drunk out of the cups belonging to a doll's tea set. Add sugar in the making as well as in the cup.

"WHO TOLD THE STORIES? or
THE TALE OF QUEEN SHAHRAZAD"

(page 13.)

Typical of my omissions is that I left out a long fable about a donkey and an ox with which the Grand Vizier is supposed to favour his unfortunate daughter on her first suggesting that she should try her luck at the palace. It is quite an amusing Aesop-like story, but it is first of all difficult to see its relevance to the matter in hand and, second, still more difficult to suppose that the Grand Vizier could have been so extremely prolix on an evening when the lives of the whole family hung by a thread. (He is definitely said to be in a great taking.) As far as I can see, its only point might be to suggest that Shahrazad's remarkable gifts ran in the family.

At the end of this introduction I have woven in both a few brief summaries of stories for which there was no room, together with allusions to the highlights of many of those which are included, and finally an explanation of the lady's methods. These, the reader may notice, were just like those adopted by Dickens and the other nineteenth-century English novelists when their novels first appeared in serial form. "See our next thrilling instalment."

THE FISHERMAN AND THE BRASS BOTTLE STORIES

(page 25.)

The first story is one of the best known of all and at once sets out the nature of Jinns—powerful and alarming beings no doubt, but, like our own giants, often to be bamboozled.

The mysterious lake and the deserted city of the second and third stories are recurrent themes. They are natural in a land where already, for over twenty centuries, civilizations with their great monuments and mighty irrigation systems had come and gone, and where sudden rains form temporary sheets of water. Travellers in such antique lands really did bring back such reports, and the story of the great black palace, and perhaps of the forlorn or wicked inhabitants who still lingered there, seemed a tale not wholly without foundation.

In a note on "Some Arab Superstitions" in the Journal of the Folk-Lore Society (the March, 1955, number), A. S. Tritton writes of traditions recorded by Ibn Shaddad (about 1285) of the province of Aleppo, some of them concerning stone monuments. Shaddad says that a black stone lion on a black pavement was found under the mosque and

339

another such lion under the citadel. These, he says, were removed with alarming consequences to mosque and fortress. Mr. Tritton conjectures that these lions may have been "Hittite monuments with hieroglyphs."

See also the note on page 342.

THE HALF-LIE
(page 53.)

This is one of the "social satire" stories and, for its contemporaries, its point was that it mocks at exaggerated mourning customs which had grown up.

Mr. Dawood includes it under this head. He also gives the long, macabre, knockabout farce about the Hunchback whose supposed corpse embarrasses many worthy citizens.

There are many such tales, in the "complete" translations, some very funny indeed but in an adult way. I have included this one, however, because it seems to stand firmly on its own nonsensical feet.

THE SINDBAD STORIES
(page 61.)

As Edward William Lane, over a hundred years ago, and now Mr. Dawood, have both pointed out, the Sindbad stories are remarkable instances of the power of travel and survival of good (and tall) stories. The tale of the island that turns out to be a great fish has a parallel in the story of St. Brandon, whose monks do exactly what the merchants did, and disturb the great creature by lighting fires on his back. The tale of St. Brandon was printed by Caxton.

The story of the Valley of Diamonds takes us back much further. There is, to begin with, a more sober account by Marco Polo of the marvellous diamond-bearing regions of Golconda which agrees as to the raw-meat method of getting the stones. But the story was already current, it seems, in the time of Alexander the Great. This great conqueror's contribution to this curious problem was ingenious. On learning (so says legend) that the real danger from the serpents was not so much their "stings" as that they were so ugly that anyone who saw them died, Alexander thought up the idea of exterminating the serpents by the simple device of providing them with mirrors.

Another Sindbad adventure is in many respects like Homer's tale of the giant Polyphemus. Mr. Dawood considers it pretty certain that

340

the relators of the Sindbad tales did not know Homer. "What they did know was the Odysseus legend." This, in the course of centuries, had, he thinks, reached the Arabs "in the form of a romantic tale of sea adventures". There was not room here for all the Sindbad stories and I have, therefore, only alluded to this one, as I prefer Homer's version. The "Old-Man-of-the-Sea", however, is so much a classic that its theme has passed into the language. It is surely one of those stories for which there is no possible substitute. There is something in it which goes to the horrid root of much human experience.

Sindbad's Elephant story seems not to be as well known to children as the others. A parallel (probably not a derivative) telling of what appears to be an ancient legend—probably Indian—is to be found in Kipling.

The grown-up reader may already have noticed that these Sindbad stories have a remarkable feature in common. Whereas in many of the other tales there is a good deal of roguery and sharp practice, the merchants, ordinary citizens, and even the rulers in this series nearly always behave not only with scrupulous honesty, but with real humanity and kindness. Why, we may ask, are they so motivated? Perhaps the exceedingly valuable but dangerous inter-continental trade in luxury goods such as silks, jewels and perfumes, and the even more important trade in spices (no refrigeration and a hot climate) would have been impossible if those concerned had not practised these virtues as a matter of course?

Be this as it may, in the Sindbad tales, the human characters may occasionally behave a little carelessly or have a misplaced idea of fun, but with the exception of some pirates in the elephant story they are all particularly honest and humane.

HAROUN AL RASHID AND THE LADY

(page 105.)

This story is extracted from the six or seven others with which it is entwined and which have (according to the translation consulted) such titles as "The Story of the Three Ladies of Baghdad", The "Porter's Story", "The Story of the Royal Mendicants", or "The Story of the One-eyed Kalendars". I have also suppressed one sister.

One or two odd features will strike the grown-up reader, especially one who consults the fuller, entwined versions.

The "Three Ladies of Baghdad" appear to exercise the duty of hospitality in a free and easy manner which must, in any Moslem society, have surely been construed as highly scandalous. Yet, at the end, all three (a kiss stolen from one of them having been forgiven) seem to have been considered highly respectable.

For example, Haroun Al Rashid might, without doubt, have taken a scandalous lady into his harem, but he is distinctly said to have married Zobaida and made her his chief Queen, while the sister from whom the kiss was stolen (here suppressed) turns out to be no less than the Caliph's own daughter-in-law and is received back into the royal family amid rejoicings.

Another odd point is that when, in most of the stories, the ladies are (as far as possible) secluded, the emancipated Zobaida, without anybody even thinking it odd, sets up on her own as an active merchant-venturer and commands her trading party.

The solution is, I suppose, to be sought along the lines that the roots of these stories go back to what the anthropologists would call a different "culture pattern"—but that none of the Moslem story-tellers whose fancy they struck (though these were apparently particularly devout) bothered to do anything about the discrepancies.

Yet another odd feature is that, whereas in "The Magic Horse", Magians, that is fire-and-sun worshippers (usually Persians), live untroubled by the wrath of Allah, and in "The Story of the Young King of the Black Mountains" it is specifically stated that Jews, Christians, Moslems and Magians all lived in amity in the city which became a lake and only suffered when the Black Arts were practised, yet, in Zobaida's story, the consequences of being a Magian were spectacularly unpleasant.

Should any particularly acute child happen to notice any or all of these discrepancies, perhaps an adult might answer that Shahrazad probably got some of these stories out of her Persian books and the Zobaida story out of one of her Arab books—an answer which is probably quite a good approximation to "the best opinion". The Arabs conquered Persia in a series of wars between 600 and 1200. In the entry by Professor A. W. Lawrence in the 1950 edition of Chambers' Encyclopædia I was struck by some remarks on the ruins of Persepolis and of Susa—vast ruined monuments in the Assyrian tradition, now excavated and visible:

> "Enormous double staircases . . . are lined with rows of processional figures, well over a thousand in all, which represent files of the king's Iranian guards and emissaries of the subject races bringing gifts. . . . Each spearman, archer, etc., is identical in face, dress and pose. Only the diversity of costumes among the subject peoples and their offerings relieves the monotony of repetition."

If what they saw was something like that, well might the sea-captain and Zobaida have believed that the wrath of Allah had suddenly turned all the inhabitants of a great city to stone figures. Mahomet having forbidden the representation of living beings, the story-tellers were unfamiliar with statuary.

ABOU HASSAN

(page 116.)

With the appearance of Haroun Al Rashid in the Sindbad and Zobaida stories and in that of Abou Hassan, we seem at last to arrive at a date. This Caliph was a historical personage and reigned in Baghdad from A.D. 763 to 809—"fifth and most famous of the Abbasid Caliphs".

But, as in the case of the great Caliph's contemporary Charlemagne, or of his predecessor Solomon, or of our own humbler Alfred the Great, or his predecessor, King Arthur, any tale—new or old—that seemed appropriate was apt to be attached to Haroun Al Rashid's name by the story-tellers.

Most of the many "Caliph" stories, of which only a few are given here, are rather more realistic and rely less on such creatures as Jinns than the rest. The Caliph, that is to say, is often told about magical events, but he does not himself, as a rule, experience them. His own adventures have a natural explanation. Haroun Al Rashid is said to have been "far the most magnificent monarch of his age". He disliked Baghdad and usually lived at Rakka, and this fact may account for the story-tellers' reiterated legends of his visiting his capital in disguise and of the rather puzzling feature that many leading citizens seem to be strangers to him. It may well have been that he either in fact did sometimes visit Baghdad in disguise or that he gave out that he did; for he would naturally want its citizens to believe that his eye was upon them.

He was a religious as well as a secular leader, as his title of "Commander of the Faithful" implies, and he repeatedly made the pilgrimage to Mecca. As for the story-tellers' accounts of his drinking wine, it may have been (or have been said by the pious to have been) wine of a kind with an alcoholic content about equal to our ginger-beer. Others certainly "passed out" in his company with or without the help of "sleeping powders" which were made from "Bang" or Hemp. But in no story does "The Commander of the Faithful" appear as anything but himself—erratic, magnificent and—alarming in an absolute ruler—with a twelve-year-old's sense of humour. His eccentric "spoilt boy" character is as consistent in these legends as Alfred's modesty or Arthur's chivalry in our own traditions.

ALADDIN

(page 139.)

This is one of the three best known stories of "The Arabian Nights". Yet it is not to be found in Lane or Burton. It does appear, however, in the edition of Dr. Madrus and Powys Mathers, who presumably got it from Galland, but they tell us nothing of its origins. I propose to follow their example, only noting that this story always supplies a particularly good headache for illustrators.

Insisting repeatedly that the principal events take place in China, the story-teller has chosen that all the names, titles, and customs without exception should remain doggedly Arabian and Moslem (King for Emperor, invocations to Allah (here omitted), the lady going to the hamam, etc., etc.). It really takes the light-heartedness of a mounter of Pantomimes (or, of course, of any child) to deal consistently with such a problem.

Let us salute Miss Baynes, the present illustrator, on her particular solution of the insoluble.

Aladdin's soporific, by the way, was, as usual, "Bang" or hashish. It was not, in the longer versions, part of the amenities of the palace or of Aladdin's personal luggage, but was specially ordered for the occasion from The Slave of the Ring.

POMEGRANATE OF THE SEA
(page 167.)

Mermaids and sea-ladies usually have a kind of wildness in their charm and Jallanar (in spite of her having justifiably hit her first admirer on the head) is more kindly and human than most; while the King seems to me a charming character.

The story has, in Lane's version, an equally long sequel in which Jallanar's son has a very difficult time when, having overheard a description by his uncle of the charms of a particularly unattainable sea-princess, he resolves to marry her. Her haughty father refusing the match for his almost equally haughty daughter, all sorts of alarms follow, including the suitor being changed into a bird.

THE PICKPOCKET AND THE THIEF
(page 181.)

In mediaeval England, when the great markets were held, a special court used to sit, just as the Cadi sits in this story. This was here called "The Court of Pie-Powder" from the French "Pied Poudré" or "Dusty-Feet". That is to say that disputants and witnesses came straight into court, just as they were, from the market. I have given here the gist of the story, which is told, with further embellishments, under the title of "The Tale of the Leg of Mutton" in Dr. Madrus and Powys Mathers, and I have added (under pressure from the indignant and right-thinking young) the compensation given to Akil's poor, ill-used old victim. The refusal of the Sultan to adjudicate is also mine and I have improved the character of the young lady. (It needed it!)

NOTES

THE MAGIC HORSE
(page 193.)

This is a Persian story and appears to belong to the time before Persia had become Mahommedan—that is, before the sixth century and long before the time of the Persian poets best known here; Omar Khayyam (early twelfth century), or Hafiz (fourteenth century).

These earlier Persian Magians were noted all over the East for their skill in the occult arts and it would seem natural to the later story-tellers to attribute to a Persian king a special interest in "philosophy, geometry and marvels". The occasion when the King sat in state wearing his Sun diadem was the Autumn Equinox, when he and his principal nobles ate ceremonial offerings of the fruits of the earth.

I have ventured to give names to the young couple. "Yusuf" means "the beautiful", "Laila" is the name of the heroine of a romantic poem by Jami which was translated by FitzGerald.

ALI BABA AND THE FORTY THIEVES
(page 215.)

In spite of its popularity for Christmas pantomimes, this famous tale needs a warning.

It is not now invariably liked by children, on account of the amount of killing involved and, owing to the nature of the plot, it is impossible to make it markedly tamer.

To my own mind, Ali Baba's own charmingly prim and sensible character and the fascinating slave-girl's courage and resourcefulness redeem it; nor did I, as a child, ever think of it as in the least too fierce. Indeed it was not till recently that I noticed that a certain child always passed it over and—though she said nothing—knowing her, I guessed at a reason. Here possibly we have one of the changes in taste of which mention has already been made.

I have included it here on the ground that, after all, it is only "bad characters" who come to a sticky end, and there is thus, to a child, nothing sad about it; also because it is so famous that any selection would seem incomplete without it.

It is amusing—apropos of our unquestioning feeling that it does belong—to note that it was not included in any of the MS. collections and that no one knows where Galland got it. That he certainly did not make it up is clear from internal evidence. Versions differ in small particulars—for instance, as to whose slave Morgiana was originally. I pre-

345

ferred the version which suggests that she had good reason to be fond of Ali Baba, for her ferocity is much better justified if it is in defence of her adoptive family.

MAAROOF
(page 251.)

This story—with its amusing "business" background and its benevolent "First Jinnee"— is included as it greatly pleases some children, just as does the Norse "Master-Thief", and for much the same reasons. If an older or particularly truthful child takes exception to the success of Maaroof's lies and general *hubris*, the adult might remark (i) that it was only when Maaroof was being sympathetic to the old ploughman that he got his second chance, and (ii) that it is not really such a shocking story, for it makes it clear that those not sure of finding a second Jinnee might do well to avoid Maaroof's example.

It may also amuse the adult to reflect that a course similar to Alee's and Maaroof's is said to be not unusual to-day. It is adopted by business men who patronize certain fabulously expensive hotels. Their argument is that, since everyone knows how expensive these places are, a business man in difficulties will reassure his associates by entertaining them there, or even by writing from such an address.

There is a sequel to the story, in which Maaroof loses and regains the magic ring, but this I have suppressed.

There is, in Lane's version, no mention of camels in this story. The treasure is carried by mules. But I have ventured to introduce camels because this is said to be one of the less ancient tales and, though camels came from further East and only reached the sort of region where the imaginary "Sohatan" seems to be situated within historic times, yet as the slowest form of desert transport (horses, mules and donkeys all travel faster) camels seem particularly appropriate to this long-expected caravan. Surprise would have been even greater than it was if only mules had appeared.

BIRD AND BIRD-CATCHER
(page 279).

This story is one of a number of Animal Fables included in The Arabian Nights. They are probably of Indian origin and this one is given at much greater length in Sir Richard Burton's last and seventh volume of "Supplemental Nights".

In the Arabic version used by him it seems to have been told in archaic

rhymed prose which he renders into a kind of medieval English as thus:
". . . there abode in Baghdad-city a huntsman wight trained in venerie aright."

Here the Trap's conversation is loaded with pious remarks which satirize the "unco'-guid" in much the way that our own puritans are satirized in Butler's "Hudibras".

Most of the "Arabian Nights" stories show very little interest in natural history, but the character and habits of this small bird seem to me to be delightfully developed.

Burton translates another such story, "The Pleasant History of the Cock and the Fox", and there is a third (given also by Lane) about an ox and a donkey, which (as already noted) interrupts the action in the introductory story of the Queen herself. These are all amusing, and so are a number of others, but I preferred this one as being the freshest and least paralleled in the fables of other nations. The Arabian Cock and Fox story, though good, is, for example, less sly and amusing than Chaucer's "Nun's Priest's Tale", if only because the part of the admirable "Dame Partelett" is omitted.

KAMARELZIMAN AND BUDOOR

(page 287.)

Lane's version of this tale is—as ever—very much longer than that given here, having not only much repetition but also a number of further complications. For instance, Kamarelziman is accidentally left behind with the old gardener when the ship sails to the Ebony Islands, there is some very unnatural history relating to the birds, and a much longer wrangle between the two Jinns who appear in the first part, with that formidable lady Meymooneh hectoring it interminably over poor Dahnesh, stunning him with a blow, threatening to pull out his wing feathers and so on, if he does not give in.

There are one or two discrepancies and other circumstances in the longer versions which suggest that it has been rather casually pieced together from several sources. I have thus not only taken the usual liberty of omitting, but also of adding two pious remarks. These, taken together, are inserted in order to suggest that three features of the tale —the rather odd disappearance from the scene of the three Jinns (who seemed, at first, to show such an interest in events), Budoor's life as a man, and the fact that Kamarelziman ends up with two wives—all have a sort of moral logic. They suggest, in short, that all these harrowing events cured the hero and heroine of ideas about the opposite sex which a Western child thinks pretty silly. Most children dislike a plot whose complication depends (as this does) on the foolish conduct of the "good" characters unless it is afterwards clearly suggested that what happened was, in the long run, "all for the best".

The "foster-brother" was no doubt a "*frère de lait*", but, if an explana-tion is demanded, it can be said that, till they are about seven, little Eastern girls (though later they will live "in purdah", as Budoor did) usually play with any little boys who happen to be about, and, if they share the same nurse, count as "foster-brother" and "foster-sister". The verb, "to foster", shows the meaning.

QUEEN SHAHRAZAD

(page 319).

In winding up the Queen's own story and giving it its happy end (all translations are unanimous in saying that the end was happy) I have deliberately echoed, without repeating, the account of her methods. I have also tried to suggest, within the framework of the fiction of her narration, both the real richness of this immense treasure-house of stories and some of the ways in which this version may be found to differ from others. I have done this because the child who has come across some other selection may thus be induced to believe that both can be held to be "The Real" Arabian Nights and that there could be (and in-deed are) yet others, with some tales included and others omitted for good, honest reasons.

Children (like Lane and Burton) suffer from the delusion that there is such a thing as "The One True", "Absolute" version of a tale or a collection of tales that they like. It is not so. Such allusions and sum-maries may help to soften that discovery. There really are more tales than can possibly be included in one book.

E2

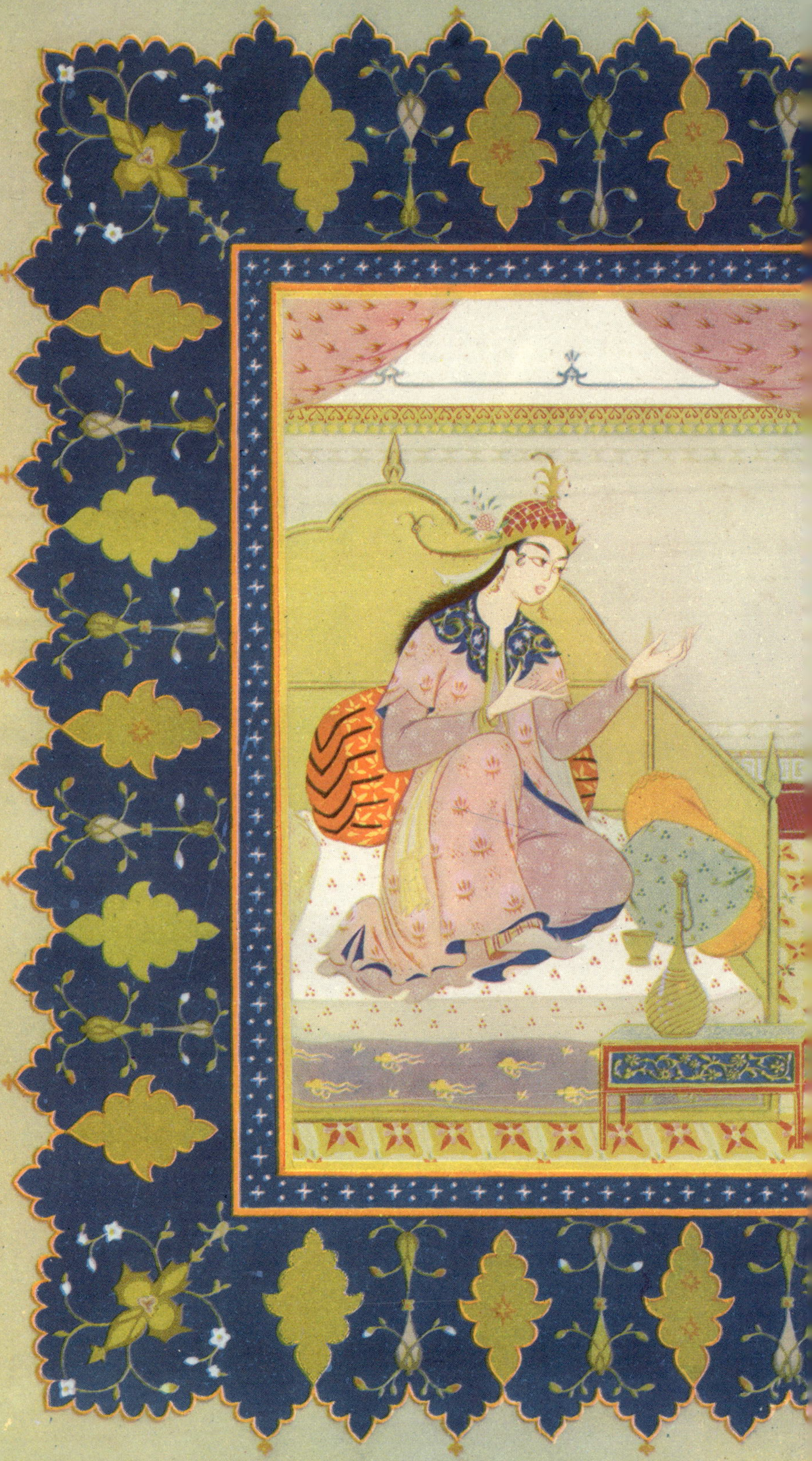